Praise for the Faire Folk Trilogy

The Tree Shepherd's Daughter

"The constant action, both magical and other e,
will keep [readers] interested in Keelie'
—*School Library Journ*

"In the recent flood of YA novel
who discover the supernatu
thanks primarily to th   ne
interesting wood magic, a   ttitude."
—*LOCUS*

"One of those remarkable tal n which the reader
becomes completely immersed … It will be enjoyed not
only in its own right, but also will have readers eagerly
anticipating books two and three in the promised trilogy."
—*KLIATT*

Into the Wildewood

"Compelling and beautifully written … a great
follow-up to an already breathtaking first novel.
Fans of the series will be very satisfied."
—TeensReadToo.com

"Fans of similar light 'chick-fantasy' novels will enjoy Keelie's
adventures in the vivid and lively Renaissance Faire setting."
—*VOYA*

"*Into the Wildewood* brings a fresh perspective to the
genre with a crackerjack plot and razor sharp writing."
—*ForeWord Magazine*

The Secret of the
Dread Forest

Dedicated to the wonderful people who volunteer their time and give their love to pet rescue, and particularly to the veterinarians who spay, neuter, and repair our broken furry friends.

Thanks to Wyndeth Davis of the National Park Service for her suggestion to include oak circles, which are now an integral part of Keelie's world.

GILLIAN SUMMERS

The Secret of the Dread Forest

THE FAIRE FOLK TRILOGY

flux
TM
Woodbury, Minnesota

First Edition
First Printing, 2009

Book design by Steffani Sawyer
Cover design by Kevin R. Brown
Cover illustration by Derek Lea

Flux, an imprint of Llewellyn Publications

Library of Congress Cataloging-in-Publication Data
Summers, Gillian.
  The secret of the Dread Forest : the faire folk trilogy / Gillian
Summers.—1st ed.
    p. cm.—(The faire folk trilogy ; bk. 3)
  Summary: After reluctantly joining her father in the Dread Forest,
home to elves and her fearsome elf grandmother, teenaged Keelie meets a
mysterious boy and learns that both humans and dark magical forces are
encroaching on the elves' enchanted realm.
  ISBN 978-0-7387-1411-0
  [1. Elves—Fiction. 2. Magic—Fiction. 3. Trees—Fiction.] I. Title.
  PZ7.S953987Se 2009
  [Fic]—dc22
                                            2009001687

Flux
Llewellyn Publications
A Division of Llewellyn Worldwide, Ltd.
2143 Wooddale Drive, Dept. 978-0-7387-1411-0
Woodbury, MN 55125-2989, U.S.A.
www.fluxnow.com

Printed in the United States of America

one

Keelie Heartwood ran, legs stretching, arms pumping, her lungs squeezed from the fear that threatened to stop her. Half blind from the tears that clogged her eyes, she tried to drown out Sean's words, playing in an endless loop in her head.

Around her the deep green of the ancient Oregon forest was a blur as she raced over the unfamiliar ground, barely noting the terrain. She listened for the cry of the hawk overhead.

Ariel came first in her life. The blind hawk was flying, and she would die if Keelie didn't coax her down. The trees here were tall and forbidding, and a collision would be fatal. She had chosen to release the nervous hawk—if Ariel got hurt, it would all be her fault.

A small stream cut deep in the loam, and Keelie vaulted it and landed, sure-footed in her running shoes, on the other side.

Stay. The water sprite's voice rose like bubbles from the fast-moving water, and though Keelie ran on, she sent back the promise to return. At least she'd have one friend here.

The Dread had nestled in deep pockets in the old woods, and her next step made her gasp as a strong eddy of the curse made her human fear spike. She squeezed her rose quartz in her fist, thinking of what Sir Davey, her Earth magic teacher, had said over and over to her this summer: *Pull on the earth, let the rocks below ground you.*

The fear ebbed and she ran on, looking up now and then for the dark wings of the hawk she'd worked so hard to rehabilitate. She could not let anything happen to Ariel. Too bad Sir Davey hadn't taught her anything about boys.

Leaves rustled on the bushes to her left, and before she could react, a lithe, brown-furred body burst through them, leaping through the air. It touched down in front of her, then leaped again. She whirled to avoid it, then stopped as another one jumped toward her. Deer. Tall and graceful, they landed on the grass of the clearing, then headed up the slope, away from her. Panting, Keelie watched them maneuver the rocks and gullies as if they were being manipulated by a giant puppeteer.

Ariel cried out above her, and Keelie looked up, dismayed that she'd let the deer distract her. The shadows had lengthened, and it would be dark soon. She needed to get Ariel and return to her grandmother's house.

She didn't want to go back, but she had to. Everyone would be waiting for her. Sean would be there. Her chest tightened, remembering the earnest look on his handsome face, the way the tips of his ears poked out between the blond locks that hung to his shoulders. The words had made sense as he'd started talking, and then they'd been lost in the thudding of her heart.

She'd thought he'd taken her aside to sneak a kiss, and so she led him to the mews, where she'd just fed Ariel. "I've missed you so much," she said, like a lovesick idiot.

And he'd looked pained and told her about Risa. Risa, the elf girl that his father had chosen for him. The one whose engagement to Sean might be announced tonight, at Keelie's welcome party.

Sorry, sorry, sorry—his words echoed with each step. She'd have to hide her feelings from everyone, especially Grandmother.

It sounded weird to say "Grandmother," a word that before had only meant Josephine, her mother's mother and the only grandmother she knew. Josephine was small and sweet, soft and full of laughter. Nothing like tall, stern Keliatiel, whose long, silvery white hair hung straight behind her, brushing the skirts of her robes. Yeah, robes. Straight out of the movies. She was the leader here in the Dread Forest, and the elves all bowed to her.

She'd made a big show of welcoming Keelie, and her house at the edge of a clearing was the site of the welcome party in Keelie's honor. The guests were all probably anxious to stare at the half-human child that Zekeliel, Keliatiel's son—the Tree Shepherd himself—had brought home. His daughter. The one who wasn't elf enough to marry Lord Niriel's son.

The thought made Keelie break into a run again. What would she say to them? And worse—how could she keep them from seeing how much it hurt her to see Sean but not to be able to hold his hand? To be called "Round Ear"? She'd seen the sidelong looks and behind-the-hand whispers around the village all week.

Keelie moved faster, looking up to try to spot Ariel again. But the sky had darkened and it was impossible to see. She tripped and landed hard on her knees. For a moment the pain was so intense that she just concentrated on breathing; then it lessened. Keelie moved one leg, then the other, carefully, testing them. Her knees burned through her jeans and her palms were scraped, but she was okay.

No, she wasn't. She rolled sideways and sat, dampness seeping through the seat of her jeans, then pulled her legs up.

Tears slid down her nose and dropped onto the dried leaves that formed the forest floor. Her hand had snapped a twig. Alder, she thought. Alder like the ones at the High Mountain Faire. Through her contact with the branch, she could see that one of the huge trees nearby was its mother. She'd never seen such a broad alder.

These trees were hundreds of years old. What must they think of silly humanity, running around trying to solve their so-called problems?

Then Keelie froze. She sensed movement in the bushes. Something was there, in the shaded crevice formed by the overhang of a massive fallen oak next to her. It was not a deer.

Keelie put her hand on the green-spotted bark of the dead giant and said the words of the Tree Lorem, which her father had taught her. "Peace to You, Oh Tree," she finished. She felt through the bark the thousands, millions of little lives that were now part of the tree, fed and sheltered because of its death. She saw in her mind's eye the storm that had felled it, felt the hot sizzle of lightning as it had burned explosively to the tree's core.

Flinching, Keelie pulled her hand away from the bark—then saw clearly the thing that had sheltered in its shadow.

It was a boy. He slept, his hoodie shielding his face, with his thin arms wrapped tightly around himself as if they could keep the damp away from his ribs. He seemed to be about her age. His torn jeans revealed one grime-spotted white kneecap, and his boots had heels so worn that it must have hurt to walk in them.

He lay unmoving, so still that Keelie wondered if maybe he was dead, but no, she'd seen him move before. She'd heard him.

A couple of the elves in the village had mentioned to her father that hikers were getting farther into the Dread Forest than ever before, now that the Dread was fading. Keelie almost opened her hand to look at her rose quartz—her ward against the Dread—but knew better. If she lost contact with the little polished stone for even a minute, the Dread would roar through her. Its terror was not real, but the panic it brought would be so deep that she would be unable to stop herself from running away. Even though she knew what the Dread was—a curse to keep humans from entering and defiling the forest—it still affected her. She willed herself to breathe more slowly.

The boy moved. His head shifted, which pulled the hoodie away from his face. He was beautiful. Dark hair fell across his brow, and his lashes were long and sooty black against his pale, pale skin. He was deeply asleep.

She saw that he was round-eared, and seemed to be as human as she was. Even more so, actually, since he wasn't half elf. Keelie touched her ear, the rounded, normal upper edge smooth under her finger, then slid a finger up the long, upswept curve of her other ear tip. So much drama over the shape of an ear.

She had the sudden urge to do a reverse Sleeping Beauty and kiss him. Would he awaken? Grant her a wish?

No, that was a genie. But at least she'd be kissed by *someone*.

The cool ground was getting uncomfortable. She got up carefully, not wanting to wake the boy. He didn't look dangerous, but she'd be sure to tell Dad about him when she got back to Grandmother's.

His presence here was puzzling. The elves didn't want humans near the forest, and relied on the Dread to keep them out. But even asleep, this boy didn't seem afraid. If he'd been affected by the Dread he would have been curled up in a ball, terrified, or running wildly toward the edge of the forest, not knowing why he was fleeing or from what.

The brilliant greens of the forest were muting to shades of gray in the gathering darkness. The boy was barely visible. As the gloom deepened, it occurred to Keelie that Ariel had not cried out in a while. Maybe she was roosting somewhere. Keelie was not excited about the prospect of spending the night in the forest, looking for a lost blind hawk, and her father would start searching for her if she was late to her party.

Wings flapped overhead and Keelie looked up expectantly. Ariel, or an owl? She stared up into the soaring canopy of the trees. Dad had been right—the Dread Forest was a forest like no other. It was his home, and now it was to be hers, too. She wasn't sure she'd call it home, though. "Home" was a word like "dad"—it had to mean something. Any place where she had to clutch her rose quartz to feel comfortable could not be home.

Of course, she'd only been here one day, so maybe she'd change her mind. She could avoid Sean, and maybe after awhile it wouldn't feel like her heart was being stapled to her ribs every time she thought about him. And she'd feel a lot more optimistic once Ariel was safe.

The dried leaves of the forest floor rustled, and Keelie looked back down. The boy was gone. She looked around for a trace of his passing. Nothing. Not a moving leaf. Where had he gone, and how had he moved so silently? It was as if he'd melted into the earth. She silently wished him a speedy journey out of the Dread Forest before the elves found him.

Keelie opened herself to the trees, asking them to find him. She felt their ancient presence, the green enormity of the mature forest, but the trees didn't answer her call. Puzzling. She could feel their guarded presence, but her connection to the forest seemed to be faltering. She came from a long line of tree shepherds, and though she'd only been able to actively communicate with trees since June, she'd gotten used to it. Was she being snubbed?

Keelie cut off her attempt to contact the trees as she heard Ariel's high-pitched call. But a chill of fear trembled through her. If the trees wouldn't speak to her, finding Ariel and getting her back into her enclosure would be a lot harder.

She took a deep breath and released it slowly, trying to regain her calm, if only for Ariel's sake. The hawk always seemed to sense her emotions; the stress she'd felt about moving to the Dread Forest had made the hawk pick at the feathers on her chest until she bled. Keelie had no feathers to pick, but she understood the feeling.

Something moved to her left. Thinking it was the boy, she turned, but instead saw raised wings settle against a large shape perched on a juniper branch, which was bent low from its weight. Keelie walked slowly toward the tree, not wanting to scare Ariel away.

The tree was near the top of the ridge, and the forest below was vast, undulating and green, reaching toward the faraway road that led toward the tiny town of Edgewood. Smoke rose from a spot near the road, and Keelie had to squint against the growing darkness to see what it was. Forest fire? She put a hand on the bark of the great fir next to her, and suddenly it was as if she were wearing binoculars.

She saw the source of the fire clearly—a giant tangle of branches and wood, heaped in the center of a clearing that had been scraped out of the forest. Big yellow bulldozers and cranes were parked at the edge of the bare earth, with a small office trailer on the other side. She would ask Dad what they were doing. The Dread was losing its strength, making the forest vulnerable to humans and their industrial ways, but this was just too close.

Maybe this was where the boy had come from.

She needed to go back to Grandmother's house, although she wished she could spend more time here. She wasn't looking forward to the elf fest.

Beneath her hand the bark warmed, and she felt the tree's awareness shift to the juniper and the bird in its branches. *Do you wish for us to send the bird to you?*

Amazed, Keelie realized that Ariel's flight had been guided by the trees. If they could do this, she could bring Ariel out every day.

The juniper's branches shook, and Ariel flapped her wide wings and glided confidently toward Keelie as if she could see again. Keelie held her arm high and Ariel landed on the leather guard wrapped around Keelie's wrist. The hawk dug her talons into the leather, shifting to steady herself.

Keelie stroked the bird's throat feathers to calm her. "There, girl, didn't that feel good?" she crooned. She couldn't get mad at Ariel for wanting to take off, when she'd done the same thing.

The strong scent of evergreens surrounded her suddenly, making her feel as if she was on a Christmas tree farm. *Tree Shepherdess, your father says it is time to return to the village.* It was a tall juniper by the path. She sensed its great age, and through it, the forest around her, steeped in layers of magic, both in the air and under the earth. She could feel the soil strata beneath her, the age-old deposits, rich in magic, and something else, deeper below, that her mind shrank from.

Soon, Keelie replied.

Now! Dad's mental voice blared into her mind. Keelie immediately shut him out. She didn't want Dad talking to her telepathically. He'd been doing it more and more ever since they'd arrived at the Dread Forest, and she was afraid that he'd look into her mind as well. What if he saw what had happened with Sean? She'd been such a fool, telling him that she loved him, that she'd missed him.

Keelie, come to the gathering! You promised you would be here and your Grandmother is unhappy. If you want to fit in with the elves you need to meet them halfway. They've come to see you.

Why couldn't he get a cell phone and text her like normal people did? And she wasn't talking about one of those elf phones that used the trees as cell phone towers, either.

She tuned him out. She didn't care if Grandmother was unhappy. Keliatiel Heartwood seemed to be glad to have her son back, but she ignored Keelie except when Zeke was around. It was as if she didn't know what to do about her odd, half-human grandchild.

Keelie started walking back to the path, working to keep Ariel steady on her arm, placing her feet carefully so that she didn't slide on the pine needles. She wondered where the boy had gone, still amazed that the Dread hadn't freaked him out this far into the forest. Maybe she shouldn't tell Dad or the others either. The boy might need their help, but they might overreact if they heard that a human had been here.

As she reached the wide, sandy path that led to the elven village, she glanced back wistfully at the gloomy forest. If the boy wasn't hurt, she wished he'd stuck around to talk a little. She was lonely. Her best friend Laurie had spent a couple of weeks with her at the last Ren Faire, in New York, but Laurie was back home in L.A. now. Their older friend Raven was in college in New York City, taking a heavy class load so that she could finish early and rush back to Canooga Springs, New York. Keelie felt totally alone.

She hadn't even seen Sean until today. Lord Niriel was in charge of the jousters, and he insisted on them maintaining a rigorous training routine even in the off-season. Sean had either been busy working out with the elven jousters yesterday or avoiding her. But Keelie had been willing to wait to spend time with him. She'd been busy with Ariel and Alora, the acorn who'd been given over to Keelie's care by the Wildewood Forest's queen. In a matter of days, the acorn had quickly grown into a seedling, and now it was a treeling. It was a total brat, too. Keelie bet that was why Dad was so insistent that she go to the party. Alora was probably throwing a tantrum.

She trudged back along the path, slowing as she saw the distinctive stone-and-timber buildings that made up the elven village. She was dreading the next few hours, and maybe the whole winter ahead. A small breeze ruffled Ariel's feathers and the hawk lifted her head to catch the cool air. Keelie was glad that, at least, Ariel had flown. It was a rare occurrence, although now it could be a daily escape for both of them. Maybe Ariel would sleep soundly tonight, dreaming of swooping down on unsuspecting field mice.

Skirting her father's house, Keelie went to the workshop

in the back where she'd built a temporary mews for Ariel out of chicken wire and boards. Once she had settled the hawk, she examined the door for holes and stared, puzzled, at the smoothly-joined boards that formed the entrance. No way could Ariel have gotten out by herself, and she was sure she hadn't left the door open.

She climbed the three worn, shallow, stone steps to the house and entered the kitchen—a broad room with a stacked stone hearth at one end and an array of copper pots hanging in the center over a scarred timber table. She hurried through to the hallway that led to the paneled foyer, and then up the curving stairs to her bedroom.

So far, her bedroom had been the best part of her new life in the Dread Forest. Dad must have had folks working on it at the beginning of the summer, back when she'd first moved in with him at the High Mountain Faire in Colorado. A canopied bed dominated the room, its posts made from twisted wisteria vines that held back billowing curtains of spangled blue and purple gauze. A cherry dresser was set up on one wall, each drawer knob a carved golden apple, and above it was a large round mirror, the frame carved with realistic-looking apple branches. She loved to run her hand over the smooth, glossy wood, which sent her images of its long-ago days on a Virginia hillside, when puffy clouds and passing deer were the only movement.

The room's sole window had an extra-wide sill, which was where she'd put Alora, the acorn treeling, in her pot. The sill was vacant now, since Alora was visiting the aunties—three ancient oaks huddled together at the opposite edge of the village green. Keelie was glad, because she'd had enough of the treeling's babyish demands.

She quickly changed out of her jeans and T-shirt and tossed on the bat-sleeved velveteen medieval dress her grandmother had given her to wear tonight. Its skirts flared out from a tight bodice, but there were no buttons or zippers. It was cut so that you had to wiggle into it, and then adjust it until it fit. She clasped a jeweled belt with a silver buckle adorned with acorns and oak leaves around her hips, and she was ready to go. There was nothing that could be done about her wild, curly brown hair without a strenuous flat-ironing session, and she didn't have time. Who cared, anyway?

There was nothing she could do to make the elves think she was beautiful, or that she was one of them. She tossed aside the wimpy leather slippers that matched the outfit and put on the expensive custom boots Lady Annie had made for her at the Wildewood Renaissance Faire in New York.

Her grandmother's house was at the end of a short path that skirted the broad green common area. If any human ever saw this place, they would believe it was part of a theme park. She could picture it now: Medieval Land, complete with picturesque cottages and small strongholds, handsome elf lords, awful, wicked grandmother elves, and traitorous jousters who made you think they loved you and then left you—

She stopped and took a deep breath. This would not

do at all. She was going to march into the party and own it. She would not look bitter or betrayed. She would smile and try not to bite anyone, no matter what they said. When she felt in control again, she walked quickly to the front of the well-lit house. She could hear the buzzing of many voices through the open windows.

Keliatiel Heartwood's house was two stories tall and made of light grey stone, its jutting upper story supported by heavy dark timbers. The path that led to the front door was bordered with fragrant herbs, and in the side yard bee skeps stood on tables, angled so that bee flight paths didn't intersect the walking trail.

Keelie stepped onto the stone stoop and placed her hand hesitantly on the glass doorknob. She took a deep breath, then staggered backwards, heart hammering, as the door flew inwards and she recognized the tall, elegant elf in the opening.

"Greetings, Keliel Heartwood. I expect you thought you'd never see me again." His deep, beautiful voice was like poisonous moss, velvety and lethal.

It was Lord Elianard, the unicorn killer himself.

two

"Lord Elianard!" Keelie stepped back, putting distance between herself and the elf lord. There was major-league bad history between them. "What are you doing here?"

"Your grandmother did me the honor of inviting me to your gathering," Elianard said. "I could not refuse." He held the door open and waited for Keelie to enter.

Revolted, she remembered him draining the life force from Einhorn, the unicorn guardian of the forest above the Wildewood Faire, using a powerful amulet that Einhorn later gave to Keelie for safekeeping. Even after Elianard failed to kill the unicorn, he'd shown no remorse, claiming that everything he'd done was for the benefit of the elves. She would be safer staying outside.

"Child, where have you been?" a stern voice said. It was Grandmother Keliatiel, the Lady of the Forest, the honcho elf in charge of all the trees and magic in the Dread Forest. The older woman stood beside Elianard, the same haughty expression on both their faces. The two elves glanced at one another knowingly, as if they'd been discussing Keelie. She wondered how her grandmother could bear to be so close to him. Didn't she care? Keelie knew that Dad had told Keliatiel about what had happened in the Wildewood.

A wave of anger washing over her, Keelie stepped back, unwilling to submit to their superior attitudes. She quelled the urge to run, although it was appealing to think of getting away from her grandmother. And away from Elianard. She could camp in the Dread Forest with Ariel and Alora. As uncomfortable as it would be, it would be better than sticking around with these hypocrites. Keelie breathed deeply, sucking in the cool evening air, easing the anger that surged through her.

Something warm and furry rubbed up against her ankle, and calm filled her as claws snagged her soft leather boot. Then a very loud and comforting purring surrounded her, cushioning her in a bubble of warm, caramel sound. Knot had arrived. Keelie glanced down to see the oversized, pumpkin-colored cat sitting between her and Grandmother Keliatiel.

He blinked up at the elven elders, then thrust a leg straight up in the air and started to wash his backside with his pink tongue. Her so-called guardian and a major pain in the backside; Knot didn't pussyfoot around.

Grandmother Keliatiel looked away, her nose wrinkled in disdain, and her heavy gaze settled back on Keelie. She felt trapped by her grandmother's piercing green stare, and crossed her arms over chest, not that the gesture would protect her.

Keelie! Dad's mental shout made her brain hurt.

"Dad, I'm here," she said aloud. Keliatiel and Elianard exchanged another glance. They hadn't heard her father's call.

A moment later, Dad pushed Elianard aside and stepped outside. He looked like an elven prince tonight, with his light brown hair tied back so that his pointed ears swept up in graceful arcs, and he wore a long green riding tunic and hose, with boots that wrapped his slender legs in soft green to his knees. He enveloped her in a hug. "You took too long," he whispered.

Dad's strong arms made her feel safe and protected. She wished that all the others would disappear, that it could be just the two of them, as it had been in Colorado and New York. Their relationship was too new and too precious to share.

Grandmother's gaze turned frosty. "Zekeliel, the child is wild enough without rewarding her for her abhorrent behavior."

Dad's arms stiffened, and he dropped them to his sides. "She is my daughter, Mother, and I will raise her as I see fit."

Elianard made a *tsk, tsk* sound. "It's exactly as I told you."

"It's worse," Grandmother said. "But now is not the time or place to discuss this matter. We have guests, and Keliel has rudely kept them waiting at her own welcome gathering."

Indignant, Keelie straightened, ready to tell her grandmother exactly what she'd learned here, when Dad placed his arm around her shoulder.

"She's right," he whispered. "Let's go inside and greet your guests."

Knot finally stopped his impromptu bath and walked in the door after them.

Grandmother Keliatiel pushed a foot into his path. "Stop, fairy. You are not invited."

Knot ignored her and sauntered past her, his tail held high. The kitty tail message was clear—*kiss this*.

Grandmother Keliatiel sighed. "Let us end this tiresome evening."

For once, Keelie couldn't agree with her grandmother more.

Inside the house, the scent of cinnamon was layered through savory food smells. Keelie's stomach growled as she stepped into the tall-ceilinged great room of her grandmother's home. This was where her father grew up, she realized. Every inch of space was crowded with the gathered elves, who ate and drank, their raised voices mingled with the sound of a flute playing softly somewhere by the main hallway on the other side of the room.

Keelie smiled stiffly at the suspicious and curious looks directed her way. She was an outsider here, worse than a stranger. A human. A half-human, anyway.

The guests held earthenware mugs and plates, reminding Keelie of the pottery she'd seen for sale at Renaissance Faires. She couldn't believe that she actually felt a pang of homesickness for her father's ridiculous curlicued wooden camper, perched on the back of his old pickup truck. Events were pretty grim if she was missing the Swiss Miss Chalet. She wanted to grab her Dad and run away to check out California's Ren Faires, far from here.

Instead, she walked forward, trying to summon the fortitude to get her through this. Maybe she'd find Knot and hang out with him. Okay, now she knew she was desperate.

A familiar-looking elderly woman with long, straight silver hair was regarding her with a steady, unsmiling gaze. Keelie stared back. She could be rude, too. The woman winked, and then Keelie laughed.

"Do you remember me, child?"

"I do, but—"

"We met in the Wildewood. The Emergency Response Team?"

"Oh, yeah. The rescue rangers. I remember now. Etila…"

"Etilafael."

"Right, thanks." The elf woman had been wearing her hair in a severe knot when she'd led a team of elven healers through the disease-ravaged Wildewood, but Keelie remembered her words: *I expect great things from you.*

"What is your sense of the forest?" Etilafael was asking her. "Have you met the great trees of the Grove? The ones called the aunties?"

"I have met them, and they are caring for my treeling, Alora. I talked to a fir on the ridge earlier. He showed me the development at the base of the mountain."

Etilafael frowned. "Unfortunate, that. The mayor of the human town has allowed construction to encroach on our forest borders."

"Do the elves own the forest? I mean, legally?"

Just then Lord Niriel, Sean's father, joined them, handsome in robes embroidered with the silver branch emblem of the jousting company he led. He bowed to Etilafael.

Keelie forced herself to relax. She wouldn't show everyone how upset she was over Sean.

Lord Niriel didn't seem to notice that anything was wrong. "Keelie, I wish to welcome you formally to the Dread Forest. I see you've made the acquaintance of Lady Etilafael, the Council Head."

Keelie glanced quickly at her new friend. The head of the Council?

Lady Etilafael winked at her again. "We were talking about the mayor's project in the clearing. Keliel wondered if we owned the Dread Forest land."

Lord Niriel's face darkened. He turned to Keelie. "Elves have lived here for hundreds of years, long before men sliced up the land and sold it to each other. But we take care of our own. We own this forest, and many others. Each elven tribe is tied to their forest, and will die for it. We cannot be apart from our forest home for long."

"Then how does my dad travel to all the Ren Faires? How do you do it, Lord Niriel?" Keelie knew they spent the entire summer going from faire to faire.

"Months are as days to us, you see. A summer is not a long time."

The passage of time was another thing that made her different from the elves. For her, a summer was a long time. How many would she have in her life? Eighty? Ninety? If she was lucky.

Dad appeared at her side with an empty plate. He bowed to Etilafael and Niriel, then gave the plate to Keelie. "I bet you're hungry."

She nodded. "A little." She curtseyed to the two elves, which felt natural in her long gown. She hoped Grandmother was watching.

Dad led her to the buffet table. She was grateful for his rescue, although talking about the forest had taken her mind off of Sean. The minute Dad had mentioned hunger she'd realized she was starving, but she wanted a huge order of spicy, tangy chicken wings and a bowl of creamy sauce to dip them in, not the rabbit food that was artfully arranged on platters on the table.

"When we get home, you can have a little something else."

He'd gotten to know her well since they were reunited in Colorado. She was certain he hadn't read her thoughts, since she'd been shielding her mind. As for his ability to communicate with her mentally, well, she had to work extra hard to block that. She'd been using the little tektite amulet Sir Davey had given her, which guarded against most types of unwanted mental communication.

"I hope Alora is still with the aunties. She wasn't in my room. Not that I'm complaining."

"Yes, she's safe with them. She's a great responsibility, I agree." He smiled and nodded at a group of chatting ladies as he led her toward the buffet table. "You are doing an excellent job of caring for her."

She was glad Alora was with the aunties, but there went her excuse to bail out early.

With Dad at her side, Keelie was greeted with guarded hellos. Other elves nodded their heads in formal acknowledgement, and she returned the courtesy. Earlier today, Grandmother had given her a dusty book to read on elven culture, full of descriptions of formal gestures. The minute she passed the elves, their talk returned to the upcoming harvest festival as if she'd never existed.

She spotted Sean and her heart started to beat with rapid hummingbird pulses. What would she do if he looked at her? She would not cry.

But she felt tears thicken her throat, and she took a

deep breath and bit into a celery stick, examining it closely as she chewed.

From the edges of her vision she saw that Sean was walking toward her, smiling. He shone in the lamplight. Tall, blond, and handsome, he had been one of the jousters at her first Ren Faire, the kind of guy all the girls noticed. And he'd noticed her, Keelie.

He'd wanted to spend time with her.

He strode up to her, weaving in between elves until he was smiling down at her. The edges of his smile trembled a little, as if he were faking it. She wanted to run away.

"Welcome to the Dread Forest." A few hours ago, those words would have seemed like a promise.

"Hi," she managed to squeak out. This had to be the most miserable social moment of her life.

"How was training today?" Dad asked from the opposite side of the table, where he was loading a plate with watercress and cucumber sandwiches. He sounded totally normal.

He doesn't know, Keelie thought. He would have warned me.

"It was tough. We're implementing some new routines," Sean said.

Zeke nodded and eyed a selection of cheeses. "Your father said he found a medieval training manual full of interesting exercises."

Sean's face lit up. "Yes, and we're almost done with the new forge. We'll be producing broadswords first."

This was like guys talking about sports, except with elves it was swords. Why couldn't Sean just leave? She didn't dare step away from her father. At least with him around, Sean wouldn't want a private talk.

"I'll be on hand when your father begins folding the new leaves," Dad said, referring to the way steel blades were strengthened at the forge.

The elves nearby nodded solemnly, and a few of them glanced quickly at Grandmother Keliatiel. Keelie wondered what those looks meant.

Sean's eyes widened with surprise. "It will be an honor to have you there."

She hoped it wasn't a duty she'd have to be a part of. It sounded hot and dirty, and she didn't think she could take the sight of Sean making swords, maybe stripped to the waist, all hot and sweaty. Of course, elves didn't sweat. But still, he'd be hot.

Keelie tingled all the way from the top of her head down to her toes. Her body was a total traitor, too. Sean belonged to someone else—so stop with the excited tingles, she told herself.

Dad leaned across the table and handed the plate of watercress sandwiches to her. "Hungry?"

She took the plate and stared dismally at the green-filled sandwiches.

Someone bumped into Sean and he turned to see who'd crashed into him.

A curvy red-headed elf girl smiled up at him, bright

green eyes twinkling. "You can bump into me anytime," she said, flipping back a lock of long, curly hair. She had *hoochie* stamped all over her, from the super-tight satin dress that emphasized her teeny-tiny waist to her overflowing cleavage.

Sean's eartips turned bright red. Keelie's heart dropped. This was *her*.

The elf girl's amused gaze turned to Keelie. "Sean darling, aren't you going to introduce me to your round-eared friend?"

Sean frowned at the girl. "Keelie, this is Risa."

"Hi, nice to meet you," Keelie's words came out so frosty that it was as if she'd actually added, *not really*.

Dad made a choking sound as he tried to swallow.

Risa placed her hands on her hips. "Have you heard? Sean and I are betrothed."

"How lucky for both of you." Keelie pulled her lips away from her teeth, hoping it looked like a smile.

Grandmother Keliatiel drifted over. "Oh good, Keliel, you've met Risa. You young people should all get together."

Keelie barely managed to nod her head. She bit into one of the watercress sandwiches, then almost gagged when she realized what she'd done.

Risa placed her hand against her mouth and giggled. "I was telling your granddaughter that Sean and I are betrothed."

Sean did not meet Keelie's eyes, which were starting to feel itchy and hot. She would *not* cry in front of all these elves.

Risa leaned into Sean and placed her hand against his shoulder. Sean did not move away. Keelie swallowed hard.

A stout elf with a small pointed beard put an arm on Risa's shoulder and bowed to Keelie. "Lady Keliel, welcome to the forest. I am Hamriel, Risa's father. I farm the south face of the mountain. The vegetables we eat tonight are from my fields." He smiled fondly at his daughter, tugging her toward him. She stuck to Sean and glared at Keelie. His smile grew forced. "Risa farms as well. She is noted for her prowess with green things. Her melons are famous."

Keelie choked out, "How do you do?" She bowed in return, noting that Risa did not let go of Sean although her father clearly wanted her to do so.

Dad walked around the table and took her plate out of her hands and put it down.

"Come, Keliel, there's someone I want you to meet." When she didn't move he tugged on her elbow. "Keelie?" His voice lowered. "Just walk away."

She heard him, but she couldn't move. Her feet were frozen to the floor, and her eyes were locked on the betrothed pair. She imagined picking up her drink and throwing it into the girl's face. Or tossing the dish of messy, smelly cheeses at her.

She wondered how much of her thoughts were visible on her face. Dad was looking worried. Then a movement by the front window caught her eye—Knot, stalking some imaginary prey. He must have sensed her stare, because he stopped and turned to look at her.

She looked right into his eyes and thought hard. She kept trying to project her thoughts until his eyes widened and his mouth dropped open, flashing kitty fang in laughing appreciation.

Keelie smiled at her father. "Dad, chill. I'm fine, really." And she was. Knot was on the job.

She followed her father to the other side of the room, not even looking back at the so-called happy couple.

Moments later a stifled scream and concerned murmurs made everyone turn.

Risa's dress had split all the way up the front, exposing her underwear. Two fat white circles lay on the buffet table—Risa's cleavage. Keelie coughed to cover her laugh. So much for the famed melons. Her grandmother and several guests were busily trying to cover the distraught girl. Sean was looking either mortified or as if he was about to break into laughter.

"Well done, Round Ear. What did you do to her?" The sweet whisper in her ear made Keelie freeze. She turned her head just a little. Sure enough, her old adversary, Elia—Elianard's beautiful, haughty daughter—was standing close enough to kiss her cheek.

"Me? Not a thing." Keelie straightened. Elia was still looking at the disaster scene and now her eyes widened. A long, fluffy orange tail stuck out from under the tablecloth.

"Oops. Excuse me while I, ah, get another sandwich." Keelie raised an eyebrow. "You want anything?"

Elia blinked slowly, letting her golden lashes rest on her porcelain cheeks for a split second. "I want exactly what you want, Keliel Heartwood."

"Tough," Keelie replied, not believing a word of what Elia said. Then she put a hand to her mouth. "Oops. Did I just say that?"

Across the room Risa was glaring at them, her eyes in slits as she looked from Keelie to Elia.

"Oh, if gazes were daggers we'd be dead, Keliel," Elia purred. "Act like you're my friend."

Friend? Elia didn't even qualify as an enemy. Keelie wished she'd never met the vain, self-centered, and dangerous elf girl, but she knew that Elia just wanted to mess up Risa's head even more. And right now, Keelie wanted that as well. She was ready. The two girls put their arms around each other's waists and smiled back at Risa, who was now wrapped in a borrowed, oversized robe. Several of the elf women looked startled to see Keelie and Elia standing so close together. Keelie's father did a double take.

Good. Let them all guess.

"I've had about as much fun as I'm going to tonight." Keelie pulled her arm free and turned away.

Elia grabbed her long sleeve and tugged her close again. "Don't leave yet. Stick around."

"She's all yours. I'm going to bed." Keelie felt queasy. She must look bad if even Elia was trying to make her feel better. No wait, that couldn't be. This was *Elia*.

Someone was plucking a lively tune on a harp, and Keelie jumped. Harps always signaled bad magic.

"Relax. Mine broke, remember?" Elia hissed.

Keelie didn't relax. Elia's magic had been potent.

Dad was with his mother, who was trying to soothe Risa, now surrounded by a crowd of sympathetic onlookers. Keelie headed toward the door, eager to slip outside.

"Now you've had your fun, so you're sneaking out, Keliel?" Risa's raised voice stopped the party noise. She was stalking toward Keelie, her hands clenched like claws.

Keelie faced her red-faced rival. "I've done nothing to harm you, Risa." If she took one step closer, she'd clock the wench.

The elf girl pulled the borrowed bathrobe tighter around her body. "You think you're so important, don't you. Tree Shepherd. Granddaughter of the Lady of the Forest. But for all that, what are you really? You just appear out of nowhere and suddenly you can do magic and talk to the trees."

Faces turned from one girl to the other, as if evaluating them. They didn't look shocked, and Keelie wasn't surprised. Maybe Risa was just saying what they had thought all along. Keelie felt her expression freeze, her cheeks cold and stiff as if made out of clay.

"Why would I hurt you, Risa? This is my party."

Risa screamed, and threw a platter of sandwiches at her. Keelie ducked and it hit the window draperies behind her. "You're evil," Risa shrieked. "Round Ears sent you to destroy us. Your so-called family is under a spell. You aren't related to them. Changeling!"

The chick had gone psycho. Grandmother's face was

pale with shock. Dad was pushing his way through the crowd toward Keelie.

A mighty bang thundered through the room, making the windows rattle. Etilafael swept forward, a tall crystal-encrusted staff in one hand. "This will cease," she commanded. "Such behavior. Lord Hamriel, remove your daughter from this house."

Lord Hamriel scuttled forward, head bowed apologetically. "Lady Keliatiel, a thousand pardons. I don't know what has come over my beloved daughter. High strung, you know."

"I am not!" Risa cried. She started to sob. "She thinks she can have my fiancé, too. Just look at her."

Knot jumped up onto the table, his puffed-out tail swishing back and forth like a pumpkin-colored toilet brush.

Risa's eyes squinted almost shut. "I hate cats. And you are no cat. It was you who destroyed my pumpkins last year with fairy magic."

She picked up a pitcher of honey wine and threw it at him. The pitcher's handle caught on a tray and tumbled across the table, drenching Knot in sticky, honey-scented wine. His back arched and he hissed at her, swatting the air with an extended paw that seemed to have claws like hypodermic needles. Seconds later he vanished, leaving a puddle of honey wine on the table where he'd stood.

Keelie took advantage of the commotion and slipped outside. Elia was leaning against the rough stone of the outer wall, laughing.

"That was perfect. How did Knot destroy her gown so thoroughly?" She bent over, trying to catch her breath. She waved at the air in front of her face, as if trying to waft more oxygen close.

"It wasn't funny. No one in that room will ever forget that scene. And it was supposed to be my party, too." Keelie tried to frown, but a smile split her face. "Did you see her bra stuffing on the table like two biscuits?" She laughed, setting Elia off again. The two held on to each other, howling, tears streaming down their faces.

"Hrm." Elianard had followed them outside, and was now clearing his throat to get their attention. A frown furrowed his aristocratic face. "Elia, it is time to go home."

Elia wiped her face with the palms of her hands. "Good evening to you, Keliel of the Honey Wine."

Keelie snorted. "And good night to you as well, Elia of the Snarky Comments."

Moments later, Knot was at her side, his fur dry and soft as if the whole incident had been her imagination.

"Well done, Snot," Keelie said, aiming a kick at Knot's rear. He purred like an outdoor motor and moved faster to avoid her boot. Weird kitty. He didn't like to be loved on, saving his purrs for when she threatened him.

She looked toward the ridge. Was the boy still out there? If he was, he'd be in for a long, cold night. It got chilly here after dark. It was a hike to get out there, but maybe she'd run into him again. She shook her head. What was she thinking? She'd had enough of boys for one night. She detoured past the aunties to pick up Alora.

"Let me stay longer, please?" The little treeling spoke aloud instead of telepathically (or in what Keelie called "tree speak"). Alora was in a new, larger terra-cotta pot that would accommodate her spreading root system. The magical acorn had grown quickly on their trip from New York to Oregon, much to Keelie's dismay.

"Nope. Time to get inside."

Thank you, Great Ones, for sharing your knowledge with Alora. Keelie knew that they probably were aware that they were called the aunties, but she didn't want to offend them.

All is well, Tree Shepherdess. The treeling learns much.

Yeah. Keelie moved her skirts aside and picked up the heavy clay pot. The treeling glittered in the moonlight, its branches hung with just about every earring and bracelet that Keelie owned; this was all thanks to her friend Laurie, who had gotten Alora hooked on her own love of sparkly jewels during the trip. In Portland, Keelie and Dad had put Laurie on a train to California, and now she was safe at home in Los Angeles, Keelie's old home, while Keelie was stuck in the north woods with a potted princess and a lying, cheating, scuzzbag former boyfriend.

She lugged Alora home, tripping over her skirts in the dark. The whole way, Alora complained about the salt content of Keelie's tears.

three

Keelie's head was pounding, and she knew it wasn't her father at her bedroom door anymore. He'd left the hall outside her door hours ago, tired of trying to coax her out. She hadn't heard another word since his boots had stomped downstairs.

She was not going out, not to a world where Sean was engaged to marry some redheaded elf witch. She rubbed her burning eyes. Her hopes for a romance with Sean were ruined, although at least Risa was the one who had been humiliated. She wondered what Risa was thinking.

Elia's presence might not be all bad—at least Keelie

had an ally against the elf witch, which made tolerating her elf frenemy not so excruciating. Of course, from Elia's point of view it might be different. She had claimed Sean O' the Woods for herself long ago, and had hated to see him with Keelie.

Sean had been a bright spot in Colorado, a distraction when she'd been overcome with grief after her mother's death. The best-looking of the handsome jousters at the High Mountain Faire, he was the only one who'd been really nice to her. He'd even kissed her, and when he arrived at the Wildewood Faire in New York, he'd acted as if he were her boyfriend. She'd hoped they could spend time together. Now she had no friends, no social life, and even her so-called boyfriend was gone. He'd lied to her, too, in not telling her about Risa.

Keelie had felt all of her hard-won cool slip away when she saw him with Risa. She was the Tree Shepherd's daughter—she could work tree magic and Earth magic. She had saved the life of a unicorn and, before that, a sprite, as well as survived a crush on a pirate and the death of her mother. But this betrayal had smashed her flat.

All she'd ever wanted was a regular life and a little happiness. Right now the only thing she had to look forward to was whatever revenge Elia would cook up against Risa. At least it was sure to be entertaining, and definitely better than being the object of the vindictive elf girl's rage herself.

Sir Davey's visit would be fun, too. He was coming for the harvest festival in a few weeks, when the elves of the Dread Forest played nice with their human neighbors in town. She couldn't wait to see him again. He was the most down-to-earth person that Keelie knew—so to speak. His real name was Jadwyn, and he was an expert in Earth magic. His lessons had helped Keelie deal with her new tree magic.

He was also three feet tall, and liked to dress like one of the Three Musketeers. One of the first magical things she'd noticed at the High Mountain Faire was that the snowy white plume on Sir Davey's hat seemed to never get dirty, even when she accidentally splattered it with mud. She rubbed the tektite that he'd given her.

The night outside her window was dark, but Keelie was used to it. Away from the cities, and with no streetlights, the faires had been lit only by the moon at night. Tonight's overcast skies meant what little light they would have had was bouncing off the cloud cover.

Dad was downstairs, worried about her, if he hadn't gone to bed already. She bit her lip. It wasn't his fault that Sean was a cheating liar. Her father wanted her to belong, to accept and be accepted by the life she'd been born into—the life her mother had taken her from when Keelie was only two years old.

She sat up, crossed to the carved dresser, and looked at herself in the mirror. Same old self. Curly brown hair, green eyes, and under the curls, one pointed ear, one round ear. At least her eyes weren't red from crying. Despite the few tears she'd shed, but she was mostly angry.

Why hadn't Sean told her about Risa earlier? She would have understood. Maybe.

"I need water." Alora said. The wide window ledge held a willow basket with twisted rope handles, the home of Alora in her clay pot.

"Alora, I watered you this morning. You won't need more until tomorrow."

"But I'm thirsty now. I want that bubbly water that Laurie gave me."

Keelie ignored her. Unlike her conversations with other trees, talking to Alora was almost normal—if you counted Alora's whining and wheedling, and Keelie's refusals to give in, as "normal."

"Just a little drink? My leaves are wilting, see?" The little oak leaves that lined the seedling's thin branches suddenly drooped. "And they're getting spotty. I think I'm sick."

Keelie walked over to the treeling and examined its leaves. She smiled. "Alora, your leaves are changing color because autumn's not far off. Soon they'll be bright reds and yellows, and then they'll fall. By next Spring you'll have all new leaves. Shiny new green ones."

The treeling had gone silent, and its little branches were quaking, making the earrings hanging from them bounce and jingle.

"Alora, what's wrong?"

"I'll lose my leaves?"

"Didn't your mother oak tell you that?"

"I never talked to her. When I was an acorn, I remember

being warm in the earth, and the sound of the forest all around me. Then I remember pushing through the earth, and there you were. And that cat."

"Didn't the aunties tell you about the seasons?" Keelie couldn't believe she was having a birds and bees discussion with a tree.

"The aunties are nice," Alora said. "They told me stories of the Dread Forest. Did you know that I have the Dread, too? I just haven't learned how to use it yet."

"You can hold off on that as long as you like." The last thing she needed was a tree radiating the curse in her own bedroom.

Alora's leaves had perked up as they talked, and Keelie realized that she was feeling better, too. Moping in her bedroom wouldn't resolve anything.

"Alora, I have to talk to my dad. I'll catch you later."

"But it's later now."

"Don't whine. I'll come to bed in a little while. You can still talk to me, in my head."

"Not so much. The farther away you go the less I can hear you. The trees around here are too big, and there are too many of them."

"So may it remain," Keelie said automatically. "See, I'm catching up." Catching up after years of living in L.A., away from the forests. She closed her eyes and tried to conjure up a mental image of where her father was, and immediately saw him at a table in the living room, a sketchbook in front of him. He was working on furniture designs. He looked up, as if he'd felt her mind probing for him, then returned to his work.

Keelie opened her bedroom door and stepped into the hallway. No strange portraits here, as at her grandmother's house. A colorful woven cloth hung on the wall, and at the top of the stairs, a kite shaped like a leaping salmon floated from its string, whirling around whenever a draft caught it.

She remembered that kite from when she was little—it had been a disturbing object when seen through toddler eyes. She always swore that her father kept a giant fish in his house, and it swam around on the stairs. Her mother had told her to stop talking nonsense, and the memory had faded, only to return when she'd walked into the house yesterday.

The stairs at the end of the hall curved like the whorl of an ear, and she walked down with her fingertips on the polished banister (mahogany, from an exotic forest, far away). In her head she practiced how she would apologize.

"Feeling better?" Her father's quiet voice interrupted the silence, but still seemed a part of it. He was so at home here. And he seemed energized, as if his home forest fed some need that had been drained during his travels.

"Not much. I wanted to say that I'm sorry, Dad. I was causing problems, and you didn't deserve it." She got it all out in one breath. Not the smoothest, but it worked.

Dad's face relaxed and he stood and opened his arms wide. She slid into his embrace and put her cheek on his shoulder, grateful for his warm, strong presence. She'd never had this before, not in her whole life. Until she came to live with him, she only remembered her mother's hugs. Mom was always busy, so, sweet as they were, the hugs never lasted long enough.

One thing that pleased her about the elves was that they lived a long time. Dad was already over three hundred years old. He wouldn't leave her like Mom had. He wouldn't die.

"We need to talk, Keelie. Sit down."

She crossed to one of the armchairs on the other side of the fireplace and sat on the edge of the seat cushion. He was going to blast her and she'd take it, but she wouldn't take back the pleasure of seeing Risa's humiliation. That had felt just right, even if it had made Risa explode.

Dad paced before the crackling fire. "Your grandmother is a strong woman, with strong opinions," Dad said. "But she's weakening. She's not as she once was."

Holy cow. If this was weak, she must have been the Terminator before. "Is she sick?"

He shook his head. "Very old. And tired. Humans encroach more on the forest every day, and the Dread is weakening. She's getting tired of fighting.

Keelie thought of the development at the bottom of the ridge.

Her father continued. "So now, as her sole heir, I must take over some of her duties. I must be at the forge when they start the new swords, preside over all public ceremonies and celebrations, communicate with the other forests and their tree shepherds, *and* serve on the Council." He turned to look at Keelie. "You know how much I hate this added business. I'd much rather stay in the forest as a tree shepherd."

"You're still a tree shepherd, right?" She couldn't imagine Dad away from the trees—although in this forest, that wouldn't really be possible.

"Yes, of course. These are added responsibilities. I still have to do my work."

"So why don't you guys just beef up the Dread? I'd have to live in a tektite tent, but that would stop the construction and logging, right?"

"Yes, it would. It's not so simple, though." He looked into the fireplace, watching the flames greedily devour the bark from the logs. "I will need your help, Keelie."

"Sure." She could oversee the studly sword-making at the forge. No problem. She pictured sweaty elf guys banging on steel. On second thought, maybe it would be a little too … rustic.

"To begin with, you're to start classes with the Lore Master in the morning," Dad continued. "And don't grumble about it. Do me proud."

The Lore Master? The Elven Lore Master was none other than Lord Elianard. "Who else is going to be in school with me?" Keelie asked quickly.

"As far as I know, you're the only one. Risa was the last baby born in the Forest, and that was years ago."

"I'll bet everyone was disappointed. Especially her parents."

Dad frowned at her. "Risa's already finished with school."

"I guess she got her Melon diploma. Heh."

"This is serious, Keelie. It signals the end of our people."

Keelie suddenly realized that she'd seen no children here. Weird. She'd never seen an elf child anywhere, now that she thought about it. "So where are all the kids?"

Her father sighed. "We'll talk about that another time. It's a tragic tale."

"You sound like a movie trailer." Keelie rolled her eyes, and then something else occurred to her. "Where do elves go to college?"

Dad shrugged. "An Elven Lore Master will teach you more than the humans' universities ever will, but I went to college because I wanted to know more about the mundane world. That's where I met your mother, of course. You'll be the only student at our school right now, and Elianard will concentrate only on you. You'll be safe, Keelie. Knot and the trees themselves will watch over you."

She hoped it would be enough.

"Elianard hates me. Why are you doing this to me, Dad? Have you forgotten what happened with Einhorn? What if Elianard tries to kill me?"

"Elianard will not hurt you. He knows his duty, and besides, he's not as strong as he once was. He has great respect for our ways—he will not go against Keliatiel's wishes."

Keelie thought of her grandmother and wondered what Keliatiel's true wishes were.

Her stomach cramped as she considered hours alone with her least favorite person. Peachy.

four

The next morning, Keelie reluctantly headed to her first class. She left the house and started across the green (which was rightly named—the grass would have made a leprechaun proud). She stopped suddenly, wondering if leprechauns were real. Given the creatures she'd seen so far, they probably were. Her life had changed so drastically from the busy and organized existence she'd once had in Los Angeles with her mother.

Keelie felt a pang at the memory of her mom, who'd died in the spring. Sometimes it felt like forever, then other times it felt as if the accident had happened only days ago.

Still other times she was overwhelmed with the desire to call Mom and share something she'd seen, or heard, or thought. Those were the moments that haunted her the most.

Keelie headed toward the other side of the village. The green was busy today, full of elves preparing for the harvest festival. A cart full of pumpkins sat on the side of the trail. Keelie glanced across the green to where the massive aunties stood, towering above the other oaks that ringed the space. Their great roots extended toward the Caudex, the petrified remains of an ancient tree that had once stood in the center. The base of the Caudex now held the Council thrones.

The Lore House was on a rise just past the last house in the village. Long and squat, it sat like a great half-timbered toad, its windows glinting in the sun.

Elianard was waiting for her by the front door, reading a book that was spread open across his lap.

"Good morrow, Lord Elianard," she said, summoning her father's lessons in elf etiquette. *Elfiquette.* She was sure no one here called it that. All the more reason to enjoy the sound of it.

Elianard glared at her with cold green eyes, showing how little he wanted to be there. "You are late." He indicated an empty wooden armchair next to his. "Sit, our first lesson will be witnessed by the trees. Tell me what you know of elven lore."

Keelie walked to the chair and lowered herself slowly

into its smooth, wide seat (oak, from this forest). "I know the Dread makes me nauseous, that Red Caps are dangerous fairies, and that unicorns are vulnerable." Green eyes met green, two shades of the forest, and held for a moment before his slid away.

Three hours later, Keelie's mind was as numb as her backside, suffering from an overdose of elf history—the migration from Europe had done in most of it.

Elianard must have noticed her glazed eyes. "What do they teach humans in your schools?"

"Lots." She tried not to sound defensive.

"Name some examples, please."

"History, math, geometry, and science."

Elianard sneered. "Science. Human scientists think they know so much about the Earth, but they don't. They think that nothing is real if they can't prove its existence. A scientist would tell you the Dread is not real." He pointed at Keelie and arched an eyebrow. "But you know differently, don't you, Keliel? As a human, you may not know what it is, but you feel its effect."

"What is the Dread, exactly? And aren't you supposed to teach me how to handle it?" She picked up the book, which Elianard had placed on a table. "I'll bet there's nothing in your lore about the Dread."

Elianard snatched the Lore Book from her and opened it to a passage written in flowing script. He read aloud: "'Building a Tolerance to the Dread. Should the Dread affect you, build a tolerance by exposing yourself to it for increasingly long periods of time. If done on consecutive days, your body will build a magical barrier against the fear the Dread's magic creates.'"

Exposing herself. She thought of herself naked among the Aunties. She didn't want the trees to see her naked.

"Duh. I *am* in the woods; I've been exposing myself to the Dread day and night." She pulled the pink crystal from her pocket. "This is what works for me."

Elianard smirked. "Earth magic. Without your quartz, without the tektite, you're open to the Dread, but soon your own magic will be able to protect you. Do not depend on objects to magnify your power. Even if your purpose is for the higher good, you'll pay a high price."

"You should know," Keelie said. Although she didn't mention the unicorn, the tension in the air was palpable.

Elianard ignored her jibe and turned the Lore Book over. He pointed to a symbol on the back—a wavy-lined, concentric circle with a thorn-wrapped acorn hanging from the outer edge. Keelie stared at it. It was the same symbol as on Elianard's amulet, which was now hidden in her room. But it was also a mirror image of one she had just seen recently.

She remembered it now. Grandmother's book.

"Look closer." Elianard said, pushing the book toward Keelie.

The symbol seemed to move. It pulled at her, and she lifted her hand, stretching her fingers out to touch it. A chill emanated from it, deepening until it made her fingernails throb. She pulled back and rubbed her fingers together.

Knot hopped into Keelie's lap, breaking her trance with loud purring and kneading her with his paws. The symbol was once again just a picture in a book. What was it about the spiral and the acorn that had put her under its spell? She reached out toward it again. Knot sank his claws into her leg. She gasped.

"Did you feel its power? Even a drawing in a book can summon the magic from within you and make it stronger." Elianard said. "I think—"

Knot's purring grew so loud that Keelie couldn't hear Elianard over the feline roar. The symbol seemed to grow, and she was lost in longing to touch the acorn. Her finger reached for it once more. What would happen if she followed the grooves, touching each curve?

Something touched her arm and she jumped up, startled. Knot tumbled to the ground.

"Is everything okay?" Dad stood over her. Relief welled up in Keelie as his hand closed around her upper arm, giving her the extra support she needed.

Knot meowed at Keelie as if he was scolding her for dropping him, then walked away with his tail bushed out. He wasn't happy. He had a cool cat image to maintain and somebody, or something, was going to pay. Some unsuspecting *feithid daoine* was going to be on his hit list, but Keelie wasn't worried—the bug fairies always retaliated.

Knot was sure to come home pink, or shaved, or smelling weird.

Elianard slowly rose from the bench and said, "I was advising Keelie to expose herself to the Dread without the shielding magic of her rose quartz. She needs to build her natural resistance, now that she lives among us. She can't rely on rocks and crystals to keep the Dread at bay." He held out the book.

Dad took the book from him.

Keelie's heart raced, wondering what would happen when she saw the symbol again. It was eerily hypnotic, and so enticing. Her fingers still tingled, wanting to touch it. Dad turned the book over and ran his hand over its smooth binding.

The symbol wasn't there.

Dad touched the embossed oak tree on the front cover, then nodded at Elianard. "I think you should try it, Keelie."

"No way am I going to walk around the Dread Forest without my quartz or tektite." She was resigned to living here, but to go without any protection was like throwing her in a lake and telling her to swim. She wasn't going to do it.

Grandmother Keliatiel appeared behind Dad. "Good morrow, Tree Shepherd, Lore Master. And Keelie. How did your lessons go this morning?"

"I'm amazed humans have survived as long as they have," Elianard said, then sniffed.

Keelie hoped this was the beginning of a cold.

"I didn't expect you to come here, Mother." Dad didn't seem surprised to see her, though. "I came to ask Keelie and Lord Elianard a question."

Her grandmother nodded her head regally. She was really beautiful, in a white-haired, elderly way. Too bad her insides weren't as nice. Definitely not a bake-cookies-and-cuddle kind of granny. "Very well. I came to inform our Keliel that Lord Niriel has generously consented to give her lessons in swordsmanship and horseback riding."

"Fencing lessons?" Keelie asked. She'd fenced at Baywood Academy one semester, but had stopped when Laurie wanted them to run cross-country instead because the shorts would show off their legs.

"No, fencing is with foils and rapiers," Dad said. "Niriel will teach you to use a broad sword."

"That sounds dangerous." The Faire jousters wore swords, and they hacked away at each other after all of their lances were broken and tossed aside. Even choreographed, it looked deadly.

"You are going to learn how to use a sword." Grandmother glowered at her. "It is part of our history and part of our culture, and I expect you to understand every aspect of our society."

Elianard stood up. "If you'll excuse me, I am expected at Lord Hamriel's house. I've been invited to a celebratory tea in honor of his daughter's betrothal." His voice was strained, as if it was an effort to be polite when saying this out loud.

Keelie winced. She wondered what he really thought about the engagement of his daughter's old boyfriend, but she thrust aside the train of thought. She'd tried very hard not to think of Sean and Risa's betrothal again, but hearing it from Elianard was like having a broad sword stab her through the heart.

Grandmother Keliatiel looked at Keelie. She thought she saw a concerned expression flash across her face, but it disappeared quickly. Dad's hand was once again on Keelie's shoulder, offering support. Keelie fought tears, imagining Knot making an appearance at the betrothal ceremony and causing havoc.

It didn't help.

Later, at Grandmother's house, Keelie slumped in a chair at the dining table as Grandmother poured tea into blue glazed pottery mugs that looked a lot like the ones Ellen the potter had made at the High Mountain Faire. The peppermint tea's aroma was bracing and delicious.

Dad passed her a plate with a slice of pumpkin bread. Keelie accepted it, but ignored it after she set it down by her cooling tea.

Outside, Ariel would be getting restless, but Keelie couldn't take her out until she'd had her fencing lesson.

Dad motioned with his head, and Keelie knew what it meant. Sit up.

She did, even though she wasn't feeling all elfy and regal.

She sipped her tea, then reached for Dad's sketch book and pencil and began drawing in a corner of one of his design pages. The symbol had been etched into her mind. Maybe if she drew it, she could purge it from her imagination.

Grandmother folded her hands together in her lap. "I understand that you feel that Sean has betrayed you, but you must understand that he faced a difficult choice. Wisely, he chose the good of his people over his desires."

Keelie drew some more. She'd heard this kind of bogus thinking before.

Dad refilled her teacup with peppermint tea. Keelie sat a little straighter.

"You see Keelie," Grandmother continued, "the elves have a different way of thinking. Our ways are a living link to history. Back in time, the royal marriages of Europe were based on what alliances were best for the countries, to keep the peace or ensure what was best for society." Grandmother waved her hand vaguely. "Elianard said you had studied history in school."

Keelie continued to draw the symbol, focusing on the thorn-wrapped acorn that dangled from its coiled end. She felt her magic flow through her.

Dad cleared his throat. "Keelie, Sean didn't know about the betrothal until he arrived here. It is something Niriel arranged with Risa's father. They think they have a chance of—"

"—of having a child, an elven child, a pureblood elven child." Grandmother's eyes sparkled with excitement at the prospect of a pureblood elf child. Sean was to be little more than a breeder.

From the corner of her left eye, Keelie watched as Dad lowered his head into his hand. At least he understood what impact the word "pureblood" had on Keelie. Her eyes focused again on her drawing. Dad had married a human—that must have really torqued the old lady's karma. Keelie's very presence was an insult to elves everywhere.

She drew some more, and the symbol had a meditative and calming effect on her. She should really be mad at her grandmother, but right now she felt detached, not a part of the scene taking place around her.

Oblivious, Grandmother continued. "Surely Keelie knows about procreation. It is my understanding that human girls know about these things very early."

"I guess *pureblood* elven girls don't learn about sex until they're over 200." Keelie shaded in the thorns on the acorn.

Grandmother's mouth sagged open, as if hearing Keelie sav "pureblood" finally made her realize the impact of the word on her son and his halfblood daughter.

"Keelie, if things were different, Sean would be here with you. As it is, elves are bound by the rules, rituals, and customs of our culture—it defines who we are, and it keeps a balance in the magic." Dad frowned at Keelie's sketch.

To Keelie this sounded like "Blah, different, blah Sean, blah rules, rules, rules."

"And besides, you're only fifteen in human years," Dad added.

Yeah, and Sean was what? Eighty? Keelie frowned. She didn't want to be here. She didn't want to discuss this at all, much less with her human-prejudiced grandmother.

"Interestingly enough," Keelie said. "When Elianard was giving me my Lore lesson today he showed me this symbol on a book. It's the opposite of the one on the book in your library, Grandmother. What does it mean?" She turned the sketchbook around so that they could see her drawing.

Grandmother Keliatiel dropped her mug and it crashed to the floor, splashing peppermint tea on her skirts. She stood and wiped angrily at them with her napkin, sneaking looks at the sketchbook in between swipes.

There was a knock at the door. Dad gently took the sketchbook from Keelie and closed it. "We'll talk about this later."

"That's Niriel." Grandmother said. "He's here to escort Keelie to her next lesson."

Keelie twirled her finger in the air. "Woohoo, can't wait. Do you think he'll know what this symbol means?"

"No," Grandmother hissed. She took a deep breath. "Do not mention that book to anyone."

"Whatev." Keelie channeled her California mall girl to create a protective barrier against her Grandmother's words, all the while thinking that she had to find out what the book was all about.

"I'll get the door, Mother. You stay here and rest."

Grandmother started to bend down to retrieve the broken mug pieces, but collapsed backward in her chair.

"I'll get it." Keelie picked up the broken pieces of ceramic and wiped up the spilled tea with the kitchen towel Grandmother handed her. Her sketch had gotten such a big reaction. What was it, and why didn't they want to talk about it?

It was unsettling to see her grandmother grow limp and need help, but she was probably faking it, Keelie thought. Looking sick to manipulate everyone to do her bidding.

"Lord Niriel is waiting for you outside." Dad nodded to Keelie, then crouched next to his mother's chair. "Are you all right?"

Keelie left, disgusted. Niriel was not by the door. She could hear Ariel's cries. The hawk sounded upset. Keelie hurried around to the side of the house.

She looked around quickly. Niriel stood near the path to the mews, watching her. He wore a sword in a scabbard on his belt and held another scabbarded sword in his hand. Keelie didn't want him near the hawk—she knew he'd been involved with Elianard's plan to use the Wildewood unicorn's magic to shore up the Dread, although she couldn't prove it. Besides, it was his idea to marry his son to Risa, so it was his fault that Keelie's heart was broken.

Ariel cried out and beat her wings.

"A pity to see something so beautiful and majestic caged.

Maybe her life would be better ended than letting her sit in darkness, listening to the wind blowing through the trees," Niriel commented.

"I think there's hope for her. I'll make her better, and until I'm proved wrong, she'll live." Keelie didn't mention the trees helping the hawk to fly. That was her secret.

Niriel bowed his head. "True, but not everyone has the habit of hope. There are some who foresee the approaching darkness even on the brightest days." He turned to Keelie's father, who had come out of the back door to check on her. "Do you not agree, Zeke?"

"I agree with Keelie. Hope conquers the darkness."

"And that is exactly why Sean and Risa have been betrothed. Their child will be the hope of the elves—the next generation. And you're not alone in being upset, Keelie. I understand Elia is unwell."

Keelie didn't care how Elia felt. Even though the elf girl had been friendly recently, it didn't mean that they were going to be buddies. She was probably plotting to get Sean back, and if Keelie fell for her charm she would only end up lonely and embarrassed.

Grandmother wanted her to learn all about elves—but one thing she knew already was that some of them couldn't be trusted. She was learning a lot, and all of it was bad.

five

"So, are you ready for your lesson? We won't go far, just to the forge." Niriel gestured toward the long buildings that housed the forge and stables.

"I'm not sure about this, Keelie." Dad looked worried. "You don't have to do this today. You've had a lot of upsets."

"I'm fine." Disgusted with herself, Keelie marched toward the path.

Niriel arched his eyebrow at her father as she passed him. "Problems?"

"No," Dad said.

She was grateful to Dad, and a sense of protectiveness

toward him welled up in her. She didn't want to embarrass him in front of Niriel. She didn't want Sean or Risa to hear that she couldn't handle a lesson. She would trudge forward and do this, even if she just wanted to return to the woods with Ariel.

"Let's get started," she said.

Niriel caught up with her, and together they walked toward the forge. "How was your Lore lesson?" His voice was deep and smooth. He looked and sounded like a movie star, but Keelie didn't trust him.

"It was okay." Okay like a snore fest.

The sound of clashing steel came from inside the forge, along with shouts and laughter. Sean was probably in there. A few weeks ago she would have been antsy, hoping to catch a glimpse of him. Today he was Risa's fiancé and she hoped he stayed inside.

"As you are aware, the forge is where the young men work metal, each making his own sword and jousting armor. We'll stay out here."

They sat on a great tree root, and Niriel launched into a long and boring lecture about the various metals in a sword. Keelie felt her eyes getting heavier and heavier as he droned on, but came fully awake with a start as he said, "And now Keelie Heartwood, you'll begin your first lesson."

He stood up and drew a gleaming silver sword, as long as her arm, from the scabbard he was carrying. "Take it." He tossed the scabbard aside.

She got up carefully and held out her hand, wondering if the sword would zap her like in the movies. Or maybe hundreds of armed men would come at her, screaming, from the woods. Instead, her fingers closed around the warm brown hilt. It was made from a piece of leather, and crisscrossed hundreds of times with a black silk cord to make a firm, hard surface.

She lifted the sword's tip, then dropped it again. It was a strange feeling, but exciting. She suddenly wanted to learn how to use this weapon. She whirled to face Niriel, and he backed quickly away.

She laughed. "Sorry. I wasn't going to hurt you."

"There are rules, Keliel, about the wielding of live steel."

She studied the blade. She knew he meant that the sword blade was naked, unsheathed, but it seemed to her that the sword might indeed be alive.

"I'm ready, Lord Niriel."

But she wasn't ready for the swift attack. His sword was out and at her throat, cold and hard, a second later. How had he moved so quickly?

She felt the sharpness on her skin a little longer, and then he released her. She stumbled forward, her own useless weapon drooping in her nerveless fingers.

"You must always be prepared for an attack, Keliel. You must hold the sword up, not like some wilting lily, and balance on your feet so that you are prepared to move, to react, without thought, without clumsiness."

She watched him leap back, then stand, knees slightly bent, eyes focused on her, a predatory smile on his face. She licked her dry lips. He'd gone from cool, handsome elf lord to dangerous animal.

"I don't think I can do this."

He stood taller, and the animal grace dropped like a discarded cloak. "Come now, where's the brave girl who led the charge into the Wildewood, who rescued Lord Einhorn? She wasn't afraid."

"She didn't have to use a sword, either." His words did make her feel stronger. She lifted the sword, which was heavy and awkward. She had a new appreciation for the swordsmen she'd seen at the faire. They made it look so easy, but this was like carrying a giant butter knife. A sharp one.

For the next hour, Niriel led her in exercises. They moved forward and backward, and she always kept the sword up, not letting it flag. When they stopped, her thighs, right arm, and shoulders were on fire.

"When do I get to hit something?" she asked, panting and leaning against a tree (oak, a young sapling).

"Oh, now we're bloodthirsty." Niriel grinned. "You can practice against a dummy, but not yet. I don't want you to fracture a bone or rupture a muscle. Little by little." He tilted his head. "I didn't think that Zekeliel's daughter would have the makings of a fighter, but you're swift, and you catch on to the moves quickly for a—" he paused.

"For a girl?" she supplied. "Or for a Round Ear?"

He rolled his eyes. "I was going to say, for a city dweller."

"Oh." Embarrassed that she'd accused him of sexism and racism, she studied the handle of her sword, remembering her lesson on its parts. The pommel was the round thing at the end, and it balanced the long part, the blade. The hilt, the part she held, was made of strong wood with steel running through it. "Is this a broadsword?"

"Yes. It does not have a basket hilt to protect your hand, and its blade is long and two-edged all the way to the hilt. This is a light one, for practice. When you have learned more, if you wish to continue, I'll let you use a heavier one."

Heavier than this? It was torture just to lift the thing a few inches.

"Tired, aren't you? We'll put our swords away and practice again in a couple of days. You might want to rub liniment in your shoulder tonight."

"Thanks, I'll see if Dad has any. Can I keep the sword tonight?"

Niriel's eyebrows rose. Maybe he thought she was going to murder his son. Or him. He shrugged. "Of course you may. Wipe it down tonight before you go to bed, and don't let it get wet or it will rust."

"Thanks." She took a deep breath. "It was fun." There. That had hurt more than her shoulder.

Niriel nodded gravely. "You must learn our ways, Keliel, but it doesn't have to be torture, you know. This is a big step. Your father will be pleased."

She noted that he didn't mention her grandmother.

Later that afternoon, Keelie sat on the ridge watching the construction going on below by the road. Above her, Ariel cried out as if warning all the songbirds she was hungry.

The discovery that the hawk could fly, "seeing" the world through the trees' vision, had eased Keelie's stress and guilt.

"You'll never catch anything that way," she called to Ariel, rubbing her shoulder. Her arm ached from the sword fighting.

She leaned back against the nearest tree (hemlock) and smiled down at the tiny people at the construction site. She imagined them as tiny people living on a puppet stage, even though they were normal-sized humans and very far away from her life in the woods with the elves.

The harvest festival was only weeks away. She couldn't wait to see Sir Davey again. The festival wouldn't be anything like a Renaissance Faire, but it would be fun to walk around the town in costume. She couldn't wait to carve a pumpkin.

Her right hand smoothed out the soil in a small area, pushing aside leaves and sticks, and then her finger began to trace a design in the earth. A spiral, starting small, grower wider. A tickle on her arm drew her attention. It was a *bhata*, crawling down the bark of the tree. It walked slowly into the clear circle and seemed to examine her drawing.

Keelie waited, examining the little creature, wondering if it was the one who had accompanied her from New York. She called the *bhata* the stick fairies, because they seemed to be a collection of sticks and moss and berries. Sir Davey said that they were air spirits who used bits of the forest to make themselves a body. Knot liked to tear them apart. They always put themselves back together again. And then they'd chase Knot, pinching and poking him with their stick limbs. She'd even seen a *bhata* ride Knot like a cowboy.

She reached a fingertip out and touched one of the thin branch pieces that served as a leg for this one. It didn't seem to notice as it concentrated on the symbol.

Ariel called from above, pulling Keelie out of her trance-like state.

"I just about hypnotized myself looking at one of those," she said aloud.

The *bhata* turned sideways and cocked a scrap of moss to one side like a bad toupee.

"I'm just saying. Call it a warning among friends." She leaned forward to smooth away the design, but the *bhata*, moving incredibly fast, stopped her by poking a stick between her fingers.

"Ouch." Keelie drew her hand back and stared at the red spot in the tender webbing between her fingers. A drop of blood welled up. "You hurt me."

The *bhata* turned from her and went back to staring at the concentric circle in the dirt. Keelie ignored it and squeezed her wound, wondering how much blood she could make ooze out. Crazy stick thing.

"You're hurt. Did you cut yourself?"

She looked up, startled. The boy she'd seen sleeping the evening before stood a few feet away, watching her warily.

"Hey. I didn't hear you come up. I just cut myself a little." He was fast and quiet. She angled her body so that he wouldn't see the *bhata*. Not that many humans ever noticed them, but she was acting more and more like a tree shepherd. "Do you live near here?"

He shook his head, his eyes never leaving her face. Or was he staring at her hand? She covered it with the hem of her oversized sweater.

"I saw you the other day. Sleeping under the dead tree over there." Keelie gestured toward it. "Were you okay?"

He cleared his throat, and a spasm crossed his face. "Er, yes. I'm fine."

Keelie didn't think he looked fine. He held his arms stiffly at his sides, his fists clenched.

Ariel called again. Keelie glanced up to make sure the hawk was nearby. She had caught a thermal and was circling high over the town.

The boy looked in the same direction. "Your bird seems to be safe." He lowered his gaze back to her hand, but then quickly lifted his head and focused on her. He smiled a little and stepped closer. "I think we need to introduce ourselves, since we keep running into each other in the forest. My name is Jake. What's yours?"

"Keelie." She wondered whether she should back away. Jake was one strange guy.

Knot appeared from beneath some ferns growing near the rock. Keelie wondered how long he'd been sitting there. He plunked himself down beside Keelie's foot and proceeded to wash his leg.

The boy nodded. "Pleased to meet you, Keelie. Do *you* live around here?" He gestured toward town.

Even though Jake was cute, she didn't think it was safe

to let him know where she lived. But then Knot sauntered over and began rubbing his head against Jake's jean-clad leg. Maybe the cat was giving her the *he's okay* sign.

"Yeah, I do. I live just over there with my Dad and Grandmother." She motioned with her chin in the direction of the elf village. It wouldn't hurt for Jake to know her family was nearby.

Knot rubbed his head up and down Jake's leg with vigorous enthusiasm. Jake smiled a little.

"So, are you a hiker? Camper?" Keelie asked.

He glanced behind him, as if he'd left his gear in plain sight.

"You don't have to worry," she said quickly. "I won't tell anyone you're here. Is someone coming back to pick you up?"

"No." He looked at her for a second, and his expression changed, as if he'd come to a decision. "I'm not a hiker," he confessed. "I'm hiding here."

Knot now sat beside Jake. The cat lifted his head as if giving him the once over.

"Hiding?" She fought the urge to scoot backward. "As in, from the police, or are you a runaway?"

"I got into some stuff I shouldn't have. Not drugs or anything," he added. "I just need a place to stay, get my head together before I make some big life decisions. Being away from people and in the forest helps center me."

Keelie understood about getting your head together. She needed to get away from people too. However, she was never alone when she was around the trees.

Ariel called from a nearby red alder. Keelie watched as

her claws dug for purchase in the branches. The hawk balanced herself on the branch as a soft wind blew through the leaves.

"She's lucky to have you look after her," Jake said.

When Keelie turned around, Knot was sitting on top of Jake's foot. The cat purred, super loud. That was new.

Relieved, Keelie relaxed. She believed Jake. "You're all wet. I've got to get back, but I'll bring you some dry clothes and a blanket, and some food. My dad made lentil stew. It's not as bad as it sounds."

"I've got plenty to eat, but the clothes would be awesome." He smiled, then looked up quickly, staring at the spot where ferns bordered the stream.

Keelie turned to look and was surprised to see Elia step out from behind a tree. The elf girl must have followed her out here. Keelie turned to reassure Jake, but he was gone. Knot was exactly in the same place and blinked up at Keelie, his whiskers twitching.

Jake must run track at his high school.

Keelie looked around again, but the only things in sight were her sword and the gauntlet she used to carry Ariel on her arm. Knot had disappeared, too.

"Who was that?" Elia was staring into the crowded trees along the top of the ridge.

Annoyed, Keelie didn't answer. Instead, she picked up the gauntlet and Ariel's jesses, which were under the heavy leather glove.

"Well, aren't you going to answer me? He looked human

but something about him was different." Elia sounded thoughtful. "I wonder how he can stand the Dread. The others must know that a human penetrated this far. Everyone will be quite alarmed. I must tell Father."

"Please don't tell him," Keelie said. "His name is Jake, and he's not going to hurt anyone. He's running away from home and hiding here."

Elia stared at her. "Don't be stupid. The Dread is the only thing that keeps humans from trashing this forest the way they destroy everything they touch." She motioned toward the construction site. "This is serious, Keelie. Look at how close they are. If we lose the Dread, nothing will stop them from building up against our land. We won't be able to keep the humans out."

She was right. And Keelie hadn't missed the fact that Elia was talking to her normally, not putting on snooty elf-princess airs. Now wasn't the time to mention Elia's role in the attack on Wildewood's unicorn, but that was a conversation that had to happen—and soon.

"I know. But give Jake a couple of days before you tell your dad, okay? I want him to have a chance."

"I don't know. I don't know about anything anymore." Elia sat on a fallen log. She spread her skirts around her, still posing even where only Keelie and the trees could see her. "I will consider it. Why are you defending this Jake?"

"Because he looks so lost." Keelie hadn't meant for the words to sound so wistful, but Elia caught it right away.

"You identify with him. Not because he's human, but because he's alone in a hostile place."

"You sound like an old woman giving advice. Or did you get your psychology degree?" Keelie thought about all of Dad's college degrees.

"You forget that in human years, I am an old woman." Elia smiled a little at the face Keelie made. "And Sean is older than me. You may have guessed that I wasn't thrilled to learn that he and Risa are betrothed."

"I kind of got that. But what I don't get is why Risa? Why not you?"

Elia's perfect posture melted. "It has something to do with the fact that Risa's mother is a brood mare. Risa has three brothers—four children—that's huge for an elven family." Elia pressed her hand against her chest. "I'm an only child."

One Elia is enough for this planet, Keelie thought.

"This boy sounds intriguing." Elia gazed into the woods where Jake had disappeared. "Can you introduce me to him?"

"I just met him. I saw him asleep in the forest yesterday and ran into him again. I think he must live in town."

Elia nodded as if she understood, but she looked disappointed. "From town. I thought he might be a traveler."

"Well, I'm not sure he's totally human. For one thing, the Dread doesn't bother him. It's fading, but it's still plenty strong." Keelie squeezed her rose quartz for comfort.

They sat in companionable silence. Knot rubbed his head against Keelie's leg. She kept a wary eye on him.

"How did your Lore lesson go today?" Elia asked.

"It was a challenge for both of us."

Knot climbed up into Keelie's lap and curled up into a round ball, tucking his head into his chest. This was scary—a loving Knot and a friendly Elia. Something was wrong with this picture.

As if sensing her discomfort, Knot stretched a paw out and sank his claws into Keelie's leg. "Ow!"

"What?" Elia asked.

"Nothing."

Elia looked at Knot and wrinkled her nose. "Better you than me."

Keelie removed Knot's claws from her pants leg. He purred.

Ariel called to Keelie. She flew from the red alder to a Western hemlock. Keelie sensed a warm and caring personality from the tall tree. Ariel would be safe in the branches.

"Your hawk seems to be doing well."

Keelie glared at the elf girl. "Some nerve. You're the one who blinded her. Why don't you remove the spell?"

Elia bowed her head and sighed. "I can't. If I try, I'm afraid it will rebound on me."

"Rebound on you? What do you mean?" Keelie asked.

"If I take the curse from Ariel, then the magic has to go somewhere."

Keelie didn't understand.

"For every magical action, there is an equal reaction. If I remove this particular dark curse, then it will return to me. I will become blind."

"There's no way of breaking it?" Keelie wasn't shocked. Her father had told her as much soon after Elia had blinded Ariel using magic beyond her skill level. No one had been able to lift the curse.

"Father has been searching all the lore books. We haven't found any answers."

"So Elianard has been searching for a way to break the curse?" That seemed hard to believe.

A loud buzzing came from the ferns underneath the alder tree.

Elia nodded and turned away. Her voice softened. "I found the curse in a book on dark magic. Father had always warned me not to use it, but I wanted to hurt you. Make you go away." Elia swung her head around, her face serious. "Remember this Keelie—the rules matter."

The buzzing became louder, and the ferns rustled with activity. A *bhata* climbed up the trunk of the red alder.

Knot swished his tail back and forth. He jumped up from Keelie's lap and ran toward the leafy undergrowth beneath the alder tree. The buzzing noise stopped and was replaced by a screeching.

Knot appeared with a bug fairy dangling from his mouth. The fairy kicked the cat with its back legs. Knot growled. The bug fairy went limp. Knot trotted down the path, his orange tail held high. Looked like it was going to be curtains for an unfortunate bug fairy.

"You know, if you give Father a chance, you'll learn a lot about the elves and the magic," Elia said.

"I don't know." The thought of being nice to Elianard wasn't a good one.

"Let's make a deal. I won't tell anyone about Jake for a few days—if you promise to give Father a chance. He's a wonderful Lore Master. No one knows more than he does about the history, the culture, the legends of our people. He can help you with your magic, too. Go to class just until the harvest festival."

Keelie didn't know if she could tolerate Elianard that long, but if it bought Jake a little more time, she would try.

"Okay! But you promise not to say anything about Jake."

Elia smiled. "Good. He can tell you about the old days."

"I heard a lot about the old days this morning."

Elia stretched out her arms, taking in the whole forest. "The old days were when the elves came here and settled in this area. Three hundred years ago, your grandmother brought her young sons to live in the forest when they were just little guys."

Keelie stared at Elia. "Three hundred years ago?" That's how old dad had said he was. There wasn't even a United States three hundred years ago. The colonies barely existed. Was everyone pulling her leg?

Then she realized what else Elia had said: Grandmother Keliatiel had brought her young *sons* to live in the forest. Dad was one.

What happened to the other one?

six

Her mystery uncle still on her mind, Keelie was both amused and alarmed when Elia walked back with her to the village. It was weird to have her old adversary as a new friend. Not that she believed her new niceness was for real. Elia was probably up to something—it would just take a while to find out what it was.

Probably something to do with Sean.

The water sprite in the brook called out to her and Keelie slowed down, looking toward the water below through the lush ferns on the shore. She heard a splash and giggle, but saw nothing.

"What are you looking at?" Elia peered over her shoulder.

"The water sprite. We've been saying hi to each other every day. I just wanted to say hello."

Elia looked puzzled. "She talked to you?"

"Yeah. I jumped over her the other day when I was chasing Ariel, and she's pretty lucky I didn't slip and land on top of her."

The elf girl made a face. "I'm heading the other way. My father's at the forge. I'll see you tomorrow."

"Okay. And remember—"

Elia rolled her eyes. "Our secret. Right. You worry too much." She smoothed her fairy-tale skirts and walked away.

Keelie hurried home, her head spinning with what she had learned. Two brothers. Dad had never mentioned that she had an uncle. What had happened to him?

She went over different scenarios, mentally play-acting how she'd ask Dad about his missing brother, but Dad wasn't home when she arrived.

She headed straight to his room to grab some old clothes for Jake. Dad's bedroom had tall ceilings and exposed wooden beams. Colorful appliquéd quilts hung from the dark-paneled walls and his bed was draped in another quilt, this one like a drift of autumn leaves across the bed. Beautiful.

The closet was tidy and held mostly denim shirts and ceremonial-looking outfits with long, full sleeves trimmed in intricate embroidery. Keelie poked around but found nothing that Jake could wear.

His chest of drawers held folded jeans and shirts, including long-sleeved thermal tees. Bingo. Keelie gathered up a couple pairs of jeans, sweats, and thermals, then a pair of thick cotton socks.

Jake needed a coat, too, but she hadn't seen one. She pushed aside the robes in the deep closet, feeling like a snoop and hoping to find winter-season clothes behind the front rod.

She froze. A low-relief wood portrait carving hung there—the image of a serene woman, with wild dark curls and a smile on her generous lips. Keelie stared at it, then ran her fingers over the familiar curve of the mouth. It was her mother.

Whoever had made this was an artist. Dad was an artist with furniture, but he'd never made anything like this. She ran her fingers lightly over her Mom's smooth cheeks, and dipped them into the hollows of her ribbon-like curls.

Mom. The artist who'd made this knew her well. Keelie felt a pang at the thought that she'd forgotten what Mom looked like. Just the little details, but all of them had been captured here. Mom's essence, rendered in wood.

No one knew Keelie like that. She wasn't loved here, except by Dad.

A sound in the hallway made her pull the hangers together and close the closet door. She clutched the folded clothes to her chest and ran to the doorway.

"Keelie, are you here?"

Dad. If she answered, he'd know she was in his room, the only bedroom on the main floor. She looked down at the folded clothes in her arms. No way she could explain this without telling him about Jake.

She waited until he went up the stairs, still calling her name, and then slipped down the hall and tossed the clothes into the bottom of the hall closet.

She took a deep breath, pasted a smile on her face and hurried upstairs. "You looking for me, Dad?"

Dad stuck his head out of her bedroom door. "I was. How were your lessons?"

"Interesting. Niriel's sword fighting was my favorite." That wasn't a total lie.

His eyebrows rose. "Really?"

"Yeah. He let me bring the sword home, too, so that I can practice." She rubbed her right arm. "Which I'll do as soon as I can move again."

He laughed. "Swords never thrilled me. And now I have to oversee the sword making," he added ruefully.

"Yeah, I don't get that, Dad." Keelie sat on her bed and motioned for him to join her.

He sat at the foot of the bed, smiling at Alora's twinkling earrings. The treeling was in a resting state, sort of a tree sleep, which meant she wouldn't interrupt them.

"Dad, is Grandmother really sick? She doesn't seem ill to me."

He leaned back against the bedpost and crossed his

arms. "She's not sick the way I was back in New York. She doesn't have a fever, but she's not as strong as she was a few years ago, and with every day she's a little weaker. Her strength is directly tied to the strength of the forest. As the Dread fails, so does she."

"But when you were sick with the elf flu it was because the Wildewood was sick. Einhorn was sick."

A vivid image came to Keelie, of Elia helping her father, Elianard, by using her magic harp to drain Einhorn's life force. A big reason why she didn't trust the new, helpful Elia. At least the harp had been destroyed.

Dad stared out the window, thinking. "We are tied to the trees. Their fate is ours. It's becoming harder to protect them, Keelie. I knew that my turn would one day come."

"Three hundred years, right?"

He smiled. "Yes. A long enough apprenticeship."

"Why doesn't your brother help out?"

Dad's smile disappeared and the green summer of his eyes grew grey and cold. "Who has spoken to you of this?"

She pressed her lips together, regretting her hasty question. Elia was holding a secret for her, and she didn't dare tell Dad the details of their conversation.

"I just heard. When Keliatiel came to this forest, she brought her two young sons. Two. That would be you and someone else."

His glacial stare continued for a few more seconds, then he sighed. "I did have a brother, Dariel. He died long ago. Do not speak of him to your grandmother. It hurts her still."

"What happened to him?"

"Does it matter? It was long ago, when this country was young."

Keelie tried to imagine what it would be like to live for hundreds of years. "Do you remember the Civil War?"

"Yes. It did not affect us much here. The Gold Rush was worse. Many came west, and the people who lived near us suffered much."

"The Native Americans, right?"

"Yes. When they were moved out, we called up the Dread to keep the others out. It was the first time the Dread had been summoned in this land." He fell quiet, remembering.

"In this land," Keelie repeated. "Elianard told me about the migration. Where did you come from?"

Dad smiled again. "Didn't you read fairy tales?"

Keelie tilted her head. "Under the Hill?"

"Wrong fairy tale. Actually, we come from many lands, but Keliatiel was born in the forests of the Pyrenees, as was my brother. I was born here."

"And your father?"

"He joined the trees a hundred years ago. His name was Zaros. You're a lot like him."

She tried out her grandfather's name. "Zaros. Why doesn't anyone talk about him?"

Dad shrugged. "He faded long ago. He was very old. We live in the now. Elves remember as trees do, but those who follow the old ways do not mourn."

So it was her human side that made her ache for her

mother's hug, made her wish she could hear Mom's annoyed call to do the chores she'd skipped.

"I'm glad we have each other, Dad."

Zeke moved closer to her and pulled her into his arms, holding her tight. "I am too, Keelie. And if anything happened to you, I would mourn forever."

"Me too, Dad." It had grown dark outside, and she still had to go back into the forest.

Dad looked around her room as if searching. "Do you feel something strange here? It's like a dark energy."

Keelie kept her eyes away from her closet, where Elianard's amulet lay hidden under the folded towels. "No, Dad. Maybe it's Alora."

Dad stood. "No. Definitely not."

Although she felt bad about being so secretive, Keelie couldn't make herself reveal the presence of the amulet. For some reason, ever since Einhorn had given it to her, she'd felt the need to keep it hidden. "What time is dinner?"

"Eight. Are you going out?"

"Just checking on Ariel and stuff."

He squeezed her shoulder and stood. "Don't be late." He closed the door behind him as he left.

Her mind reeling from everything she had learned, Keelie sat for a moment then got up, anxious to get the clothes to Jake. He was probably shivering, waiting for her.

"The aunties said that Zeke's brother died many rings ago." Alora's voice piped up. The room jingled as she moved her jewelry-laden branches.

"What else do the aunties say?"

"Water me."

"I'm sure they didn't ask you to water them."

"I'm so thirsty."

Keelie sighed and got up. The watering can was by the door, still half-full. She started to pour the water on the soil around Alora's slender trunk, then stopped. She needed to hide the amulet better, and what better place than under Alora? Keelie reached into the towels and pulled it out. She put the amulet on, shuddering as the cold, thorny acorn touched her chest.

She wrapped her arms around Alora's pot and heaved it up, then carefully walked to the hall, bracing herself against the wall when she got tired.

"What are you doing, Keelie? Are we going shopping? Laurie told me about shopping. I need new twinkles for my branches."

The treeling didn't know the word for the finery she wore, so she projected the effect she wanted, twinkling her branches covered in gems.

Keelie snorted. "No, we're not going shopping, but you are about to get a major twinkle, and it will be our secret."

She carried Alora's pot outside, past Dad's workshop. The treeling talked nonstop. By the time she set the pot down, Keelie was ready to heave her over the closest hedge.

Inside the workshop she found a large clay pot that Dad had prepared to allow for Alora's growth. It was half full of rich soil. Keelie dragged it outside, then took the amulet off and dropped it into the pot, digging it in with her fingers.

Alora watched, quiet. Keelie turned to her. "I want you to take care of this necklace," she whispered aloud. She was glad the treeling could hear and that she didn't have to send the message telepathically, in case other trees overheard.

"It's beautiful," Alora whispered back. "But very cold."

"Must be the magic. I'm going to repot you."

A surge of treeling happiness filled her mind. Alora was glad to get a new pot *and* a new necklace. Keelie tilted Alora's pot and tapped it all around, loosening the soil, then grasped the treeling low on her trunk and pulled a little. She came up easily. Keelie dangled the little tree over the new pot, letting the roots barely touch the soil.

Alora giggled. "That tickles. Hurry, Keelie. My toes are cold."

"You don't have toes. You have rootlets."

Alora made a rude noise.

Keelie grasped a handful of soil and dribbled it around Alora's roots, repeating until Alora could sit comfortably. Then she grabbed the old pot by the rim, upending it into the new pot so that all the soil fell in. She tucked Alora snugly into her new home.

"Remember, no one must know that the necklace is under you."

"Okay, but I must have a gift for my silence."

A bribe. Twice in one day. "What do you want?"

"More twinkles. Twinkles that show."

"I'll get you something."

Alora hummed happily. Keelie left her there for the time being and went to wash the dirt from her hands, smiling at Dad in the kitchen. "I repotted Alora. She's outgrowing the old pot."

"That's great, Keelie. I'm pleased that you are so responsible with the Great Tree's gift." He was chopping onions and tears glimmered in his eyes. Keelie used the kitchen towel she'd dried her hands on to dab at his eyes.

"Onions are killer, aren't they? My Grandma Jo always said the stronger the onion, the better the flavor."

Dad smiled. "I'll remember that." He started to pluck tiny leaves from a branch of thyme, letting them fall on the diced onions.

Keelie got the clothes from the hall closet and went out the front door to avoid running into Dad again. She sent a thought to the trees.

Oh guardians of the Dread Forest, show me where the human boy is.

She got back confusion and doubt. She tried again. *The human boy named Jake. I was with him.*

We see no one but you and the elf, the aunties trilled.

Had he left and gone back home? She'd been worried all this time for nothing.

I see him. It was Alora.

Get over yourself, Keelie answered. *This isn't how you'll get another twinkly.*

But I can see him, she insisted. *He's a dark cloud, and he was a dark cloud when you spoke to him with Elia.*

A dark cloud? Keelie shrugged. Maybe he had some kind of magic doohickey that let him withstand the Dread, and it made him invisible to the trees.

"Show me where he is, Alora."

"Take me with you."

Keelie gritted her teeth. She had to get back home in time for dinner or Dad would get suspicious. She walked around the side of the house, and with the clothes pulled tight to her chest, she picked up the new, even heavier pot, and staggered to the cart Dad used for hauling firewood. She wrestled Alora's pot into the makeshift rickshaw and pulled the cart into the dark forest, with Alora guiding her.

She had almost arrived at the stream when Alora announced, "There he is."

Keelie squinted into the darkness and saw a dark, fog-like swirl low to the ground, like a shadow serpent coming toward her. It slowed, and then stopped, and Jake stepped out of it, the fog clinging to his skin like damp cloth.

This was not human behavior. Her life was getting really complicated.

seven

Keelie jumped behind the cart, her heart thumping hard against her rib cage as her brain tried to reason out what she'd just seen. Watching Jake materialize out of thin air had to be right at the top of the list of the weird things she'd seen in the past several months. Keelie didn't know whether to run or stay. She took a deep breath of the soothing scent of the surrounding evergreens, trying to calm herself. Something warm and furry rubbed against her ankle. She glanced down, saw Knot, and relaxed a fraction, feeling safer.

Mist swirled around Jake's feet. It was as if he had a

fog machine hidden in his ragged boots. Fat water droplets dripped from the trees, making little puddles on the ground. She stared up at him. His eyes were bright green like an elf's, but the veins in his eyes bulged bright red, blood red. His skin was as white as the snow atop the highest Cascade mountain peaks.

The mist twirled around him like a vapory snake, and its tendrils reached out for her. Keelie stepped back. Behind her, a loud stick snapped. A jolt of panic filled her and she almost tripped, hitting the cart heavily.

"Don't knock me over," Alora said in a frightened voice.

Keelie's palms were sweaty. Little beads of condensation had formed on Alora's leaves. Keelie closed her eyes and connected to the forest's magic, trying to find an answer from the trees. But there was no answer. She envisioned the green around her, and a wave of energy flowed from her to Alora. The clay flower pot glowed with a golden light. It wasn't hot, but bright. Uh-oh! Keelie sensed that the amulet was reacting to her tree magic. She could only hope there wasn't going to be any big problems because she did. The comforting scent of loamy soil filled the air, which glittered with gold and silver flecks.

Keelie could see the *bhata* all around them, and out of the corner of her eye she saw the water sprite's huge eyes peering at them from the stream bank.

"Keelie, don't be afraid." Jake said. His voice sounded as if he were faraway or not altogether there, as if bits and pieces of him were still forming. The mist encircled him, and sparkles like silver glitter revolved around him. Jake closed his eyes, and when the sparkles disappeared, he looked like a normal boy, like he did the first time she saw him sleeping in the woods.

"I think we're both more than mere humans. So who's going to explain first?" Keelie asked.

Silence.

Knot sat down on Keelie's foot, a heavy lump of fur. The cat's purring filled the silent forest, accompanied by an occasional plip-plop from the water dripping from the trees.

"Gentlemen usually go first." Keelie prompted.

"Who said I was a gentleman?"

"Well, what are you?"

"What are *you?*"

Keelie sighed. "We could play this game all day, but if we're going to get anywhere, somebody has to 'fess up first."

Alora's face pushed out from the bark on her trunk and she piped up. "I'll start. I'm Princess Alora, the Princess of the Great Oak of the Wildewood."

Jake bowed elegantly. "It is the greatest honor and pleasure to meet you, Princess Alora."

Shocked, Keelie looked at the little treeling, then at Jake. Only tree shepherds could hear trees talk, even when they spoke aloud.

Alora lifted her little branches to her face and giggled, her twinkles glistening even in the dark shade of the trees.

Keelie noticed that Alora's face seemed more human—her nose more pronounced, her eyes more expressive, and her mouth rounder with human-like lips.

She looked from Alora to Jake. "You can truly see her? And hear her?"

Jake nodded and shoved his hands into his pockets. He seemed like an ordinary teenager—just one who talked to trees, like she did. She glanced at his ears again, wondering if they'd suddenly turned pointy, but his head was blurry in spots. She rubbed her eyes and turned to Alora. When they got back home, she was going to scold the treeling for revealing herself to someone she didn't know. Time for the stranger-danger talk.

Alora leaned back and lifted a leafy branch as if she was about to share a secret with her best friend. She whispered, "He's nice. Don't worry—we can trust him."

Jake grinned.

Keelie didn't grin back. She studied him. He was still pale, and his curly hair was wild. The blur was still there. Tree magic wasn't helping, so she touched the rose quartz at her belt and reached for the Earth magic it could summon. The blur vanished, revealing pointed ear tips. "You're an elf."

He frowned. "Not so much, anymore." He looked at Keelie, and then down at Knot. "Once a long time ago, but…"

"But—what?" Keelie encouraged him to continue. She

wanted to know what happened to him, and if maybe they were related.

Knot meowed. Jake kneeled to pet the cat on the head. To Keelie's surprise, Knot didn't hiss or swat at him, but purred. He was still sitting on her foot, which felt like it was going to sleep.

Jake nodded. "If you think it's best."

Knot meowed. So, apparently, the cat could talk to Jake but not to Keelie. Not like she wanted to speak *meow* anyway. Maybe she should kick him off her foot, but she liked having him there.

Still camping out on her foot, Knot placed his paw on Jake's hand. Jake stood. "I will tell you my story, Keliel Katharine Heartwood."

She gasped. "How do you know my full name?" Unfair, he knew about her, but she didn't have a clue as to his real identity or to what he was. She looked down at the cat. "You told him."

"I've been watching you as you run through the forest chasing the hawk. I heard the elves talking about Zeke Heartwood's Round Ear child."

Even though she didn't show it, a sharp pain stung Keelie in her chest. Despite everything she'd done for the elves, they still called her Round Ear. Although she promised Dad she'd tried to fit in with them, she didn't know if they'd ever accept her as one of their own. She straightened, mentally preparing herself for any more insults Jake might have heard the elves say about her.

"What are you?" Keelie asked. If Jake was half-human, she hoped her fate wouldn't be to turn into mist and lose her great tan, because she was more determined than ever to hang onto humanity.

Jake spread his arms and stood before them, like a storyteller at a theme park. Alora leaned forward as if she was about to hear a really good tale.

"I was once an elf," Jake began, "but I was born with wanderlust. I had to see the world, and I traveled. When I returned home, I discovered that logging companies were going to build a railroad through the Dread Forest. The elves were sick and the Dread was receding. A wizard who'd discovered the secret of the Dread made a deal with a railroad baron, to remove the Dread so that humans could enter."

"No way," Alora shouted. She put her branches to her mouth.

Jake nodded. "The wizard said he could find a way into the forest and make it so the workers wouldn't be afraid. They wanted to bring iron in. It would've killed the fairies, and the forest would have died, too. The trees would've been poisoned by the coal. My people, tied to the forest, would be lost and forlorn on Earth. We'd traveled from Europe, and found our home here. Where else could we go? To join our kin in Canada? Each elf becomes attuned to a place where his soul lives in harmony with the forest. This was our forest."

Keelie nodded. Dad had told her so. Alora leaned closer to her, and the treeling's branches scratched her face.

"Do you mind?"

"Oops, sorry." Alora sounded a lot like Laurie.

"There seemed little choice," Jake continued. "I had to stop it."

Keelie couldn't imagine a railroad through this forest. She shivered with fear for the trees.

"I had knowledge of our lore, and I knew that during the Middle Ages, an elven alchemist had tapped into the fairies' dark magic to stop an army from taking over our lands. It stopped the army, but the alchemist was transformed by his use of the forces of darkness."

Keelie looked at Jake. "Transformed, how?" She bet he'd turned into a Red Cap; nothing could be darker than that little minion.

"He turned into a vampire. A creature of the night—a creature twisted by dark magic despite his willing sacrifice to save his people."

Keelie flinched. "Vampire?"

Jake was by her side in a blink. He placed a cold hand on her shoulder. "You're so warm."

She looked up at him, and he held her gaze, his eyes bright green, but rimmed in red. A zing went through Keelie. Alarmed, she mistrusted the warm feeling she got from his gaze. Something about him touched her heart and made her feel all bright inside, but his words had been frightening. Dark magic. She shrugged his hand off and backed away until she felt the reassuring roughness of bark from the oak behind her.

"You're the one who saved the Dread Forest from the railroad all those years ago."

"Bingo."

"You used dark magic, and now you're a vampire, just like the alchemist."

"Yes. And I was banished by the elves because of it."

Keelie's chest ached as she thought of him, homeless and wandering, far from the forest to which he was still tied.

Jake turned away and gazed down at Alora. "Let me carry her for you." He reached for the flower pot. Keelie stepped between him and the cart, not trusting his intentions. Maybe he would be drawn to the dark magic of the amulet hidden between Alora's roots.

"You can trust him." Alora's little voice was confident.

Jake bowed his head. "Princess Alora of the Wildewood Forest is safe with me."

Alora might be safe, but Keelie wasn't safe from a sudden awareness that she liked Jake, even though he was cursed. He had saved the forest from the railroads, so he knew how to work dark magic. Keelie thought about the design on grandmother's book and wondered if there could be a cure for Ariel's curse in there—if she was willing to use the amulet. Maybe Jake could show her how. Such a tiny amount of dark magic wouldn't have the same dark consequences.

Jake's eyes darkened. "Remember always, Keelie, even

though we think we're justified in using dark magic, there is a price to be paid for such knowledge and actions."

Had he read her mind? He was watching her like a predator watches its prey.

"If you saved the Dread," Keelie managed to ask, "why did the elves treat you so badly? Surely they understood your sacrifice?" There were parallels to their stories, and she shivered thinking of her own brush with dark magic.

"For the safety of the other elves and the forest." Jake stayed close to her. "Cold? Or are you afraid of me now?"

Keelie thrust her chin up. "No. If Knot trusts you and Alora trusts you, then I'll have to trust you." She was taking a risk trusting the opinions of a trickster cat and a newborn sapling.

"You're a rare being among the elven, the humans, and even among the fae, Keelie Heartwood. Most people would be afraid of me."

"I think it's because I've seen dwarves, elves, and water sprites. However, if you ever wear a red hat, then I'm going to run from you."

Jake smiled. "I'll pull Alora's cart for you until we're almost at the village."

In a way, it was like a guy offering to carry her books, except in Keelie's case, it was her tree.

She couldn't say no, even though she suspected that he'd feel the amulet's presence. She surreptitiously unclipped the rose quartz from her pants loop and leaned over to tuck it into the soil, whispering the shielding spell Sir Davey had taught her.

Above her, Alora giggled. "That tickles."

Keelie straightened, and the second her finger lost contact with the Earth magic–shielded soil, the Dread slammed into her. She forced herself to straighten, knowing that the urge to run screaming was just an illusion.

They walked slowly, and Jake chatted about elves while Keelie concentrated on acting normally. The faint sound of village life grew louder. Music, talk, the clanging of the blacksmith's hammer—all meant that soon she'd stop feeling so awful.

A tiny, sane part of her mind thought that they were acting like friends, until Jake asked about Elia.

"She's Elianard's daughter, and we've had some run-ins," Keelie said through gritted teeth. "He's my elven lore teacher." She made air quotes around "elven lore." "You shouldn't trust Elia. She seems nice now, but she's done some awful stuff."

"She's not so bad. I see the beauty in her heart." Jake looked a little moonstruck. "I can see that she loves her father very much. She's loyal."

Keelie snorted.

Jake stopped walking, and as soon as he released the cart handles Keelie felt in Alora's dirt for her rose quartz.

"What are you doing?"

"Getting my house key." Her fingers closed around the smooth stone and she almost sobbed with relief. An empty pillowy feeling in her head took the place of the squeezing fear.

Keelie turned to Jake. "I think Elia saw you, but she said she'd give you a few more days before she tells the other elves. So you've got to go somewhere else, or we've got to figure out a way to convince the elves to let you stay in the forest."

Jake shook his head and stepped back. "They'll never reverse the banishment. And things will go badly for you if you tell others about me."

"Is that a threat?"

"It's the truth."

"I'll speak for you," Alora said. The treeling seemed a lot taller, and now she was making dreamy tree eyes at Jake. He didn't notice, but Keelie wasn't surprised. It was a guy thing.

"I wish it would make a difference." Jake looked at his feet.

Dad's voice echoed from the trees. "Keelie?" He did not sound happy.

She sighed. "That's my dad. When will I see you again?" When she turned around, Jake was gone.

eight

"Keelie, where have you been?" Dad asked.

"I've been—"

Alora cleared her throat. "She took me out for a ride."

"Yeah, she wanted some fresh air." Keelie wondered why the treeling was covering for her after having whined so much. Maybe it was because she and Jake seemed to have some kind of flirty connection. "I hope it's okay that I took the cart."

Dad arched an eyebrow. "You walked the tree?" He studied Alora as if seeing her for the first time in a long while. "You've grown a lot since this morning." He bent to examine her leaves.

Keelie hoped he didn't sense the presence of the amulet. She'd picked a lousy hiding place.

The tree preened, shifting her weight forward in the flowerpot and making the cart roll forward. "It's the air here. It's done wonders for me."

"What about me?" Keelie asked.

"Oh yeah, you." Alora twirled her trunk around so she faced Dad. "Keelie's helped, too, even though she's complained a lot."

Keelie narrowed her eyes. "Next time there's a thunderstorm I'm going to put you outside."

Alora placed her branches on where her hips would be, if she had hips. "You wouldn't dare. I'll tell the aunties."

"Time for dinner. We're dining with your grandmother," Dad said. "Would you join us Alora?"

"What do trees eat? Leafy green salad?" Keelie had been looking forward to ditching Alora for a little while, and she also had to find a new hiding place for the amulet before some internal elven-magic detector went off to alert them.

"I don't have to eat anything. And it would be a nice change to enjoy some civil conversation," Alora replied. She crossed her branches over the place her chest would be if she had one. She turned her face away from Keelie and sighed.

"Fine, don't look at me. No big loss."

Dad leaned forward as if to take the big pot. "Can I carry the princess for you, Keelie?"

She was about to say "you sure can," but a cold tingle shot through her fingers. The amulet.

"I have it, Dad. I don't want the princess thinking she can charm her way through life."

Surprised, Dad cleared his throat. He'd used his elven charm on a certain city council woman back in the Wildewood. "Let's not keep your grandmother waiting."

At dinner, Dad sat at one end of a long dining table (oak from Sherwood Forest), which looked like it came from a castle's great hall. Grandmother sat at the other end. Keelie was across from Alora, who played with her twinkles. Everyone ate in uncomfortable silence. Yep, they knew how to have a rip-roaring good time here in the Dread Forest. Keelie figured medieval monks vowed to silence would've been a jollier bunch than these somber elves.

Keelie thought about Jake. It wasn't fair that he had to live as a vampire because he'd used dark magic to save the Dread. There had to be a cure for him. Elianard had tried to drain Einhorn's magic but the elves hadn't ostracized Elianard, unless Dad just hadn't told her that he'd been punished somehow.

And if she could find a way to save the Dread, maybe the elves would finally accept her. Maybe even her Grandmother would approve of her, and Dad and she could be a happy family without all the tension.

"How did your lesson go with Niriel?" Grandmother asked.

"Fine." Keelie answered. She didn't want to talk about Niriel and the sword fighting. She did want to know more about the time the Dread disappeared.

Dad ate his food and gazed out the window behind Alora. Grandmother delicately cut her tomatoes with a silver knife etched with scrolling leaves and vines.

"Were you both here when the wizard put a spell on the forest and made the Dread disappear, back when the railroad tried to come through?"

Grandmother dropped her knife, and it made a loud clank on her plate.

Dad lowered his fork. "How did you know about that?"

Keelie had to think fast. "Elia and I were talking."

"Why were you talking to her?" Dad stared at her as if she'd started speaking French.

Grandmother hummed with approval. "I think it's wonderful Keelie has made friends with Elia; she'll be a good influence on Keelie."

"I'm not so sure about that, Mother. Be careful around her, Keelie. What did you two talk about?" Dad asked.

"Sean."

A surprised look crossed Grandmother's face.

"Oh." Dad looked puzzled.

Keelie decided to drop her question. Dinner continued in uncomfortable silence.

Knot sauntered into the room with his tail held high,

strutted past Dad, and sashayed over to where Grandmother was sitting. Loud purring emanated from underneath the table.

Grandmother's back stiffened. "Zeke, your beast is rubbing his head against my leg."

The purring became louder.

Keelie bit down on her lip so she wouldn't smile. Or laugh.

"Mother, he likes you."

The purring became even louder.

"Zeke!" Grandmother backed up in her chair, looking ready to jump backward.

Waves of purring vibrated the table.

"Knot. Stop it." Dad said in a firm, *I mean it* tone. Keelie had been on the receiving end of that, many times.

Alora's eyes widened.

Knot exited from underneath the table. His orange fur puffed out like a manic hairball. Keelie knew if she were to pet him she'd receive a static electricity charge. His eyes were totally dilated, black rimmed in green. Okay, something was weird about this.

"Zeke, don't you have something to say to Keelie about a certain situation?" Grandmother suggested.

"Mother, I don't want to discuss it now. Let me choose the time."

"Zekeliel. Now is the perfect time. I can't take another minute of his meddling, and if he's not around, then they won't know what is going on. It's time you were able to raise your daughter as an elf and not a human." Grandmother motioned with her hand. "And a whatever."

Keelie wanted to know who was meddling with what. Why didn't Grandmother want to keep this secret? She wondered if Grandmother and Dad might know something about Jake. Had Jake told her everything?

Keelie looked from Dad to Grandmother and back to Dad. A thick wall of tension formed between them as they glared at one another.

"I'm tired, Zeke, and you promised me you'd talk to Keelie about this. And now she's asking about the railroad—what if she discovers ... "

Hating that they were speaking about her as if she weren't at the table with them, Keelie was about to shout when Alora shook her head. Keelie stared at the treeling. Frost had formed on the flowerpot, and the treeling was growing right now—at that moment—right there at the table in front of Grandmother and Dad. Dirt crumbled around the base of her trunk as she widened and rose. If they discovered the amulet, it was going to be bad news for Keelie. Fortunately, Grandmother and Dad were having a stare down.

"Fine. Have it your way, Mother." Dad sounded frustrated, and worry lines formed around his mouth like he'd swallowed something distasteful. He templed his fingers and leaned his forehead against his hands as if he was gathering his thoughts before he spoke. He lifted his face toward her. "Keelie."

"Yes?" She kept her gaze focused on him. She suddenly felt sorry for Dad—he seemed so serious. He'd had a lot of responsibility dumped on him since he'd arrived. She missed him. It was like there were two different versions: Faire Dad and Dread Dad. She'd take the Faire Dad any day of the week. He smiled at her, and then for a brief moment, he was back. But then like a shimmering mirage in the desert, the friendly, relaxed Dad dissipated and the serious elven father replaced him.

"Keelie, your grandmother—" Dad glanced over at Grandmother Keliatiel as if confirming this was something she wanted to do.

She nodded. "You agreed, too, after all the trouble he's gotten Keelie into."

"Keelie, your grandmother and I have been discussing Knot. We don't think he should be your guardian anymore."

"What?" Shock riveted through her and her chin felt like it had dropped to the floor.

"You heard your father. We don't think this..." she pointed at Knot "...creature should be your guardian."

"I can't believe you said that," Keelie said.

"You heard me."

"Yes, I heard you, but I'm not believing what I'm hearing." Keelie's shock ebbed into surprise.

Knot's eyes narrowed into slits and his tail swished like an angry cobra, ready to strike. His claws extended from his paws and he glowered at Grandmother, who glared back at him. He hissed.

For a moment, Keelie could've sworn she heard Knot say in a human voice. "You wouldn't dare."

Dad and Grandmother stared at him.

Knot meowed.

Grandmother quickly overcame her surprise and stubbed her index finger on the table. "See, they're interfering with Keelie. They have their own agenda."

Dad turned away from Knot and back to Keelie. "You have to listen to me because I can't have you running into dangerous situations like you did with the Red Cap and with the unicorn. There are dangers in the Dread Forest."

"I'm fine in the forest. Knot accompanies me everywhere I go. If I run into trouble, he'll be there to pee on anything or anyone who is a problem. I'm learning that being a tree shepherd has unusual complications, but Knot has been there for me."

Dad remained somber and stiff, looking more and more like Grandmother Keliatiel. "He has a conflict of interest when it comes to your interests."

Duh! Keelie could've told him that within the first five minutes she met Knot. However, the sadistic hairball had been there for her, and no way was she going to have another guardian. Knot had been her mother's guardian and he was going to remain Keelie's. A fierce loyalty for the feline rose within her.

"Knot will stay my guardian," she said flatly.

"Do not talk to your elders like that, young lady. Just because you're half human doesn't excuse disrespectful behavior," Grandmother said.

Keelie pushed her chair back and stood up, not even looking at her grandmother. She stared at Dad. "I don't care what Grandmother Keliatiel says about Knot. I don't care she doesn't like him. He stays with me."

The sound of tapping against glass filled the room. Keelie looked up and saw the twiggy faces of the *bhata* pressed against every window in the house. Somehow they'd heard her, and had responded.

"Zeke, what is going on?" Grandmother sounded nervous.

"I think they're sending us a message."

Knot hopped onto the table, walked over to Dad, and swatted him on the cheek. A red scratch mark formed on Dad's face. Unmoving, he narrowed his eyes at the cat, and Knot stared right back.

Then the windows opened as if by invisible hands, and about a hundred small *bhata* riding on squirrels streamed into the dining area. The wooden floor was a moving mass of fur and sticks. The only thing missing was Snow White. Keelie should've been freaked out by the squirrels, but she wasn't.

Grandmother Keliatiel placed her hand over her mouth to suppress a scream. You would've thought living in the forest she wouldn't have any heebie-jeebies about squirrels. From Grandmother's reaction to the woodland animals,

Keelie concluded this wasn't an everyday occurrence in the Dread Forest.

A squirrel skimmed over Keelie's foot. The animal's fur was creepy and woolly against her skin. She jumped back. Okay, that was a little too close for comfort.

A *bhata* with holly leaves for hair climbed up Alora's flowerpot and began digging into the soil. Alora shrieked at the *bhata* and pounded it with her branches. "Make it stop, Keelie."

She raced around the table, grabbed the *bhata* by its stick feet, and held it upside down, pointing her finger at it. "Stop."

The *bhata* blinked at Keelie with round brown eyes the soft color of ground nuts. She turned it right side up and placed it on the table.

"Go!" Keelie pointed toward the open window. It bowed its head and climbed down onto the ground, leaving a trail of holly berries in its wake. At least she hoped it was holly berries.

The squirrels and the *bhata* surrounded Dad. Knot's eyes remained dilated, making him look like a possessed kitty from a horror movie.

Dad bowed his head to the cat. He said, "I understand. All will be well with Keelie."

Dad turned to Keelie. "Knot will remain your guardian."

"I knew it. I knew it. We're too late. This all started with Katharine, and her mother before her. Of all the mundanes,

Zeke, you had to pick the one with…" Grandmother looked at Keelie and her voice faded away.

"What started with my mother and Grandmother Josephine?" Keelie asked.

Grandmother Keliatiel shook her head. "Nothing you need to know about. The damage has been done."

"Mother, enough," Dad said in a deep voice.

Keelie and Alora stared at one another. Grandmother Keliatiel sat back down in her chair.

Keelie watched, dumbstruck, as the *bhata* and squirrels departed through the windows.

Knot's fur glowed pumpkin orange, as if he were ready for Halloween. Walking across the table, he strolled over to Keelie and placed his neon paw on her hand. His footpads felt cold against her skin. She smiled at him.

He hissed.

"Don't think this changes anything," she said.

He purred.

He hopped off the kitchen table and walked down the hall to the bathroom. She heard him scratching in his litter box.

Alora shook her leaves. *What a cat!*

Grandmother looked disgusted.

Keelie didn't know what the *bhata* had to do with Knot, or what her mother's mother had to do with anything. She knew that Dad and Sir Davey could speak to the cat, although they'd never admitted it nor told her what he was. She must be asking all the wrong questions.

The next morning, Keelie went down to the village green to practice her new skills with the broadsword. She swung it around in a high arc over her head, trying to ignore the sharp pain in her muscles. She was surprised at her arm strength today. Even though she didn't want to learn from Niriel, Keelie liked the idea of using a sword to bash her enemies. It would be cathartic, even if her enemy was just a straw dummy. And the pain would fade as her skill increased.

She hoped the workout would release some of her anger against Grandmother and Dad. At breakfast she'd wanted to discuss what had happened last night, but Dad wouldn't talk. As usual, he clammed up and expected her to understand everything by osmosis. Grandmother, on the other hand, was mad; she had lost the argument and Keelie had won.

Keelie thrust her sword forward. Knot would remain her guardian. He was observing her from the cart. She watched him, but pretended she wasn't looking at him. He looked like a normal orange cat, except for his size.

He turned around and blinked at Keelie. He seemed to be saying, *Caught you admiring me.*

"As if." She pointed the sword at him.

He purred. Psycho cat. Keelie lowered the sword.

Knot swished his tail back and forth, then lifted a paw and started washing it.

Keelie wished she had a lesson today. She was ready to do battle.

"Keelie."

She froze at the sound of Sean's voice. She placed the sword tip against the ground and held onto the pommel as if supporting herself. She didn't want to talk to him. Not after his betrayal. Not after his betrothal to Risa. She didn't want to turn around. She couldn't look at Sean. Her heart hammered against her chest.

"Don't ignore me, Keelie."

She pivoted, facing him with the sword raised and pointing at his heart. It hurt to see him, knowing how she'd kissed him, how she'd pined for him in the Wildewood. A small part of her was still fond of him, and it hurt to think he'd discarded her feelings so easily.

Keelie pulled the sword away and dropped the tip. "I think the time for talking has passed." Maybe she was more like Dad than she thought.

Sean stepped closer, and pain flared in his eyes. "I told you that it was my father's idea to marry Risa. We have to breed true. I have to do what is best for my people."

My people. Even Sean—the one person who had treated her as an equal—thought she was different.

Anger surged through her, and she pulled the sword from the ground. Green magic washed over her as she felt her magic flow through her body. She was so tired of hearing the same elven rhetoric over and over—Dad telling her she had to be more elven, her grandmother telling her what to do. Keelie knew in her heart she would never measure up to their expectations—because she would always be human. She gripped the pommel tightly in her hand.

"Go away, Sean." She aimed the tip of the sword at him again.

Suddenly, a burst of green magic flashed from Keelie's hand and traveled up the sword blade. The steel sparked and sizzled, giving off the sharp, acrid-sweet smell of hot metal. As the magic moved quickly up the sword, the steel blade transformed into wood.

Sean stepped back, his mouth open in shock. "How…?"

Keelie's hand opened and the sword fell to the ground, tip first. It stood, the hilt swaying. Smoke curled from the earth around the blade, and she felt the throb of green magic around her and, strangely, from below as well.

Sean stared at the sword as if he was trying to reason out what just happened. It was still, now, its metal hilt bright silver against the gray wood of the blade.

A loud buzzing erupted all around them. The *feithid daoine*. Hundreds and hundreds of the bug fairies flew as if from out of nowhere and surrounded Sean. He swatted at them.

Several *bhata* lowered themselves from a nearby tree and reached for the sword. Keelie understood. She reached out gingerly and wrapped her hand around the hilt.

"Don't touch it," Sean cried.

But Keelie drew the sword from the earth and lifted it high above her head. The *bhata* swarmed down the tree's branches, obscuring her arm and the sword, and then climbed back up and disappeared into the leaves, taking the sword with them. A bit of silver glinted through the green, then it was gone.

"My father said the fae are uncontrollable and do what they please, without regard to the consequences. You shouldn't have let them have that sword."

"It felt right to me." Keelie frowned. "And who are you to tell me what to do? Why do you care, all of a sudden?" She took a step toward him, her finger pointed as her sword tip had been moments earlier. "You want to talk to someone who cares? Go find your so-called fiancé!"

An angry buzzing from above suddenly turned louder and a swarm of *feithid daoine* descended over them. Keelie threw her arms over her head, but the bug fairies whizzed past her, headed toward their target. Sean.

He yelled and ran, his golden hair surrounded by a cartoon tornado of wings and chittering, insect-like fae.

At her feet, Knot swatted at a huge *feithid daoine*, and it made a clacking noise with its wings before lifting up and joining its friends. Moments later, the bug fairies disappeared, gone as quickly as they had appeared.

Sean stood on the other side of the clearing, seemingly unhurt, although his hair was tied in several hundred itsy bitsy, intricate braids, with flower-colored ribbons at the end.

He touched his head gingerly. "What happened?"

"The *feithid daoine*. I think they like me, and thought

you were going to hurt me." She tried not to laugh at his pink porcupine 'do, although she was glad he wasn't hurt.

"I saw you—" Sean looked puzzled, his fingers still twirling his tiny braids as if he hadn't quite realized what had happened yet. "I swore I saw the sword turn into wood."

"Are you sure?"

He shook his head, dazed.

Keelie suppressed a laugh. "That's a good look for you. I'm sure Risa will love getting those braids out."

He stumbled away, one confused elf.

Keelie looked up into the trees, but the leaves were still. She opened herself to her tree magic, carefully, afraid something else would turn to wood. The trees were vigilant, but there was no talk, no sign of trouble. Just the throbbing below-foot, as if a giant engine ran the forest.

She had to call Sir Davey to tell him what had happened. How could steel turn into wood? She couldn't ask Dad because then Grandmother would find out. It seemed she heard everything that was spoken in the Dread Forest.

Keelie was sure that the elves could feel the presence of the amulet's dark magic. If they saw this, she would be accused of using it. She needed help, and she wasn't going to find it in the Dread Forest.

nine

Keelie paced back and forth in her room, hands clenched at her sides. "If Sean tells Niriel about the sword and Niriel asks Dad about it, then I'm going to be in big trouble. I have no idea how I did it, but maybe the amulet is starting to affect my magic."

Keelie turned to the treeling, expecting an answer, then noticed that the soil in Alora's pot was disturbed around her slender trunk. Keelie bent over and rearranged the soil, grimacing as some fell to the floor.

Alora's face pushed through her bark. "Nobody has ever transformed steel into wood. The aunties are saying you're the first tree shepherd ever to do anything like that. The first elf, even."

"Dad will wonder why. Everyone will. What's happening to me, Alora?" Keelie walked over to her bed with its green cotton spread.

Knot was sleeping on her bed, feet stuck up in the air. Some guardian he was. She stared at him, thinking of Jake, the sword, and all the fairies' strange behavior. She realized that she was biting down on her thumbnail and held her hand out to examine her pink nails and ragged cuticles. She had never bitten them before, and she wasn't about to begin now.

She paced again. She had to find a solution.

She had to call Sir Davey. He could help her—he knew about this kind of thing. But all the phones in the elf village were plugged into the tree network and if she called, Dad would know. She had to go into town. She remembered seeing a pay phone at a diner next to the tattoo and piercing shop.

"Stop! You're making my sap whirl around in my head."

"You don't have a head. You have a trunk."

"That back and forth thing you're doing with your walking branches. Stop it."

"My walking branches?" Keelie looked down. "You mean my legs."

"You're driving me crazy, and my roots are cold. I feel like I have frost inside of me."

Cold? Keelie suddenly noticed that Alora's leaves were beginning to curl around the edges.

"I'm sorry, Keelie. I don't feel well." Alora's rough bark face drooped. "That magic twinkle is bad."

The amulet had to go. She should have moved it earlier, but she'd been distracted by the sword. One crisis at a time.

Something tapped at the window. Keelie jumped, heart racing. She relaxed when she saw several *bhata* looking in at her.

Having the stick people around seemed normal now —it showed how far she'd come in the past few months. Her breath caught as the brass latch clicked and the window opened by itself. The *bhata* crept in, then jumped, landing on her bed. Knot opened one eye, and flexed his paws as if kneading the air.

Keelie recognized the larger *bhata* with the holly leaves. It didn't have as many berries in this leafy arrangement as it had last night.

Either the *bhata* were brave or stupid, because they stayed close as Knot now rolled over onto his side. The cat sat up, then reached out a paw and swatted at a skinny *bhata*, knocking it off the bed.

"Enough." Keelie pointed her finger at the cat. "You may be my guardian, but you're not going to bully them while I'm around." She placed the *bhata* back on the bed. It rubbed its head.

Knot yawned.

Keelie wondered why the *bhata* were here. The leader pointed at the bed. Maybe it wanted something. Walking over, Keelie kneeled, then bent over until she was face-to-face with it. "Show me."

It climbed down and reached toward Keelie. She held still and felt its stick arms trace down the side of her face. Purring filled Keelie's ears. She looked up. Knot leaned over the edge and watched with bright intent green eyes.

She knew they were here to help her. She closed her eyes and a sepia-toned vision filled her mind: the *bhata* were carrying the wooden sword over their shoulders and were taking it deep into the dark labyrinth of the forest. Then she saw a cave, huge and hidden from the eyes of humans and elves. She had a sense of deep magic.

Keelie opened her eyes. She looked at Knot, wanting confirmation that letting the *bhata* take the sword was the right thing to do. They'd probably hidden it somewhere safe, where Dad and Grandmother wouldn't sense it.

He purred and swatted another *bhata*, knocking it off the bed. No answer there.

Keelie bowed her head to the lead *bhata*, "Thank you."

The *bhata* leader bowed as much as his stick body allowed, and the others, which had gathered around Alora and were poking in her dirt, retreated to the windowsill. Alora was strangely silent.

With quick movements, the stick fairies jumped out of the window and disappeared into the canopy of the trees surrounding the house.

She wondered if she should have asked the *bhata* to hide the amulet, too, but knew she would have to do that herself. It was too important, and too dangerous, to keep in the house where her father and grandmother might sense it. Plus, it was making Alora sick.

"Alora, are you okay?"

The little tree's branches quivered. "No."

"Don't worry, I'll move that bad twinkle."

Keelie turned back to tell Knot, but he wasn't there. She found him waiting by the door and went to open it. One minute she was dealing with ancient secrets and powerful magic, the next she was doorman to a cat. Knot swatted at her leg before he strode out.

"Ungrateful beast."

His purring drifted back to her as he walked away. Keelie smiled. At least things were good between her and Knot.

Time to find a better place to stash the amulet. She pulled a pair of sterling silver earrings studded with tiny amethysts from her nearly empty wooden jewelry box (reclaimed cedar from an exotic Asian forest) and dangled them in front of Alora.

"Oh, pretty! Are those twinkles for me?" The treeling's slender branches strained toward the earrings. Keelie smiled. Amazing how the promise of jewelry brought such a quick recovery.

"They're yours if you swear you won't tell anyone about the bad twinkle. I'm going to take it out of your pot."

"I won't say a word. Not to anyone."

"You can't send thoughts about it, either. Not even to Jake."

The treeling was silent for a moment. "Jake is your friend, but he thinks you're scared of him."

"Then Jake would be right. He's kind of scary, Alora." Keelie hooked the earrings over two of Alora's branches, then knelt to dig out the amulet while Alora shook her leaves to make her ornaments bounce and jingle.

The amulet was deep in Alora's roots, and Keelie pried them gently to one side, pulled the prickly metal acorn out, then carefully tucked the soil back around the roots. When she finished, she saw that the treeling had fallen into a peaceful sleep.

Keelie took the amulet to the bathroom and washed it, wondering at how it remained untarnished even after days in dirt. She slipped the cord over her head and put the heavy metal amulet inside her shirt, its now-familiar chill reassuring. No one would find it here. She shrugged on a hoodie and quietly made her way down the hall.

Good thing Dad and Grandmother were at an afternoon Council meeting in the village. She could hide the amulet in the forest. She just couldn't risk leaving it around the house anymore—there was much she didn't know about it. What if it called out to Elianard, who'd once worn it?

She planned to bury it near the work site below the ridge, where the iron and steel earth-moving equipment might mask the amulet's magic. The elves wouldn't think to look for it there, not even Elia. She didn't trust the elf girl. Lately, she didn't trust anyone.

In Dad's ornate little camper, Keelie found a flashlight. She clicked it on. A dim light shone on the ground. The batteries were weak, but it would do in case she was out after dark.

Keelie climbed the trail that bordered the ridge. As she approached the top, she saw the earth-moving equipment below, in the clearing at the edge of the forest. It seemed awfully far away, and in the dense woods there was no clear path to the bottom.

A twig snapped behind her and she turned, looking for any drifting tendrils of fog that might signal Jake's presence. The only thing out of place was a big orange blob at ground level, sneaking from tree to tree. Knot was following her, either out of catlike curiosity or because he was taking his guardian duties seriously.

Keelie walked a little farther, looking for a path down the mountain. Ahead was the sound of rushing water, and she paused as a new thought struck her. The stream would make a good hiding place, too, and it was closer. She turned away from the ridge and hurried toward the sound of the water.

Up here, the stream was split into two by a huge granite boulder, an island of stone in the middle of the rushing shoals of water. A lone cypress grew on the boulder, its roots entwining and encircling the rock. Definitely a great place to hide the amulet.

Keelie climbed down the steep bank, then stepped onto a small flat stone, trying to find another way to cross to the boulder and still stay dry. A loud splash erupted behind her. She turned and saw the little sprite that she'd seen and talked to earlier.

The water fairy at the High Mountain Renaissance Faire had resembled a catfish, but this one was different. She had huge dark eyes, a wide mouth, and a trout tail, which shimmered iridescently. Yarn-like hair flowed down into the water.

"Hi," Keelie said. "Can you tell me what's the best way to get to that big rock?"

The sprite swam closer, reaching out a web-fingered hand to hold onto the rock that Keelie was on. "You can see me?" it said, looking up both stream banks, as if to make sure no one else was around.

"Of course!" Keelie knelt on the rock, thinking it was rude to tower over the little sprite. Cold water seeped through her jeans. "Don't the other elves see you?"

The sprite rose, leaning closer, her upper body leaving the water. Yep, definitely a girl. "No. They hardly ever come up here, and when they do, I go upstream because they like to pee in the water." She made a face, her broad mouth turned down, then turned her head from side to side, studying Keelie from her broadly set, dark purple eyes. "You're different from them."

"Different? How?" Keelie wondered if the sprite could detect her human half.

A loud purr rumbled behind her and Knot rubbed up against her backside, then leaned hard against her just enough to make her lose her balance. Startled, Keelie tried to straighten, but it was too late. She fell into the water with a large splash. The water was only knee-deep, but very cold, and she was drenched and taking deep, sharp breaths, as if that would warm her.

The water sprite swam up to her and put a clammy little hand on her arm. "Are you all right?"

Keelie nodded rapidly, more because she was shivering than from agreement. "I'll live." She turned to glare at Knot.

The water fairy's eyes grew wider when she saw the cat. "You!"

Knot raised his right paw, extending claws like a badass with a switchblade. He glared at the water sprite.

"Knot, I'm going to kill you." Keelie stood up, water rushing from her drenched jeans. She gasped as the air hit her cooled flesh. Maybe she should sit in the water some more. It had been starting to feel almost warm.

Knot lowered his paw and hissed at the sprite, who laughed melodically with a sound like wind chimes. "I know him," she said. "He must like you, because he's never this affectionate with anyone else."

"Pushing me in the water is showing affection?"

The water sprite nodded. "He did that to his other girl. Has he licked your eyeballs yet?"

"No." His other girl? "When did he do this to his other girl?"

The water sprite did a back flip, smacking her tail on the water. Keelie thought she had left, but she surfaced again. "I cannot tell when. Three snows ago."

"Three snows." Keelie was disappointed. She thought that maybe the sprite meant her mother. So who was this girl that Snot the cat had antagonized? Someone he loved. Maybe Dad knew.

Knot was washing his tail, as if he found the water sprite and Keelie boring. Keelie was cold, and her underwear was soggy. She needed to hide the amulet near the boulder.

"I need to hide something, but I don't want the other elves to find it. Can I hide it in your stream?" Keelie pointed to the boulder. "I want to bury it under there."

Knot jumped from rock to rock until he was on the little island, beside the cypress. His gaze held hers and she seemed to know he approved.

"Oh yes," the water sprite said. She sounded pleased that Keelie had asked for her help.

Keelie pulled the amulet's cord over her head and handed it to the water sprite. Despite being wet and soggy, she suddenly felt warmer.

The water sprite accepted the amulet in her small

webbed hands, then quickly disappeared beneath the water.

Without the amulet, Keelie had a stronger sense of the trees around her. She could feel the cypress.

Do not speak to others of what you've seen, tree, she commanded.

My name is Orim, and I have held this great rock for eighty rings. Do not tell me what to do, little Tree Shepherdess.

Knot sharpened his claws on the cypress's trunk.

Oh, that hurts. Make the bad fairy stop and I won't tell anyone your secret.

Keelie gave Knot a thumbs-up, and he stopped and started to lick his paw.

Your secret is safe with me.

Minutes later, the sprite returned.

"It is done. The amulet is in a crack in the rock, below the water's surface."

Keelie bowed her head. "Thank you."

The water sprite smiled. "It was my honor to help you, sister."

Sister? The sprite must be very lonely to claim kinship with Keelie. She'd have to come back and see the water sprite more often, especially if the elves couldn't see her.

Keelie left the stream and found her way back to the trail, her wet jeans slowing her walk. The afternoon shadows were lengthening, and the forest seemed very still. She looked around, trying to figure out why she felt that something was wrong. Fog crept along the ground, obscuring the forest floor.

Was this Jake?

Tree Shepherdess, stop him. The anguished cry came from a nearby tree, but she couldn't tell which one. Other trees joined in the cry for help.

Stop who? Where are you?

The trees' fear clouded the images they were sending her.

To her left, Keelie noticed movement, and then a dull silver glow came from an evergreen. For a moment the tree glowed like neon light. Then it started to fade, as if something was pulling the light out of it.

Help me. The evergreen pleaded in her mind. The fog was becoming thicker.

Keelie closed her eyes and centered herself. Green magic filled her.

Dad. She saw him, sitting at a long table, the faces of other elves around him.

Keelie? He frowned. She hardly ever initiated telepathic communication between them.

There's something draining the life force from one of the trees. I'm going to stop it, but I may need your help. She sent him a mental image of the area, hoping he'd recognize this section of the forest.

Keelie, stay away from it. I'll be right there.

I can't stay away, Dad. The tree's fading. I have to go to him.

She closed the mental communication with Dad.

When Keelie opened her eyes, she could see with her tree sight—she could see the faces in the trees, just as she had in the Wildewood. They were frightened, although some seemed angry.

The fog blanketed the forest, rising from the ground, making it hard to see even with her tree vision. She didn't know how she was going to stop the predator, but she'd improvise.

She walked silently, focused on the glow from the evergreen, but it was getting dimmer. She sent encouragement to the tree. *I'm on my way.*

She knew from the other trees that this was Ernem, and he was fading quickly, soon to be a part of the Great Sylvus. Keelie hurried. She could finally make out a smoky image, blending with the shadows of the trees, that was absorbing the evergreen's energy.

"Stop it, Jake. Leave him alone!"

The smoky, hazy form turned to her. Keelie's heart pounded hard and fast. She didn't see a corporeal image, but she could make out a human form inside the haze. It looked larger than Jake. Could there be two vampires in the forest?

She had no more time to think about what it might be. The smoky form whirled, batlike, in the air above her, and then flew straight for her.

ten

Terrified by the shadow swooping toward her, Keelie ran, the sound of rushing water filling her ears. She was now close to the creek again. She didn't see the sprite, which was wisely hidden away. Knot was gone, too—some guardian he turned out to be.

The aunties called out to her, their voices heavy and ancient. *Cross running water, Tree Shepherdess. The evil will not follow.*

The darkness touched her back, cold, and Keelie hurried down the bank of the stream and then launched herself into the air, briefly flying like Ariel before crashing down on the boulder. She grabbed at Orim's trunk and held on.

Dad's mind touched hers. *Keelie?*

I'm okay, Dad. I'm in the creek.

Don't move. I'm on my way.

Bhata scrambled in the treetops, their borrowed limbs clicking like chopsticks. Keelie pulled herself to her feet, holding onto Orim's trunk. She winced at the pain in her knees but sent soothing thoughts to the tree, who was alarmed at all the commotion. Then a movement on the opposite creek bank caught her eye, and she stared.

It was Jake, standing in front of a large deer. The animal was in some kind of trance. A wave of silver energy flowed from the deer to Jake. His eyes were closed, and his body glowed with the silver light that filled him. He was draining the life force from the deer.

"Stop it!" She jumped into the creek and picked up a fallen branch, lifting it like a sword, thinking only of saving the deer. She held the branch high over her shoulder, ready to wield, and forded the creek, water squishing through her already-wet tennis shoes. "You have some nerve, trying that again."

Jake opened his eyes. They widened in surprise as he saw her climbing up the bank below him.

Dad's voice filled her mind. *I'm almost there.*

"Stop it *now*. Let it go." Keelie motioned toward the deer. "You're killing it."

"I'm not." Jake gestured with his hands as if to break an

invisible tether. The deer blinked, awareness returning. It pawed the ground then bounded away.

Relieved that it seemed to be okay, she turned to glower at Jake. "What were you doing to that deer? The same thing you did to the tree? And why did you attack me?" She lifted the branch, ready to defend herself if he jumped her.

"What are you talking about? I wasn't harming the deer. What attacked you?"

Keelie scrambled up the bank and stormed over to him. "Game time is over. You're going to answer my questions. I saw you in the forest draining the energy from a tree, killing it. Why would you do such a thing?"

His eyes darkened to flat black. "You saw someone draining the life force of a tree? That's not possible."

"It's possible, and it happened. I thought you were different. Haven't you learned anything? Of course the elves will kick you out of here if they find you. You're a monster." She held the stick like a baseball bat.

Jake flinched. "I don't need blood, just energy. I only take enough to sustain me—I would never drain another creature of its life force." His gaze held hers. "You have to believe me, Keelie. I'm not evil. And I don't do trees."

Keelie didn't believe him, but Knot was weaving in and around Jake's legs. There should be a warning label: Do *not* use your cat as a guidepost in decision-making.

"Where have you been?" Keelie glared at the hairball. "You abandoned me."

He sat down and blinked at her—Kitty for *you're fine, quit your whining.*

Green energy filled her as Dad connected telepathically. *Keelie? Where are you? You're not by the tree.*

I'm okay, Dad. I was scared and ran. I'm in the woods, not too far from the creek.

Stay there. Don't move. I'm on my way. Keelie felt a mental hug from her father. Like he used to do.

Keelie looked at Jake. She didn't know why she didn't want to reveal his presence to the elves, especially if he was a danger to the forest. "I don't know what's going on, but we need to talk. Knot seems to trust you, so I will, too—for now." She pointed to the direction the deer had taken. "You're going to have to explain what is going on in this forest. For now you need to get out of here. My dad is on his way, probably with help."

Jake's tense posture eased. "Thank you," he whispered. "I will tell you everything." He was gone with supernatural speed.

Seconds later, Dad was there. He grabbed her and wrapped her in a hug, almost squeezing the air out of her lungs.

He released her and brushed her hair from her eyes. "Thank the Great Sylvus you're safe."

She smiled up at him. It was like having Ren Faire Dad back.

"What happened?" His eyes searched her face.

Keelie swallowed. She couldn't tell him about Jake—she'd promised him a chance to explain himself. She didn't like keeping secrets from Dad, but she felt sorry for Jake. Earlier in the summer, she'd accused Dad of keeping elven secrets from her, and now she was the one with the secrets (of course, she hadn't told him about the Wildewood unicorn at first, either). But when she had some time, she had to figure out why she couldn't let him in.

Branches swayed as a wind began to blow through the trees. Keelie could hear murmurs and scratchy whispers—the trees were speaking to each other. The green leaves on the hardwoods flipped, showing their undersides as they liked to do when a storm was coming.

Dad closed his eyes. He was talking to the trees, although Keelie was blocked from the conversation. When he reopened them, his eyes glowed bright green. He stared at Keelie in shock. "It can't be."

Keelie shuddered. So he knew about Jake now. This was her chance to explain, but she couldn't.

Deep male voices boomed nearby. Keelie recognized Niriel's, then heard someone shout, "Milord, over here."

Dad touched Keelie's arm. "Say nothing. Let me answer the questions."

She nodded. No problem there.

Dad's face was drawn and tense. He kept Keelie close to him, his hand grasped tightly around her upper arm. She watched as he scanned the forest. Maybe he thought the fog thing would return.

She heard the pounding of horses' hooves upon the ground before she saw them. The entire Silver Bough jousting company thundered up on horseback, swords drawn, ready to go to battle, led by Niriel. Sean, whose hair still looked a little bedraggled from his recent *bhata* encounter, was at his father's side.

Keelie hoped he had a lifetime of bad-hair days for breaking her heart. He didn't make eye contact, but Niriel stared at her as if she was a disgusting peasant and he some feudal lord coming to punish his errant servant. He reined in his horse near them. The big beast snorted and bobbed his head.

"Something evil plagues the forest, the Dread fades, and your daughter is at the middle of it," Niriel said coldly. "Explain why you're here in the forest."

"I could ask the same of you, Niriel. Why is the entire elven patrol riding in the forest?" Dad looked regal in his elven clothes, a match for Niriel or anyone in the jousting company.

Niriel motioned with a gloved hand. One of the jousters rode forward. Keelie recognized him from the Wilde-wood Faire, where he'd escorted the elf girl playing the role of Maid Marian. He handed a burlap bag to Niriel, who scowled and curled his nose as he reached into the bag and pulled out a stiff rabbit coated in mold. It stank, and looked flat as if all the air had been sucked out of it.

Niriel threw it down at Dad's feet. The rabbit's head broke off and rolled away. Dust billowed out from the body, releasing more of the rotten odor. "We have a vampire in the forest, and when we find him, his fate will be quick. We'll destroy his cursed soul."

A cold fist squeezed Keelie's heart. *Jake.* She looked at the rabbit. He'd told her he didn't totally drain the life energy of animals, but rabbits were so little. Maybe he hadn't meant to kill it.

Dad looked from the rabbit to Niriel. Keelie saw he was forcing himself to keep a stolid face and not wrinkle his nose in disgust. "Has the Council sanctioned this hunt?" His voice sounded calm.

Veins bulged in Niriel's neck. "Etilafael has called for a meeting this evening. I'm sure as soon as she and Keliatiel understand the danger we're in, they will approve extending the protection of our jousters to all our lands, as they were of old. Not only are we facing an ancient evil, but the Round Ear town mayor has canceled the harvest festival and declared the lands next to ours open for recreational use for all."

"I wasn't told of this arrangement." Dad frowned.

Niriel leaned forward in his saddle. "The Round Ears are now allowed to bring their machines on the park land..." He snapped his fingers as if it would summon lost words. "ATVs, I heard one Round Ear call them. On our land."

"The Dread will keep them out." Dad still sounded calm, but Keelie noticed that his left hand was squeezing a piece of wood. He was tense.

"The Dread is failing," Niriel said. "I will propose to the Council that we use the book."

Keelie wondered if Niriel was talking about the book at her grandmother's house. She glanced quickly at the spot where the sprite had put the amulet. The sprite splashed in the water, but no elf glanced her way. All eyes were on Dad and Niriel. Poor sprite.

"The old ways will not work. There would be repercussions from the humans and others if we use the forbidden magic." Dad's voice grew harsh as he struggled to maintain control.

Keelie had never heard her father refer to "humans" in such an angry way. It shocked her to her core. Had he forgotten she was half human?

It seemed Niriel hadn't, as he looked from Dad to Keelie. "Yes, I agree, but seeing that you care for them so much, what do you suggest, Tree Shepherd? Will you send your Round Ear child to tell them to stop invading our land with their destructive ways? What about the trees—how will you protect them? Because mark my words, once they allow the humans access, the loggers will follow."

Dad pulled Keelie close and wrapped his arms around her protectively.

"Names can't hurt me, Dad."

Before he could respond, a ripple of fear filled the air. It came from the trees, and the first wave was followed by a stronger one that made the rose quartz in her pocket grow hot.

The trees swayed as if a strong wind was blowing

through their branches. In her mind, Keelie heard panicked cries from the trees.

Tree Shepherd, protect us.

The weight of their pleas pressed in on her. The jousters looked up into the green canopy above as if they too could hear them. The horses whinnied and pawed at the ground. Sean made soothing noises, trying to calm his horse.

Niriel smiled wickedly. "It is your duty as Shepherd to heed their call." He held his gaze hard and fast on Dad.

Dad lifted his right hand, palm outward, then moved it quickly to his right in a cutting motion. A green light enveloped him and Keelie felt chlorophyll fill her body. She could see frightened faces in the trees, their eyes filled with anxiety and apprehension.

Dad's loud telepathic message rang through the forest. *I will protect you.*

The aunties, the most ancient oaks of the forest, chimed in, their voices united. *Calm yourselves. Listen to the Tree Shepherd.*

"I have not seen you use your power often, Zekeliel. I have to ask myself why you don't use it more in our times of need. Your daughter, as well. My son has told me interesting stories about your daughter's magical capabilities."

Keelie's chest tightened with fear. Had Sean told him about the wooden sword?

"Everyone has a story about my daughter's magical abilities." Dad's smile was tight. "She is a tree shepherd. The trees accepted her from the beginning, and she came to them in their time of need."

"And now she can prove herself to us during our time of need?" Niriel looked at the other armed horsemen.

"You want her help, yet you call her a Round Ear. She doesn't have to prove anything to the elves." Niriel started to stammer a reply, but Dad was on a roll. "And whose time of need do you speak of, Niriel? The trees? The elves?" Dad lowered his head and aimed a hard look at Sean's father. "Yours?"

Niriel's eyes narrowed. "I speak for this forest. Our home. I will call a meeting to propose that we use the book's magic to protect what is ours."

"Then we will discuss it with the Council, not here in the open forest where all can hear." Dad toed the rabbit carcass. "My daughter's magic is not open for discussion by you or by the Council. This conversation is over. I have tree-shepherd business to which I must attend."

Niriel bowed his head elegantly. "Later, then." He tapped his feet against his horse, turned around and motioned with his hand for the jousters to follow. Sean looked at Keelie and then rode away with his father.

Dad tugged on Keelie and she trailed after him as they walked down the path to the ailing evergreen. She'd never heard Dad speak so forcefully in front of another elf. Okay, he'd spoken to Grandmother the other night when she challenged him about Knot's guardianship. He'd taken on Elianard several times. But this time Dad had radiated power.

Keelie remembered that she hadn't seen Elianard today. Not that she wanted to, but normally he would be right in the thick of things with Niriel, demanding use of the book. Maybe Elianard didn't do horses.

She walked alongside Dad in silence. She was surprised that her magical abilities hadn't gone unnoticed by the elves here. At the High Mountain Faire she'd taken part in the Tree Lorem for the Queen Aspen, but most of the elves had been sick at the Wildewood Fair, where she'd really used her magic. In typical elven fashion, it sounded as if they were finding ways of using her without acknowledging her. She didn't like that idea.

They soon found the tree, which was scared out of its trunk. Keelie summoned her tree magic, and as green energy filled her, she could see its face. Thin, long-nosed, and with worry wrinkles lining his barky forehead, the poor thing was jittery, his eyes darting back and forth as if he were on the lookout for more trouble.

Dad circled the tree, examining it as a doctor would a patient. "Whatever drained it will be back." He spoke aloud to Keelie, then said in mental tree speak, *Fear not, Ernem. We will protect you.*

Ernem shuddered his branches. *It was terrible, Tree Shepherd.*

Dad sent reassuring images to Ernem. *I will place a strong spell of protection around you. Sleep.*

The nervous tree closed its eyes. His branches drooped and he succumbed to slumber.

"How do we do put a spell of protection on a tree?"

"It's a combination of Earth magic, securing the tree's roots in the earth, and harnessing sunlight to create a shield around it."

"Harnessing sunlight sounds dangerous. Should I get some SPF 45, sunglasses, and a hat?" Mom had always made her be careful about UV rays. Not to mention that Keelie had no clue what she was supposed to do.

Dad leaned against the sleeping tree, which was now snoring very loudly in tree speak. Keelie was glad she didn't hang out in this part of the forest because there would be problems between Ernem and herself if she had to listen to him snore all the time.

"I need for you to use your rose quartz. Place your hand with the quartz on the ground—like you did with the power plant. Just open the channel, and I'll control it."

"I don't know if I can do that." In the Wildewood, her use of the crystal on the ground had unleashed enormous energy, enough to save an entire forest and also to knock out a power plant.

He nodded and smiled. "Sure you can. Except this time, I will use sunlight to transform the energy around the tree as a protective shield. It will give Ernem time to heal."

She pulled the rose quartz from her belt loop and sat down cross-legged on the ground. She placed her hand flat on top of the quartz. She could feel the energy of the earth humming underneath her hand.

Dad placed his left hand on the trunk of the tree. He

held up his right hand and it began to glow with green light. A slanting beam of sunlight swirled around him as it filtered into the green energy pulsing from him. Soon yellow sunlight and green magic whirled and twined around Dad and Ernem.

The rose quartz underneath Keelie's hands pulsed and grew warm. She could feel power surging up from the earth and through the crystal. Keelie shot Dad a panicky look. What should she do with this power?

Dad nodded and she felt him draw on that power, and like sucking a milk shake through a straw, a thick stream of power rose through the quartz and to her father, joining the sunlight and green magic.

Keelie watched, awed, as her father wove the three streams of energy into a strong net which settled on the ground around them, then sank out of sight. She felt it pull tight around Ernem's roots.

The rose quartz grew hotter. When it started to burn she dropped it, and just like that, she was free of the Earth magic. Then the Dread closed in on her with suffocating swiftness. She scrambled for the rose quartz and gasped with relief when she found it. She made a mental note to get a second one as a backup.

Her father still held the magic, and now the green magic and golden light rotated counterclockwise in a single coil of energy, focused through the rose quartz.

Keelie was about to rise but Dad shook his head. "Stay."

From beneath Ernem's roots a veil of green rose, flecked

with yellow sparkles that glittered like teeny, tiny suns. It rose higher and higher, enveloping the tree, Dad, and Keelie.

"Wow!"

Dad smiled, his casual, laid-back self again. "We do good work, daughter. Ernem will heal and be protected." He patted the trunk reassuringly.

It had grown dusky while they worked, and she held the light pink crystal in front of her to illuminate the area around them with its glow. "That kind of recharged its batteries."

Dad laughed. "In a way, I guess it did."

"How did you use the energy that I summoned?" Healing Ernem and protecting him made her want to work more in the forest with Dad.

"It takes practice, but I don't think it'll be hard for you to learn. You have more ability than anyone I've ever worked with, including my own father."

Before she could ask about her grandfather, Dad's relaxed demeanor vanished and he grew stern again. Oh great, he was back to being Dread Dad. The vision of them working together in father-daughter harmony disappeared.

"It's time to go home, and it's time for you to tell me exactly what you saw—I think you're keeping something from me. "

"Okay, Dad. But not in front of Grandmother."

"Why not? She's the Lady of the Forest."

"Because—" She fell silent.

She couldn't see a way out, but she'd have to figure out a way to save Jake—even though she knew the punishment would be extreme.

eleven

Back at the house, Dad called for Grandmother Keliatiel. She didn't answer.

Keelie looked up at the empty space above the fireplace. Mom's carved portrait would look good up there. She crossed her arms over her chest. She didn't know why she was thinking about Mom right now, because Dad was about to demand answers about the vampire. She didn't know what to do.

Dad returned to the living room. "Your grandmother tells me that the Council is reconvening tonight. An emergency meeting." He pointed at Knot. "Keep guard."

Knot hissed and walked away.

"Don't take that attitude with me," Dad called after him. "As long as you remain her guardian, then you obey me." He turned to Keelie, agitated. "He always took your mother's side, too." He motioned toward the chair. "We need to talk." He was wearing pants underneath his robes, but he maintained the same regal air that he'd had when confronting Niriel in the forest. It was like her father was transforming right in front of her eyes, turning into a Council elf.

Keelie remained standing. "What do you mean, Knot always took mother's side?"

Dad ran his fingers through his hair. "Keelie, I don't have time to explain. I have to go to the meeting too, and I need to know what you've seen."

It angered her that Dad thought he could just not talk about Mom. Hide it all away, like he had hidden her portrait in the closet upstairs. No, Keelie wasn't going to do this anymore. It was time Dad talked. If he expected Keelie to tell him what she knew about Jake, well, he could talk first. "I want to talk about Mom."

"Not now. I need to know what you know. You saw an entity sucking a tree's life force. Can you explain everything you saw?"

"Didn't Ernem tell you?"

"He did. He said it was a vampire. But I want your version too, Keelie. He's a jittery kind of tree, and he didn't see much because of his panic."

"I got that same vibe from him."

"Tell me what you saw, and we'll see what we can do. There's so much you don't know, Keelie."

"Yeah, because you don't talk to me … because you don't explain anything to me." Anger and grief burned through her heart like hot molten steel. "You didn't contact me for thirteen years. You let Mom take me away without fighting. Then you drag me back here to the Dread Forest and make me live with a grandmother who makes it really obvious that she hates humans. You keep going to Council meetings with the other elves. What do you talk about? How to handle your Round Ear child?"

Dad's face paled and his ear tips reddened. His expression was pained, but Keelie was glad she'd finally let her father know how she felt. It was time for them to deal with some real things.

Dad opened and closed his hands, making fists. "Your mother chose to take you away, thinking that it would protect you. But we stayed in touch, in our way." His voice rose. "Katy left me, but I've honored her wishes." Dad looked past Keelie as if he were seeing the image of Mom standing in the room. "If she had stayed, I would have chosen to age as she aged. And when she died, I would have faded."

Surprised that Dad was even talking, Keelie reeled at the fact that Dad had been willing to end his life when Mom died. She would have been all alone.

Dad turned back to Keelie, his face angry but also filled

with pain. "Your mother ran from me, Keelie, and took you from my life. She wanted me to promise not to come to you, but I sent gifts, and she sent me photos of you."

Mom was no ogre. If only she were here to give her side of the story. Keelie wanted to protect her, but without the truth, she didn't know how to answer. Mom had taken so many of her secrets with her.

"And I couldn't have come to you even if I'd tried. You were under the protection of the Shining Ones."

Keelie was confused. That's what the trees had called her friend Raven in the Wildewood. "What are the Shining Ones, exactly?"

"The Shining Ones are the high fairies."

"Like the *bhata*, the *feithid daoine*?"

"Yes, but more." Dad looked up at the ceiling as if seeking some help from the universe. "There are different kinds of good fairies, just like there are different kinds of bad ones. The Shining Ones are the high court."

"Like a fairy queen and king?" Keelie remembered images from her Arthur Rackham fairy-tale books.

"The very ones." Dad's mouth was stretched in a solid line. "And they're not very nice." He seemed to state that as someone with personal experience.

"And that's why I want to get rid of that cat. It's a spy." Grandmother appeared in the doorway. Her eyes were bright and her head held high in indignation.

"Mother, I think you've interfered in my life enough. I will do as I see fit in this matter. I was given the message that Knot stays, and Knot stays. If you hadn't interfered, then Katy might have let me be part of my daughter's life."

Stunned, Keelie whirled around and stared at her grandmother. She seemed indignant now, but hurt, as if Dad's words had pierced her heart.

"I didn't know she would take the child," Grandmother said. "I couldn't let you fade. I'd lost one son. I couldn't stand to lose another."

Dad glared at her. "I lost my child because you couldn't bear to let me go."

Grandmother Keliatiel walked closer to Dad, her hand stretching out for him. "I insisted Katharine leave Keelie with me. I told her I would raise the child. She was half elven—she would have magical powers. Katharine said she'd make sure Keelie never discovered she was elven. She would only know the human world, but Katharine did not tell us she was kin to the Shining Court."

The Shining Court? No way. Grandmother was making up stories to excuse her behavior. Keelie could see it being played out as Grandmother told the story: Mom packing her bags, telling Dad not to find them, and leaving with toddler Keelie in tow. Mom had done exactly what she'd threatened to do. That much was probably true, minus the fae kin.

A knock at the door startled them.

Dad stood. "We have to go to the meeting."

Grandmother sat down carefully. "I don't know if I can attend."

"You must, Mother. Niriel is going to try to convince you to use the book."

Grandmother was silent for a moment. "He wouldn't dare."

"He spoke of it in the forest. He brought the entire Silver Bough, armed, with him."

"He dares raise an army? The book stays in my house." Grandmother squeezed her hands into angry fists, then dropped them and leaned back. "I'm too tired to deal with this, but I will need to be there to argue on the side of reason."

Keelie wondered if she should mention the amulet, but decided against it. They were talking about the book; they knew nothing of the amulet.

Dad walked over to Grandmother Keliatiel and held out his hand. "Let's go. You can rest when we return."

He pulled her gently to her feet and offered his elbow. She linked her arm through his and leaned against him, looking defeated and old. Even though the old woman had never been nice to her, Keelie's heart ached to see her like that.

Dad stopped at the door. "You're to stay in this house and not go anywhere, please."

Keelie stood there. They'd just had this big argument, and they were going to leave her. Elves!

Dad must have sensed her feelings. "We'll talk later."

It wasn't the resolution Keelie had wanted after such a big argument. But she had a lot to think about, and being away from Grandmother Keliatiel was exactly what she needed. She shouldn't feel sorry for the woman who had driven Mom away. Not that Mom hadn't had a part in her own exodus from the elves.

Keelie leaned her head in her palm as if she could push the thoughts back into her mind. It felt as if they were spilling out of her forehead. If she ate something, maybe she could think better.

She was just finishing a bowl of leftover vegetable soup when she heard Ariel banging her wings against the mews walls. It was time to feed the hawk. Dad had said to stay in the house, but even though the mews were outside, they were technically part of the house. It would be cruel to allow the hawk to go hungry.

Keelie grabbed a rat from the refrigerator where she'd left it thawing that morning. She smiled. Grandmother became squeamish whenever Keelie served rat. Mom would've run in the opposite direction. Keelie smiled sadly imagining Mom's reaction.

Using a flashlight, she walked to the mews. The waxing gibbous moon shone down on the house.

Ariel's milky eyes seemed cloudier tonight. Behind her, in the dark of the side of the house, a stick snapped. Alarmed, Keelie shined the flashlight in that direction. Her heart raced as she searched the area. Nothing.

"Hey girl. It's going to be fast-food rat tonight, Ariel."

Tendrils of fog drifted around the mews. Keelie froze in mid–rat toss.

Fog swirled around, then began to solidify.

"What the...?" She was ready to run as adrenaline pumped through her body.

The fog dispersed and there stood Jake with a goofy grin on his face. "Too bad it's frozen rat, otherwise I'd have a snack. The energy from the ones in Seattle is sort of slimy from the pollution they absorb through their bodies."

"I don't even want to know. What are you doing here? And can't you just walk?"

"This is faster."

"If the elves find you, you're going to be in trouble."

Jake waved his hand nonchalantly. "They're all at the meeting except that girl Elia and her father. It will take hours. Your father may not be home until tomorrow afternoon."

Keelie cut her eyes over to him. "How do you know so much?"

"I hang out. Watch." He extended a hand, pale and long-fingered. For a moment nothing happened, and Keelie wondered if she was supposed to do something, but then a dark mist seemed to seep out from his skin like a microfine spray of ink. The mist thickened until she couldn't see his hand anymore, and then he dropped his arm. The mist moved, showing that his arm was gone, turned to black fog.

Keelie's mouth went dry. "Can you do that with your whole body?" Her voice came out papery and rough. She held the rat, a heavy weight in her hand.

"Yes. I've been practicing for a very long time." He looked into her eyes, and they were no different than they were before. Jake's eyes, not some monster's. Her breathing slowed, and with it her heart. She'd just thought he summoned the fog to hide himself in, not that he could actually turn into mist.

She hoped he hadn't been watching her shower.

"I've seen evidence of that creature that chased you in the woods. Can we talk?"

"Let me feed Ariel first. And yes, let's talk—I have a few questions for you." She went to the mews, where Ariel eagerly pounced on her rat and nibbled at it with her beak. Keelie turned away before Ariel got to seriously digging into her rat supper.

She walked around the side of the house and saw Jake on the porch, in a rocking chair that Dad had made. She smiled, trying to act as if everything was normal, and sat on the porch swing (cedar from New England).

The stars twinkled in the night sky, visible in small open patches in the tree canopy. Keelie could see the silvery outline of Jake's face in the moonlight.

He rubbed the smooth arm of the rocker. "Your father has a great talent for wood." He sounded wistful.

"I know. People love his stuff at the Ren Faires." She stroked the swing's arm.

"Do you miss being with other humans?" Jake asked.

Keelie shrugged. "I do. I miss the friends I made. It was like leaving another family." Then she gestured with her hand to encompass the house and the woods beyond. "But we came to the Dread Forest. Home Sweet Home."

"It's not so bad. Give it a chance. There's a lot going on right now."

"There's always something going on. Ever since I arrived at the High Mountain Renaissance Faire, it's been one freakin' dysfunctional adventure after another."

"Adventure nonetheless," Jake said.

"I can do without all the excitement, thank you."

"You are spoiled, Keliel Heartwood," Jake said sharply. Red flashed in his eyes. "You have a home. Your home travels with you. From your mother's heart to your father's love. Think before you speak. Think of what others may have lost."

A pang struck Keelie's heart. "Was it really awful being exiled?" she asked.

He turned his face from her. "For almost seven of your lifetimes, I have wandered the earth, banned from my forest and my family. Do you know what that's like for an elf?"

Keelie thought of the trees, whispering her name as she slept. She thought of Dad fixing oatmeal, of the bright colors of the Ren Faires, and the deep and varied greens of the forests she had seen. "I'm starting to know." She put her hand on his arm. "I'm so sorry."

Jake smiled at her, the red fading from his eyes. "You said you had questions. What are they? I'll answer them to the best of my ability."

"If you're a vampire, why aren't you like Dracula? Or like Edward Cullen?"

"It's all about the way you're transformed. Bloodsuckers are changed by a bite from another vampire. My change was brought about by using dark magic, magic that caused harm to bring about change. Let's just say there are consequences for using dark magic."

"But what if you use just a little dark magic, for a good cause?"

Jake shook his head. "It doesn't matter if one's intentions are good. There are rules to magic. It's like physics. You can't choose to skip gravity."

Keelie's mind spun. "When you saved the Dread Forest, did you use the book of magic?"

"I tried, but it didn't work exactly like I thought it would."

"What happened?" She needed to avoid whatever he'd done that had failed.

He shook his head. "Things didn't go according to plan, and I tried something different. By the way, I found more dead rabbits in the woods, and a dead deer, too. There's another vampire out there. We have to find out who it is. If it keeps killing, its blood thirst will deepen and it'll become a full-blown nosferatu."

"So there are two of you running around the Dread forest." Bad news.

"The other one needs help, Keelie."

"I need help, too." Elia stood in front of the porch. Her gown was torn, and she had scratches on her face.

"What happened to you?" Keelie asked.

"I was near the construction site, and I tripped and fell into some briars."

Jake jumped up and guided Elia to his chair. She accepted the help meekly.

Near the construction site? That sounded very un-Elia.

"I've seen the fairies around you. I know they protect you," Elia said to Keelie. She leaned forward shakily and ran her fingers through her tangled golden curls, raking leaves and twigs out to drift to the porch floor. "You have to go to them and ask them if they can heal him. He didn't mean to hurt anyone. He just wanted to save the forest. Our home."

"Heal who? Save what?" Keelie was totally confused.

Elia lifted her face to Jake. "You did the same thing, once. There has to be a way to cure him."

Jake shook his head and gazed at Elia with sympathy. "I'm sorry. There are ways to deal with it, but he is on a course that was set when he tried to kill a unicorn."

"What are you talking about?" Keelie stood up, not wanting to be left out of the conversation. And she wasn't sure she liked the way Jake was looking at Elia—as if she'd hit him with a baseball bat.

Elia's eyes were rimmed with tears. "You have to help him, Keelie. You know what it's like to lose a parent. I can't lose him. He's my father. I'm begging you for your help."

Keelie stepped back. "Wait a minute. Are we talking about Elianard?"

The elf girl nodded miserably. "My father is turning into a vampire."

twelve

Elianard was the vampire. She should have known. But she couldn't believe Elia was asking her to save Elianard, even if he was her father. She grasped the side arm of the porch swing to steady herself.

"I don't know how I can help." Keelie looked at Jake, who returned her gaze without any expression. "I think you two had better go. Grandmother and Dad will be returning soon."

Elia nodded. She wiped her eyes and sniffled, then glanced at Jake to see if he was looking. Keelie felt the outrage build. Faking it again. Could she ever believe the elf girl?

Jake sat down next to Keelie, glancing over at Elia before putting his head close to Keelie's. "She needs your help. You're a tree shepherdess, but it means more than helping trees. Do the right thing."

Jake's voice was soft, but sounded old, as if he carried centuries of wisdom. If she closed her eyes, he'd sound like Dad.

Ariel cried out, and her wings beat against the cage. She turned her head from side to side, as if she might see again if she kept trying. It tore Keelie's heart in two. Elia had laughed when she'd cursed Ariel. She'd gotten into a lot of trouble for using magic she couldn't undo, although the punishment, whatever it had been, would not help Ariel to see again.

"The wizard at the rehabilitation center couldn't break the curse on Ariel. Elia is the one who ruined her forever. And she helped Elianard try to kill a unicorn. She doesn't deserve my help." Keelie stood up, but Jake grabbed her arm.

"People make mistakes, and it would be a mistake not to help Elia."

Keelie glared at Jake. "Did you know her father threatened to kill Dad?"

Elia wailed, probably sensing that Jake was starting to see Keelie's point. "I'm sorry," she said. "I wish I could take back what happened in the Wildewood. And I wish I'd never cursed the hawk. It was wrong. You're more powerful than anyone thought possible for a Round Ear." Too late, Elia realized her mistake.

Keelie jerked her arm free of Jake's. "Even now, they think of me as something less than them, yet they expect me to save their asses when they get in trouble. Maybe this time I won't help." She took two steps toward the front door.

"Keelie." Jake's tone was commanding. "Not helping someone is as bad as cursing them. It can lead you down the path to darkness."

Keelie stopped—her hand level with the knob, not looking back but feeling Jake's gaze boring into her back. "If Elia can find a way to break the curse on Ariel, then I will think about helping Elianard."

With that, she bolted up the stairs two at a time. She needed to talk to someone who wasn't an elf. Or a vampire. Someone sensible. And how dare Jake take Elia's side? And they kept looking at each other as if they were in love or something. Disgusting.

Sir Davey could help her. Maybe she could call him on Dad's tree-connected cell phone.

Alora was watching her. The treeling's branches were crossed over her trunk, and Keelie imagined her impatiently tapping her roots in her flowerpot. "The aunties told me what happened to Ernem. I sense him. He sleeps peacefully now."

Keelie nodded. "Then you know we ran into Niriel

and the jousters, and that Dad and Grandmother are at an emergency meeting."

"I know. Maybe you should listen to Jake."

"Why?"

"He has a good heart, like you."

"So, you're saying I should help Elia."

Alora's face pushed out of the trunk's bark. "In the forest, if one tree is sick, then its sickness can spread from leaf to leaf, eventually killing the whole forest. If by saving one tree you stop the disease, then you can save the forest."

"Thanks for the tree philosophy lesson. I need to talk to Sir Davey." The treeling might be right, but Keelie didn't want to help Elianard. There was too much history between them. She went downstairs and searched for Dad's phone in the kitchen, but she couldn't find it. Maybe Dad had it in his room.

She found Mom's carved wooden portrait leaning against the wall of Dad's bedroom. Dad must have pulled it out after their talk. Fresh pangs of grief constricted her heart. She walked over to the picture and ran her hand over her mother's face. "What should I do?"

Mom had run from the elves, which meant losing Dad. Keelie didn't want to do that. She didn't want to be out of her father's life. But if she wanted to be part of his life, that meant being part of the elves. She still felt that urge to run back to California—if she could, she'd run back to her old life, back with Mom. But Mom was dead now, and Keelie didn't know if she could do that because it would mean living without Dad. She sat back.

There was one thing she could do. She wasn't going to let Mom's memory be shoved back in the closet. Keelie picked up the portrait. She wrapped her arms around it. "Come on, Mom."

She carried it down the stairs and placed it on the fireplace mantle. Front and center. The focal point of the Heartwood home. If Grandmother fussed about it, Keelie would set her straight. "Love you, Mom."

Fatigue overcame her. She yawned. If she took a little nap, she wouldn't be so tired when Dad and Grandmother came home from the meeting. Assuming they even came home. Keelie had decided she needed to tell Dad everything she knew about Jake. Her father would help her find a solution to his situation.

As for helping Elianard, Keelie didn't know. She'd healed an owl and restored Einhorn the unicorn, but she didn't know if or how she could help Elianard. She couldn't doom him to a lifetime of darkness just because she didn't like him, however.

Keelie lay down on the sofa, sinking her head into the plump cushiness of the pillow. Something heavy landed on her stomach, knocking out her breath. She opened her eyes. Knot purred as he tucked his front paws underneath him. Keelie yawned again. "I wish you could talk to me. I wish I could talk to Laurie."

His purring grew louder as Keelie drifted off to sleep.

Keelie was in the lunchroom at Baywood Academy, eating fish sticks. Gross! Processed fish sticks at that. Laurie sat across the table from her, silver tree earrings dangling. Ashlee scooted her green peas around her plate, then looked up, her mouth agape at something next to Keelie.

A loud purring vibrated around her. She turned her head, and almost fell out of her chair when she saw that a huge fluffy orange cat holding a plastic lunchroom tray stood there. The cat wore a musketeer hat, and had a sword belted around his waist and floppy boots on his back paws.

He motioned with his furry head toward the empty seat next to Keelie. "May ow sit 'own," he asked in what sounded like a thick Scottish accent. He sounded a little like a kitty Sean Connery.

Keelie nodded. "Knot? What are you doing at my school?"

He winked at her. It was Knot. This was too creepy. He plunked his tray down next to hers, moved his tail to one side, then sat in the chair next to her. He opened his milk carton with his claws and drank greedily, long pink tongue thrusting into the carton's opening. Dribbles of milk trailed down his chin. He wiped it with the back of his paw, then licked his paw clean. "Me-ow. That is 'owd."

"What are you doing here? What am I doing here?"

Keelie looked around, wondering what else was strange. This was a dream, right?

Knot ate his fish sticks, watching her.

Laurie and Ashlee stared at the cat.

"What are they doing here?" Keelie pointed at her friends. "And I knew you could talk."

"It is yeow subconscious placing yeow in a happy place." Knot motioned with his paw at Laurie and Ashlee.

They stared back. "What did you say we're doing here?" Laurie was confused. Ashlee seemed to be in a catatonic state.

Knot pointed at Keelie's fish sticks. "Do yeow want those?"

"Have at it." Keelie shoved the tray over to him. "Why are we here?"

She had to wait for him to finish eating because he'd crammed six fish sticks in his mouth.

He pointed to her milk. She gave it to him.

"This is your cat?" Ashlee finally managed to squeak.

Keelie nodded. "Normally, he isn't this big." She turned to Knot. "Why am I having this dream?"

"Yeow needs to remember dark magic is not bad or good, but if the heart of the user is bad, then yeow magic will be bad. If the heart is good, dark magic can make user dark. If good magic is used by bad heart, then bad things can happen. If good magic is used by good heart, then good happens. Yeow are good. Yeow understand?"

Keelie looked up. Ashlee and Laurie had disappeared. Sadness filled her. She missed her friends.

"I'm not going to use dark magic. I'm not like Elianard. Is this about me not helping him?"

"Yeow can think yeow will use dark magic for good, but meow can be bad."

"I've seen Star Wars, and I'm not going to turn to the dark side, Yoda cat."

"Meow said too much already. Queens will be mad at meow." Knot gazed at Keelie. "But meow will protect Keelie no matter what." Knot's purring became louder.

"So let me get this straight. In kitty language, meow means me? So cats go around saying, me, me, me? That figures."

Knot winked and the lunchroom began to fade...

Keelie woke up and blinked at the sunlight that filtered through the windows. "What a dream." She looked around for Knot, but he'd disappeared.

She stood up and walked into the kitchen. "Dad, are you back?"

No sign of anyone.

She ran upstairs and peeked into his room. It was tidy, just as it had been before. Jake had been right about the meeting lasting all night. She looked out the window and there was no dark fog, which meant that Jake wasn't hanging around outside.

Keelie remembered the fish-stick dream. Knot had warned her not to use dark magic. Although it was just a dream, it still reminded Keelie that she had to decide if she was going to try to help Elianard. She thought about Dad. He would want her to help. It would be the right thing to do. She would have to trust that.

But first, she had to figure out how she'd transformed the steel sword into wood. She was sure it hadn't been with Earth magic, and it hadn't felt like a mix of earth and tree magic, either. If it was some safe method that involved the amulet's power, then maybe she could use it to heal Elianard and Ariel.

She wanted to talk to Sir Davey, though, before she told Dad. It meant she was going to have to go into town and use the pay phone near the Magic Forest Tattoo shop. Keelie walked back into her room. Alora was sleeping, so Keelie knocked on her trunk. "Hey, wake up."

Alora shook her branches and her eyes opened. "What?"

"I'm driving into town."

"You're not supposed to drive unless you have an adult with you."

"I didn't say I was going by myself."

Outside, Keelie found Elia sleeping on the porch swing with a blanket draped over her. Jake must have brought it to her. Flames of jealousy flickered behind Keelie's eyes. Elia was as beautiful as a princess in a fairy tale, but inside she was a warty frog.

She shoved Elia's arm. The elf girl opened her eyelids

halfway and lifted her head. "What? I didn't eat all the goat cheese."

"Goat cheese?"

Elia sat up, the blanket falling down. Her gown was rumpled and wrinkled. "I was dreaming."

"Where's Jake?"

"He went into the forest. He's going to keep an eye on father for me." She yawned and stretched.

"You two seemed to have hit it off."

Elia smiled. "He's so kind and considerate."

"Totally. Not your type. I don't think elves and vampires are a matched item."

Elia scowled. "Like he's your type."

Keelie chose to ignore that comment. "I need to go into town, and you need to go with me."

"Why?"

"Because I'm not old enough to drive by myself, and I need an adult."

"Are you going to help my father?" She sounded wary.

"Are you going to break the curse on Ariel?"

"You know I can't."

"I'm not saying I'm going to help Elianard, but I can try, and I need to talk to someone before I can do anything."

Elia nodded. "You need to talk to the dwarf."

"His name is Sir Davey."

"I know. One of his names, at least."

"Then call him by his name."

"Okay, okay. Being nice doesn't come naturally to me. It's early, and I haven't had any tea or oatmeal."

"You're not going to get any, either. Meet me by the camper in fifteen minutes, dressed in these." Keelie tossed her a bundle of clothes.

Elia sat glumly on the passenger's side, wearing the jeans and T-shirt Keelie had given her. She looked about twenty-two—old enough to be an adult driver.

Keelie cranked the pickup truck's engine and it chugged to life. She pushed down on the gas, and they were on their way.

"I'm sorry about what happened to Einhorn." Elia turned to her.

"Me, too." She didn't look at Elia.

"I walked away, you know. I refused to help Dad kill him."

"I know."

"I'm sorry about the hawk."

"Me, too."

Keelie kept looking straight ahead, negotiating the curves on the road.

"I've changed, Keelie."

"So you say, Elia, but I don't trust you."

"I know."

Keelie pulled into a parking space in front of the tattoo shop and turned the car off. She was a natural behind the wheel. Dad would be pleased, once he got over the mad-on about her taking the Swiss Miss Chalet without permission.

Outside, the "Piercings Available" sign glowed blue against the brick wall. Keelie touched her belly, so far still free of any embellishment.

A corner of Elia's mouth lifted. "I had mine done at the Ren Faire by a silversmith."

"You've got a piercing?" Keelie sighed. It was so unfair.

Elia arched an eyebrow and raised her shirt to expose a silver ring glinting in her navel. Keelie figured everyone on the planet had a piercing except her.

She looked at the tattoo shop. If she got her belly button pierced, no one would know but Elia, and she'd keep her mouth shut because she needed Keelie's help. Keelie'd wanted a piercing for so long, but although Mom was close to letting her have one before she'd died, Dad had resisted. First things first, though. She had to call Sir Davey.

Elia pointed toward the diner. "I need some food. They serve good oatmeal here."

"Fine, go get your breakfast. I'll make my call. Take your time." And if you're not back when my call's done, I'll go and get my belly button pierced, she thought.

Keelie punched in Sir Davey's number. His phone rang several times. Finally, his greeting kicked on. "This is Sir Jadwyn. Prithee leave a message."

"Sir Davey, this is Keelie. I need to talk to you. Now. Please pick up."

"Hello?" The mellow baritone was not quite right.

"Sir Davey?"

"No, this is his brother, Alvain. Davey's away mining for diamonds in Arkansas. Can I take a message?"

Disappointment flooded Keelie. "When do you expect him back?"

"Oh, I'd say in a few days. Once those boys start digging, they get busy and lose all track of time. I stayed home to sort the geodes—that's dragon eggs to you—for the Northern California Renaissance Faire in a couple of weeks."

"Tell him Keelie Heartwood called, and I need to speak to him as soon as possible."

"Well, hello, Keelie! You're Zeke's girl. He talks about you all the time. I'll let Davey know you called, and that it's urgent. Is there anything I can do to help?"

She didn't know Alvain, or how much he might know about Earth magic. "No thanks. I really need to speak to Sir Davey."

As Keelie hung up, she pressed her head against the phone. She didn't know what she was going to do. Sir Davey was out having a Snow White Hi-Ho moment in an Arkansas diamond mine. And he never mentioned he was going to the Northern California Renaissance Faire. Or that he had a brother.

It stung her, as if he'd betrayed her. He could've told her about California, but he probably thought that she would have begged him to take her along. And he would have been right.

So here she was, stuck saving Elianard and being nice to Elia, who had managed to turn Jake's attention away from Keelie.

She looked at the Magic Forest Tattoo shop. She deserved a belly button ring. The world owed her a belly button ring.

Keelie marched in. A high wooden counter (yellow pine, Georgia) ran along one side of the shop, plastered with pictures of possible tattoos, everything from tribal designs to beautiful colorful renditions of dragons. There seemed to be a lot of fairy drawings.

A scary-looking dentist's chair with a tray table next to it was on the other side, along with a low counter covered with bottles and jars.

A purple-haired woman with a fairy tattoo on her arm looked up from a three-ring binder of tattoo samples and smiled at Keelie. "Just looking? It's all right to look. I won't bite."

"I'd like to get my belly button pierced."

Her pierced eyebrows rose. "How old are you?"

Oh, great, here came the "you'll need your parent's permission to get a piercing" comment. "Eighteen."

The woman lowered one of the eyebrows. "I was sixteen when I got my first tattoo."

"Two years younger than me." She was pleased that her voice sounded steady.

The woman walked around the corner of the counter. "Are you hiking in the forest?"

"No, I'm visiting with my grandmother."

"I have a lot of hikers come in to get a tattoo as a re- minder of their spiritual and mystical experience in the Dread Forest."

"Really? I thought most people were afraid to go in the forest." Keelie wondered how long the Dread had been fading if people were finding it "mystical." Sounded like a bunch of New Age hooey to her, the kind Laurie's mother would fall for. Of course, Keelie talked to trees and fairies, so who was she kidding?

The door opened and Keelie was surprised to see Elia walk into the shop.

"There you are." Elia looked around curiously.

Keelie turned away and looked at the glass case where an assortment of belly button studs and rings were dis- played.

Elia walked over to the woman. "Hello, Zabrina."

"You know each other?"

Zabrina nodded, and Keelie noticed a shimmer around her. She felt a surge of magic from the woman, a bright and sparkly feeling, like bubbles across her skin.

"You're not human."

"You're not eighteen." Zabrina snorted. "And you're one to talk—you're not totally human either." The tattoo artist waved her hand and the shimmer grew, ringing outwards through the air in ripples. Her eyes were silver now, ringed in purple, and her skin glowed bright.

Keelie felt the magic lap against her, as if it couldn't penetrate her own. "What are you?"

Zabrina smiled and lifted her chin proudly. "My father is one of the high court—my mother is human."

"The Shining Ones." Keelie gazed at her.

"And you're Zeke Heartwood's daughter."

"Yes. But how did you become a tattoo artist? That seems like the last thing a fairy would do."

"I'm good at it, and I have to eat, too."

"Don't you go and live in the woods with the other fairies?"

Elia snorted. "The Shining Ones stay to themselves. If they have half-human children, they don't acknowledge them. That's the way it is." She gave Keelie a meaningful look that said, *that's the way it should always be.*

Keelie blushed. She'd thought she could begin to like Elia, but the elf girl was reminding her of exactly how hateful she could be.

Zabrina sighed. "It is so. Still, the magic calls to our blood, and we have to be near it. That's why some of the hikers leave with a special feeling. The magic in the forest calls to them."

Keelie thought back to the sprite in the woods. "Do you see the Shining Ones?"

Zabrina nodded. "Sometimes."

Keelie turned to Elia. "Do you see them?"

She shook her head. "The fairies don't like elves—they prefer human company. They don't show themselves to us."

"Shows they have good taste."

Elia scowled.

Zabrina smiled. "Do you still want your piercing?"

"You bet I do."

Zabrina handed Keelie a clipboard. "Read this carefully, then sign. I'll get everything ready. Won't take long."

Keelie read the disclaimer and signed it, then sat in the chair.

"I'll just tilt the chair back so that you're lying down." Zabrina hit a lever on the side of the chair and Keelie watched Elia's face rise into view.

"Are you going to watch?"

Elia grinned. "Maybe it will hurt."

Zabrina glared at her. "It will not. Keelie, undo the top of your jeans and unzip the zipper a bit." She sat on a rolling stool and scooted over. "Don't worry, it doesn't hurt. Did you decide on a bar or a ring?"

"A ring."

"That's the best choice. It's easier to turn it at first and keep the area clean." She snapped on rubber gloves, then got a big cotton swab and poured a solution onto it from a tall bottle. "This will disinfect the area." She rubbed Keelie's belly button and the skin around it. It felt cold.

"Is that Sean?" Elia's voice made Keelie turn her head to look out the door; then she felt something like a bee sting her belly.

"Ow. I don't see anyone."

"My mistake." Elia smiled.

"Okay, all done." Zabrina was wiping up a couple drops of blood from Keelie's belly. Where a naked belly button had once been, there was now a little silver hoop.

"That's it?"

"Yup."

Keelie got up carefully, her belly sensitive, and paid for the piercing. She looked down at the silver ring and the slightly swollen, reddened skin around it. Finally. She couldn't wait to tell Raven and Laurie, and to buy all sorts of cool jewels to wear.

Zabrina gave her a bottle of antiseptic and directions for taking care of her new piercing, and the girls left the shop.

Keelie looked at the elven girl's haughty, aristocratic profile. "Sean wasn't really out there, was he?"

"No." Elia was looking straight ahead.

"You said that to distract me?"

Elia shrugged.

"Thanks." The elf girl had actually done something nice for her. Amazing.

They wandered around town, stopping outside a hardware store to admire some metal sculptures for sale; Keelie thought they resembled the water sprite. There was a second-hand clothing store. They stopped in at the diner for some coffee and herbal tea but didn't stay long, since Elia was anxious to return home. Keelie's belly button itched and she had to fight the urge to scratch it.

Elia shook her head when she saw Keelie rub the skin around it. "It won't heal if you touch it."

"I can't help it. It feels hot." They returned to the Swiss Miss Chalet, waved at Zabrina in the tattoo shop's window, then climbed into the truck and drove back up the hilly road to the Dread Forest. Keelie fished in her pocket for her rose quartz, to keep the Dread at bay, and hardly felt it when they passed into the area protected by the spell. But her piercing felt as if it were on fire.

"Something's wrong," she said, teeth gritted. She pulled over to the side of the road.

Elia looked at the dashboard as if expecting mechanical problems. Keelie put the truck in park and lifted her shirt.

She stared numbly at her belly. Elia cried out, her eyes wide and her mouth opened in an "O" of shock as she stared at Keelie's belly button ring. It had turned to wood.

thirteen

Keelie couldn't believe it. She ran her hand along her stomach, touching the belly button ring that had been sterling silver just an hour before. The itching was getting worse. This wasn't supposed to happen—getting her belly button pierced had been a long-sought-after goal. Now she had a rash to go along with her transformed body jewelry.

"I've never seen that happen before." Elia frowned. "You've really got this tree shepherd thing in your blood." She seemed to be assimilating the fact that Keelie was actually half elf, as if this was the first time she'd really considered it. Keelie wanted to smack her on the forehead and say, "Duh!"

She turned the truck around and headed back toward the Magic Forest Tattoo shop. Zabrina couldn't believe her eyes. "Weird, man." She used wire cutters to break the wooden ring. "You need an enchanted silver ring. Let me see what I can do."

"I can't afford another one."

"This one's on the house." Zabrina held the splintered wooden ring up to the light, examining it.

"Does this happen to all the elves?" Keelie glared at Elia. She could've said something about the ring maybe turning into wood if she suspected this would happen.

"I've only seen this once before," Zabrina said.

Keelie lifted her head from the piercing chair. "When?"

"The transformation of one material to another should be impossible." Zabrina looked at the ring closely. "Hard to tell by the wood grain what type of tree this is supposed to be."

Elia leaned forward. "Our lore has no tales of elves who can change silver to wood."

Zabrina held out the ring. "Apparently Keelie can."

Elia looked at Keelie with cold, calculating elf eyes.

Keelie sat up. "What happened before? To who?" She pointed to the wooden belly button ring. "Did someone's ring turn into wood?"

Zabrina frowned. "It was one of the dwarves. He works at the hardware store, and he's a really great artist, too."

Elia scowled. "A dwarf. There's a lot of them around here."

Zabrina lifted her hands. "I only know what I saw. This kid came in wanting an eyebrow ring."

"What happened?" Keelie's heart raced with the thought that there might be someone else out there like her.

"Pierced his eyebrow with steel. It transformed into a small piece of clear quartz—a teeny, tiny shard of crystal no bigger than the eyebrow ring. He didn't get the rash."

Keelie leaned back against the chair, wondering where that guy was now. She didn't want to give up on getting her belly button ring. "Let's try the enchanted silver. It's my tree shepherd ability mixed with my human blood—that's all I can figure."

"Hey, honey, magic manifests itself in funny ways. Watch this." She pointed to her fairy tattoo. Small sparkles surrounded the tattoo, and like an animated drawing come to life, the fairy flew from Zabrina's skin and hovered near her. The fairy darted about the shop, then flew back to Zabrina's arm and became a tattoo again.

"That's neat." Keelie wondered if Dad would let her have a free-range tattoo like that.

"I think so. Kind of freaked me out when it first happened, but I've grown fond of her." Zabrina swabbed Keelie's belly button and the skin around it with a clean cloth. "I named her Molly. Okay, let's get you fixed up."

Keelie winced as the new ring was inserted, then sighed, relieved it was over.

"Now that, I've never seen. Another first." Zabrina frowned at Keelie's belly.

Keelie looked down and was surprised to see that the piercing had healed around the new ring and the rash had disappeared.

She had to find Sir Davey right away. First the sword, and now the belly button ring. Dad had to know, but she couldn't tell him without having a plan. Keelie didn't like the fact that Elia knew about this, but she was careful not to show it.

On the way back home, her skin didn't itch. Good to know—she had to go with enchanted silver jewelry in the future.

Elia remained silent. Keelie knew she had to be worrying about her dad. "What do you think they'll do to Elianard when they find him?"

"They'll banish him like they did with Jake." Elia sounded glum. She leaned her head against the window and stared out at the passing woods.

"Are you going to stay with the elves, if a cure can't be found for your dad?"

Elia blinked several times. "I have nowhere else to go. I guess could go to the far north, to the elves who live in the Northwest Territory; my mother was from that clan."

"Your mother?" Keelie had never heard Elia mention a mother. Then again, she would have to have had one, unless Elianard had cloned a female version of himself.

"Where is she?"

"She faded after I was born." Elia sighed.

Keelie didn't feel like she had a right to push for more

information. She knew what it was like for people to want answers, the details, how you felt when someone close to you died, like your mother. Prying people lived vicariously through the grief, imagining how they would react when their own loved one died.

Keelie drove on. She and Elia had more in common than she wanted to admit—a scary thought.

It was noon when they got home. Dad was sitting in the rocking chair on the front porch. His ear tips were red and his face solemn, lips pursed in a thin line. "Elia, Lady Etilafael has asked for you to come to her house. She needs to speak with you. Your father is ill, child."

Elia nodded, ducked her head, and walked rapidly toward the elven village.

Keelie felt sad for her. "Maybe I should go with her."

Dad stood and pointed toward the door. "Others will care for her. You—go inside. Now."

Still thinking about what was facing Elia, Keelie went into the living room and sat down in a comfy chair with plush, soft cushions. This was usually Dad's chair, but she knew she was in for a long lecture and she might as well get comfortable.

Dad paced back and forth in front of her. Knot sat on the arm of chair, purring happily like he couldn't wait for the lecture to begin. The only thing missing was fish-flavored popcorn. She remembered the fish sticks from the bizarre dream. She glanced at Knot, and he purred even louder.

Instead of looking at Dad, Keelie studied the way the orange tabby stripes swirled in Knot's fur. Strange—this was the first time she'd noticed a spiral pattern. As if sensing her thoughts, the cat turned around and blinked one eye, as if winking at her. Then he lifted his leg up in the air and began washing his behind.

Gross cat!

"Keelie, what were you thinking?" She startled and looked up. Dad had stopped pacing and now stood in front of her.

"What was I thinking in reference to...?" She waved her hand in a circular motion.

She hoped Dad would just get mad, give her a lecture about driving, punish her, and move on, because the skin around her belly button had started to itch like it had before, but worse. She wanted so badly to scratch it.

He arched an eyebrow. "In reference to going into town, especially after the incident in the woods. You know the danger. And I can't believe you disobeyed me after I told you to stay here while I was at the meeting." He shook his head. "I should've known I couldn't trust you to listen to me."

"Dad, you can trust me." His words hurt, and the skin around her stomach was itching in a bad kind of way. It was stinging now.

"No, Keelie, I can't. You lie to me. You disregard my rules, and you don't trust me. Why were you in town?" He stared at her, expecting an answer. His eyes were a combination of sad and mad.

This was it. She was going to have to tell him about the sword and the belly button ring. She couldn't put it off any longer. She was going to have to trust him. She looked up at the wooden portrait of Mom.

"I wanted to call Sir Davey."

Surprised, Dad stopped pacing. "Why?"

She inhaled and then, with a deep breath, the words rushed out. "I needed to talk to him because I have a problem."

"You could talk to Sir Davey, but you couldn't talk to your own father?" He looked hurt.

"You've been busy. You've been Elf Dad."

"Elf Dad?"

"You're different here. It's not the same as it was at the Ren Faires. It's like you're more elf than my father."

It felt good to tell him.

"I've been busy. I have responsibilities here that I don't have out in the world. I'm here, now, Keelie." He sat down on the sofa. "What were you calling Sir Davey about? Let's talk."

"I can turn metal into wood."

Dad blinked several times. "You can turn metal into wood? I don't understand."

"When I was practicing with my sword the other day, Sean showed up. He wanted to explain to me why he was betrothed to Risa. I was mad, and I pointed my sword at him, but then this tingle went through me. And the next thing I knew, the sword had turned into wood. I'd show it to you, but it scared me so I gave it to the *bhata* to hide until I could figure out what was happening."

Dad paled. "The *bhata* came at your call?"

"Yeah. Those little guys follow me around. They're really nice."

"So, you chose to seek out Sir Davey's counsel rather than mine." His face was unreadable.

"Yes. Because I thought it was Earth magic."

"But you kept it a secret."

"There's more."

Dad ran a hand over his face.

"Today when I was in town, I went into the Magic Forest Tattoo shop." Keelie started to lift her shirt. "And I got my belly button pierced."

Dad slumped in the chair. "I'm too old to be a father. Keelie, honestly, I don't mind that you got your belly button pierced. Let's talk about the *bhata*."

"No wait, Dad." Keelie lifted her shirt to reveal the red blistery swath circling her belly button. The enchanted silver ring had indeed turned to wood, and now little green buds were beginning to form. It was a solid wooden ring with no clasp.

"Whoa!" Her father's eyes bugged out. "What magic is that?"

"I seem to have an allergy to metal." She lowered her shirt. "I need to get this ring out. Otherwise, I'll have a tree blooming from my navel." Images of Pinocchio's nose came to her.

Dad's face became even paler, and the vein in his neck

was pulsing very hard. He squeezed his hand into a tight fist. Keelie didn't know if this was a good thing or a bad thing. It was a good thing he was trying to remain calm, and it was a bad thing if he was envisioning squeezing her neck.

"Funny, all these years I thought I had an allergy to wood—now it turns out to be metal." She was trying to lighten the mood.

He didn't seem to appreciate her attempt and pounded his closed fist against the arm of the sofa. "Keelie!"

"Yes." She swallowed. Maybe she wouldn't have to worry about a tree growing out of her stomach because she'd be dead before she ended up full of roots.

He ran his hand down his face again. "I've never seen this before."

"You can't fix this?" Keelie's voice held a hint of panic.

Dad stood up and waved his arms in front of him. "I don't know what to do."

That statement hit her as if a redwood had landed on her. Dads were supposed to know what to do, especially magical tree shepherd dads.

"Come on, I have an idea."

"Where are we going?"

"To the Magic Forest Tattoo shop, and you're going to tell me everything on the way there."

As Dad drove the Swiss Miss Chalet, Keelie told him everything that had happened, from the sword to the piercing. "Zabrina said a guy came in for an eyebrow ring piercing, and instead of turning to wood, it transformed into crystal."

Dad nodded. "Was there anything else unusual about this guy?"

"Zabrina said he was little, a dwarf."

The car swerved as her father reacted to her words.

"Keep your eyes on the road." The memory of coming down the Wildewood mountain was still fresh in her mind.

"We'll have to find this dwarf. Maybe he has some insight about the transformation of one material into another. But right now, we need to get this ring out."

Keelie nodded. The leaves were beginning to unfurl.

"We'll fix it." He patted her on the arm. "We'll figure it out."

Comfort ebbed over her. Keelie was glad she'd talked to him.

"Dad, about Jake. Like I said, I just want him to be safe. I don't want the elves to hurt him."

"I know, Keelie. Me neither."

At the Magic Forest Tattoo shop, Zabrina's mouth fell open in shock when she saw the tree ring. "Kid, this is an original." She put on her rhinestone-encrusted cat-framed glasses and examined Keelie's stomach. "I've never seen anything like this." The wings of Zabrina's fairy tattoo fluttered. Dad's eyes widened in surprise as the two-dimensional fairy tattoo floated off Zabrina's arm and hovered over Keelie's shoulder, joining them in staring at the little branch growing from her navel ring.

"Can you take it out?" Keelie tried to keep the panic out of her voice.

"I can try. I'll be right back." She exited through the

beaded curtains. The fairy tattoo smiled, bent her head coyly, and batted her eyelashes at Dad.

Dad turned around and stared at the equipment on the other side of the shop, then at the artwork on the wall. "What is she?"

"She's half fairy."

Zabrina returned with her wire cutters. "If this doesn't work, then we'll use this." She held up a huge bolt cutter.

Keelie gulped.

Dad's eyebrows rose. Zabrina offered the bolt cutter to Dad. "Here, hold this."

After cleaning the area with disinfectant, Zabrina placed her glasses on her nose. The rhinestones sparkled brightly. "Aha, here it is." She inserted the wire cutters and pushed down on the handles. Keelie braced herself for pain. There was a loud click, and Zabrina held up the broken tree ring. "Here you go."

"Well done." Dad looked at her with an admiring but inquisitive gaze. "Was there magic in the ring?"

"Nope." She pointed to her glasses. "These help me see any glamours or illusions." She held up the wire cutters, the broken tree clasped in their grip, and pointed at them. "This, however, is not an illusion. Your daughter transformed silver into wood. If I were you, I'd figure out why, and very soon."

fourteen

Grandmother Keliatiel rushed outside to greet them. "Where have you been? I've been worried."

"I had to run to town," Dad motioned toward the house. "Mother, you need to rest."

"Why did you have to go into town?" Keliatiel waved her hand. "Never mind. Etilafael needs to speak with you on a matter most urgent. It's about Elianard."

Dad nodded. "I'll go talk with her."

"She's at the Council house."

"Keelie, I need to go, but when I return, we'll figure

out this problem. Mother, you need to rest. You know you shouldn't be up."

"What problem? Perhaps I can help Keelie. I do need to speak to her."

"No. I want you resting," Dad insisted. "I'll be home as soon as I can."

"I need to go check on Alora and Ariel," Keelie said hastily. "I'll see you later, Dad." She waved at him as she headed up the stairs.

He smiled. "Hopefully sooner than later. Stay by the house, and don't go into the woods."

Upstairs in her room, Keelie listened to Alora's complaints. "Why didn't you take me to town? I've been stuck in this flowerpot. The aunties told me they wanted me to visit. So you need to take me to them."

"I can't take you into the woods. Dad told me to stay by the house." Keelie was determined to be good.

"But the aunties said it was important for you to come. They want to talk to you—in person."

"I can't go and see the aunties." Keelie lifted her shirt, relieved to see that the rash was gone. A circle of green now ringed her navel—chlorophyll poisoning. Of course. Coffee would take care of it.

"You have to go and see the aunties!" Alora insisted.

"I can't. I told Dad I'd stay near the house, and I will."

"The aunties have something to show you." The treeling lifted her face up.

"If the aunties want to talk to me, then they can telepathically tell me whatever they have to say."

"Fine, try it," Alora grumbled. "I know it's important."

"We'll see." Keelie opened her senses and sought out the aunties.

Old ones, I'm here.

A stern voice rang in Keelie's head. *Shepherdess, we seek an audience with thee.*

Yes, do not keep us waiting. The Tree Shepherd comes to us when we command, another haughty voice chimed in.

We are most insistent you come now. Quit being an impertinent little acorn, a third voice demanded.

Impertinent little acorn! Demanding old biddy trees. Who did they think they were? The queens of the forest? Keelie had met a tree queen before, and she hadn't acted like this.

I can't, Keelie replied. *I promised Dad I'd stay here at the house. There are dangers in the forest.*

There was a knock at Keelie's bedroom door. "Keelie, I really must speak to you." Oh joy. It was Grandmother Keliatiel.

I must go. She closed her mind to the aunties.

Alora shook her branches disapprovingly. "They're not going to be happy with you."

"Tell them to get in line."

Keelie opened her door. Grandmother stood there, tapping her foot impatiently. "I wish to speak to you downstairs."

"I'll be right there."

Grandmother leaned closer, peered at Keelie, frowned. "Are you all right? You're looking a little green."

"I'm fine. Just tree shepherd stuff."

"Your grandfather always turned green after using magic, when he was your age."

"Really?"

Grandmother nodded. "Yes, he would have green fingernails and toenails, too. And the veins in his eyes would be green." She smiled at the long-ago memory.

"Wow. When was that?"

"Let me think." Grandmother wrinkled her brow and stared at the ceiling. "Was it after *As You Like It?* Yes, I think it was."

Warmed by her grandmother's conversation, Keelie grinned at her. Maybe things were thawing between them. She opened the door a little further and leaned against the doorjamb. "I love *As You Like It*, too. Where did you see it?"

"Gibbons' Tennis Court. I think it was in 1669. Or was that in 1730 at Drury Lane?" Grandmother's eyes lost focus as she remembered.

Keelie couldn't imagine remembering all the facts that a multiple-century lifespan would cram into a person's skull.

"We treated your grandfather's headaches with an herbal tea given to us by the..." She stopped as if a forbidden name was about to escape from her tongue. "I need to speak with you, downstairs. Now."

"Can't we talk here?"

Grandmother glanced at Alora, almost too quickly to be noticed. "Downstairs, please."

"I'll be down in a minute. I have tree shepherd business with Princess Alora."

Grandmother scowled. "Well, hurry."

Keelie closed her door and leaned against it, as if willing Grandmother to go away. She heard footsteps on the wooden floor, leading away from her room.

"I need to see you downstairs." She mimicked Grandmother's stern voice.

"The aunties are mad at you. You need to go and see them." Alora glared as she crossed her branches over her chest.

"Well, they're not the first. Lately everyone needs to see me privately. I just can't go out. It's too dangerous."

"You're in trouble with them."

"I'll talk to them later."

Keelie went downstairs and found her Grandmother sitting in the chair with the big cushy pillows.

"We need to talk about that." Grandmother pointed toward Mom's wood-carved portrait. "You must persuade your father to remove it. When I insisted, he refused. He said you wanted it in view, therefore it stays. Is this correct?"

Warmth and love for Dad filled Keelie. "Yes. I want it here. It's beautiful." She gazed lovingly at the sculpted lines of Mom's face. "And I miss her so much." Pain made the words come out in a whisper.

"No doubt you do." Her grandmother's voice was emotionless. "The craftsmanship is superb. But I think the living room mantel is hardly the place to display it. Why don't you move it to your bedroom? I think it makes Zeke think too much about Katharine."

Keelie stared at her Grandmother in disbelief. "Yeah, so, he loved her. What's your problem?"

"And she broke his heart." Grandmother looked angry.

Keelie suddenly realized something. "When you look at me, you see her don't you?"

"You have her way about you." Grandmother frowned and examined the armrest of her chair.

Keelie looked up at Mom's portrait as if it would give her strength. "The portrait stays."

"You dare defy me?"

"Yes, I do. And I think you need to understand. I'm staying. Dad loved her, and he loves me."

"Keelie, this is not a request, it is an order. I want you to tell your father that you would like him to remove this portrait. Say whatever you wish." Grandmother made a cutting motion in the air. "I just want it done."

"No." Anger burned Keelie's cheeks. "I won't. You may run this forest, but you don't run me."

Grandmother pointed a thin finger at Keelie. "Oh, but I do. You are my blood, for good or bad, and I am the head of this family. I will not lose Zeke, not even to his daughter.

I've lost one son, I won't lose the other. I want the portrait gone tonight."

Wind blew outside, and Ariel called out plaintively from the mews.

"No." Keelie shook her head. It hit her, once again, that her grandmother would never accept her. Like the elves, Keliatiel couldn't overlook the fact that Keelie was half-human; but her grandmother had an additional reason for not wanting Keelie around. She was afraid of losing Dad.

Ariel cried out again.

Grandmother leaned back in the chair. Her voice was high with tension and anger. "That hawk has been shrieking all day. Go and take care of it. I don't know why you even keep it alive."

"How can you be so cruel?"

"You think me cruel, child?" Grandmother closed her eyes and then opened them. "I am tired. Maybe I've seen too many cruel things and had too many cruel things happen to me, and they've hardened my heart. You count your years in decades, Keliel, but I'm hundreds of years old." She shifted in her chair. "I've lived through a long swathe of the history of this world, times where I've seen firsthand the cruelty of the human race. You think me unkind and unloving to you, child. It may be that time has warped me." She sighed. "Let my experience guide you. You can't heal that hawk. There is no way to break the curse. She can't fly, and by nature's design a hawk is meant to feel the wind in her wings. Be kind to her, Keliel. Let Ariel die."

Keelie recoiled. "No!" She jumped up, ready to argue.

The elderly elf continued as if she hadn't heard her. "Your father is going to have to lead the elves, and he can't live in the past." She stood and walked to Mom's portrait. "You can't live in the past, either." She turned to Keelie. "Be kind to your father, too—let him be free of the past. Allow him to let your mother go."

With tears brimming in her eyes, Keelie spun on her heels and walked out the front door, letting it slam. She'd missed lunch, but the confrontation with Grandmother had killed her appetite. She ran to Ariel's cage.

The hawk beat her wings against the wire. "I would never kill you, Ariel. Never. Never. I'll do whatever I have to do to save you."

The hawk cocked her head to listen. Her milky white eyes staring at nothing. She beat her wings against the cage. Keelie stepped back and looked up at the pale sky. The wind rustled through the trees. "Calm down girl. Do you want to fly with the trees to help you? It's just so dangerous out there."

She shuddered at the thought of Elianard catching Ariel and drinking her blood. A breeze rustled the branches above them. Ariel lifted her head and called out again.

Ariel *had* been flying, though, aided by trees. Wasn't that enough? And was death freedom, or did you simply cease to exist? Keelie thought about Mom. She wasn't here anymore and all Keelie had were memories. She couldn't touch her, talk to her, or see her. She lived in fear of not remembering what Mom's voice sounded like. Keelie wiped away the tears dripping down her face and leaned against the bars of the cage. "Ariel, I don't know what to do. I refuse to just let you die."

"May I make a suggestion?" a voice asked. Keelie turned around as Niriel stepped into the mews. "She's a beautiful bird. Sad her fate is to be condemned, blind, and held captive in a cage. Her only other option is death."

Keelie groaned inwardly. Here was the last person she wanted to see, and he was being as rude as Elianard had always been.

Niriel's sad smile twitched at one side, as if he was having trouble keeping up the empathy. He was a total fake. "Too bad you don't have the knowledge to save her."

"Dad says elven curses can't be lifted."

Niriel arched an eyebrow and gazed up at the house. The light in the living room was on. He rubbed his chin as if something was bothering him.

He knew something.

"What is it?" Keelie demanded. If there was a way to break the curse, she wanted to know about it. She wouldn't let Ariel die.

"Long ago, we elves had the knowledge. We were powerful then, and wielded magic easily. We have since lost the knowledge held in our great books of magic, shared with the Shining Ones. The amulet key has been lost as well."

Keelie immediately thought about Elianard's amulet, which she'd left with the sprite. It was a key? To what? Her skin was cold where it had lain against her. "But that's dark magic."

Niriel shrugged. "To save a little bird would require just a little magic. Too bad we no longer have the knowledge." His voice was deep and warm, its tone comforting. Keelie felt sleepy. Her little bird needed just a little magic. She'd thought the same thing.

Something sharp sank deep into her leg. "Ow!"

At her feet, Knot glared up at her, his ears pressed against his head. She pushed at him with her foot. He purred.

When she looked up again, Niriel had disappeared. Ariel spread her wings wide, as if telling Keelie that she wanted to fly.

She'd used a huge amount of magic at the Wildewood, and it hadn't hurt anything. Using a little dark magic wouldn't be noticeable, and if it meant Ariel would fly unaided again, it would be for a good cause. Ariel would have a chance to live a normal life. Surely, Dad would understand why she did it.

Keelie looked around the side of the house, but Niriel was nowhere in sight. Good. Grandmother was resting and she could get the book, then run to the stream, get the amulet from the sprite, break the curse on Ariel, and still have time to put the amulet back before anyone noticed that she was gone.

She went into the house, ignoring Ariel's cries behind her. "You'll be free soon, my friend," she whispered.

fifteen

Keelie hurried to her room and changed into hiking boots, then crept along the hall, listening for her grandmother. She needed to get to the forest quickly. If she didn't do it right this moment, she was afraid she'd never find the courage. Dad would have to forgive her for using dark magic. He would understand her reasons.

As she made her way down the stairs, she heard the front door open.

Dad walked in and Keelie stepped back into the shadows. If he saw her, she'd be in trouble.

His shoulders slumped. Grandmother greeted him at

the door. Dad wrapped his arms around her. "Mother you need to sit."

"How is he? Is there hope?"

"No. He has chosen to fade. He sealed his fate when he tried to kill Einhorn in the Wildewood. Strangely enough, though, Elia said Keelie has something that could cure Elianard."

It had to be the amulet. That was what would cure Elianard.

"Keelie?" Grandmother inhaled and let loose a plaintive cry. "Poor Elia. She's desperate. She'll do or say anything to save her father. What will happen to her?"

"She will stay with her father until he fades. After that, she does not know what she will do."

Keelie listened, her heart breaking for Elia. Her mother was dead. Now, her father was dying, or fading, as it was for elves. Keelie knew what it was like to lose one parent, but to lose both? At the thought of losing Dad, fear squeezed its cold hand around her heart.

"Mother, I wish to check on Keelie." Fatigue was in his voice. It had been a long day. "Please go home and get some rest. I'll be over as soon as I can."

As Grandmother gathered her shawl and headed for the door, Keelie rushed back to her room, Dad on the stairs right behind her. She barely made it.

Alora, who had been sleeping, lifted her leafy head, "The aunties say the humans are in the forest."

Dad walked into Keelie's room. "What are the aunties saying, Alora?" His eyes were bright with concern.

"Humans are in the heart of the forest. Their machines are so loud."

Dad closed his eyes and Keelie knew he was telepathically contacting the aunties. When he opened them, they were bright green. His face flushed red.

"The Dread has been broken." Dad clenched his fists. "There are some teenagers with ATVs creating havoc. The trees are frightened. It could be like in the Wildewood—they could become angry and turn against the humans."

"Dad, can I help?"

"Not now. I want you to watch over your grandmother."

"Dad, I need to help you. I need to be out there helping you with the trees."

"Keelie, I know, but I need you to stay with Grandmother." He clasped her shoulders. "That is how you can help best."

"Why should I help her? She ordered me to tell you I wanted you to move Mom's portrait." Anger filled Keelie.

Dad's mouth was drawn down in sadness. For a moment he was silent, then he sighed. "Keelie, her health is connected to the Dread. She magically and physically tied herself to this forest. It takes a potent form of magic to renew the Dread, and we don't have the power to renew the forest without it. The Dread is fading, as is your Grandmother. 'As the forest goes, so go the elves' is more than a philosophical statement, my daughter. And if my mother fades, then it will be my turn to tie myself to the forest.

Horrified, Keelie stepped forward. "If something happens to the forest, then the same thing will happen to you?" Images of the High Mountain forest and the Wildewood forest flooded Keelie's mind. "Dad, why would you tie yourself to a dying forest?"

"I choose to hope, Keelie." Dad walked to the doorway. "But now, I need to go stop the humans. If the trees panic and humans are harmed, it will bring doom on us. Go to Grandmother's house and sit with her."

Dad walked downstairs.

"I told you to talk to the aunties," Alora whispered softly.

Keelie ignored her and went downstairs, then outside, walking quickly to her grandmother's house. She found Keliatiel sitting on the couch in the vast great room, where the dismal welcome party had been just a few days ago.

Grandmother looked frail, her eyes closed, her shawl clutched tightly around her shoulders. She opened her eyes when she heard Keelie come in. "I want to go to bed."

Keelie nodded. This would work out great. She helped the old lady up and followed her toward the stairs. As she passed the library door, she glanced quickly at the low bookcase in the center of the room. But the book was not there anymore.

Grandmother's bedroom was dominated by a huge, dark-wood bed carved with flowers. As Keelie settled her into the sheets, she brushed her hand over one of the bed-posts, then pulled it away quickly, shocked at the bed's age. It was from a walnut tree, even older than the Sherwood oak that formed the table in the dining room.

Keelie used her already-heightened tree sense to search Grandmother's room for the book of magic, but it was not here either. Had Keliatiel hidden it? She sat with her grandmother until the old lady's eyes closed. Outside, the sky had darkened. Grandmother looked pale, almost transparent. For the first time, Keelie wondered if she was going to die, to fade.

She walked through the dim house, trying to sense the forbidden book. She felt a glimmer of its dark magic, and turned to search the dining room with her mind. It was like a game of Marco Polo—she could "feel" she was getting closer to the book as she walked in certain spots. It felt strongest in front of a tall cabinet with locked doors. Keelie turned the key in the lock, but it wouldn't open.

She heard a moan, and hurried back to her grandmother's room. Grandmother opened her eyes and blinked several times. Keelie bent down. "Can I get you anything?"

Keliatiel reached out and smoothed back the hair over Keelie's ears. Over her pointed ear, first, then over her round ear. "Keliel, I'm sorry, child, for speaking so unkindly to you earlier."

Sympathy and sadness welled up in Keelie. "Dad told me that you aren't feeling well. I get crabby when I'm sick."

Grandmother lifted her head, then lowered it as if even

that small movement had taxed all her energy. "As a baby, you would scream very loudly when you were upset. Zeke said you reminded him of me when circumstances didn't go as I planned."

"You mean you get mad when you don't get your way."

Grandmother nodded. "Despite my differences with Katharine, she was a good mother. I tried to understand why she took you away, but anger and bitterness clouded my judgment. It still does. I could have taught you so many things."

"I'm here. You can still teach me."

Grandmother closed her eyes. "We'll see. I don't remember ever feeling this tired. We'll talk later."

Keelie knelt on the floor and leaned her head against the bed, the edge of the mattress pressing into her forehead. She closed her eyes. She felt so helpless—she needed to do something. Getting up, she returned to the cabinet in the dining room, frustrated by the lock. Was there a charm on it? A curse? She didn't know enough about magic to tell the difference. She needed a better key.

She froze. A key. And she knew just where to find one.

Keelie ran back to her house to wrestle Alora down the stairs and over to her grandmother's.

"Where are we going, Keelie?"

"To open a cabinet."

"Is that fun? You don't sound like you're having fun."

Keelie plunked the heavy planter down in front of her

sleeping grandmother. *Watch over her. You're going to contact me if she wakes up.*

Alora scowled. *I'm not the one who's supposed to be watching. If you'd listened to me, then you wouldn't have to sneak out to talk to the aunties.*

An image of the sprite popped into Keelie's mind.

What? You're not going to the aunties? What are you going to do, Keliel Tree Talker?

I'm going to see the sprite. I'll be back. If I hurry, then I can be back before Dad returns.

I don't like this. You need to go to the aunties. They can advise you. They know everything that goes on in this forest.

No, Dad is with them. He has enough to do to stop those kids with the ATVs. I'll be back.

This was becoming a pattern. If someone had told her a year ago that she'd be hiking in the woods day and night, she'd have laughed at them.

The moon was bright in the dusky sky as Keelie ran back to Dad's house and grabbed a flashlight from the Swiss Miss Chalet. Playing the beam over the path, she could see numerous tire tracks in the dirt. It angered her to think about a bunch of idiots on ATVs wheeling through the forest. There had to be a way to restore the Dread. If not, more and more humans would come into the forest.

Hearing the creek, Keelie called out for the sprite. "Are you there?"

The little sprite rose up from the water. "Here I am."

Keelie knelt down. "I need the amulet."

The little sprite tilted her head. "Are you sure?"

"I'm sure. I need it now."

The sprite shook her head disapprovingly. She disappeared underwater with a silent splash, and returned with the mud-encrusted amulet. As she lifted it up in her hands, the mud washed away and its silver thorns glinted in the moonlight as if winking at Keelie.

Keelie reached out for it. Her fingers touched the sprite's wet, clammy skin. Clasping the amulet, Keelie felt cold, as if she had plunged her hands into a bucket of ice water and the chill had permanently settled in her bones.

"Thank you."

The sprite smiled, wide and lipless, then sank back out of sight.

As Keelie made her way back through the woods, her heart raced with anticipation. She had the amulet—she should be able to unlock the cabinet.

The wind blew through the trees, leaves rustling against one another. She caught whispered tree conversations. *What is the Tree Shepherdess doing? Where is she going?* She hoped Dad wasn't listening to the trees tonight.

Some form of healing magic had to be in the book. She wasn't sure how to use it, but Einhorn had given her the amulet for a reason. He knew Keelie was the one who could resist dark magic. After all, she'd defeated the Red Cap when she barely even knew how to use her tree magic.

She reached out to the trees on the edge of the forest. *Where is my father?*

He is with the queens, the ones the little princess calls the aunties. Do you wish to speak to him?

No. Fear rushed through Keelie. If they contacted Dad, he would come back.

As you wish, Tree Shepherdess.

Keelie crept into her grandmother's house.

She held the amulet to the locked cabinet door. She didn't know how she knew what to do—it was as if she were being guided by the amulet itself. The spiral on it began to glow, starting on the outside ring, then circling deeper and deeper until it reached the center. From inside the cabinet, a bright gold light shone, matching the light coming from the amulet. The lock on the cabinet clicked, and the door swung open.

The book floated out. Keelie reached for it with an outstretched hand, holding the amulet with the other.

The concentric spirals on the book started to rotate, and then the book fell open. Alora's voice was loud in her head. *What are you doing?*

Keelie barely heard her. She was lost in a trance. The pages of the book flipped open. Keelie looked down and there it was—a spell to heal blindness. She read it, wondering why the strange script made sense to her.

She remembered the dream and Knot's warning not to use dark magic, even for a good cause. But she must heal Ariel. She could control the magic. The wind was blowing and she heard the trees. *No! Tree Shepherd, hurry.*

Keelie ran outside to the mews, the book tight to her chest and the amulet thrust forward in her hand. She shouted the words of the spell. Dark storm clouds formed, blotting out the moon. The wind increased, and a cold eeriness wrapped around her as a golden undulating light flowed from the amulet and snaked its way to Ariel, enveloping the hawk in bands of light.

Gold light shone from the hawk's eyes. Ariel flapped her wings, her beak open, but made no sound.

Keelie held the book close. The magic was now reaching into her, the end of that serpentine light now entering her wrist and moving up her arm.

A dark fog surrounded her. The book was knocked out of her hand.

Keelie looked up into Jake's pale, horrified face. "What have you done?"

sixteen

Keelie dove to snatch up the book and held it tightly against her chest, turning to keep Jake from grabbing it.

"Stupid girl, you've cursed yourself." He was angry.

Then Elia's voice rang out in the darkness. "Let go of her, Jake. She's got to help my father."

Jake ignored Elia. "The magic didn't heal Ariel. It transformed her." He turned to Elia. "And it won't help your father, either." His eyes flashed red, reminding Keelie that he was neither elf nor human.

Keelie shrank away from him. She wanted to feel the magic course through her again. She hugged the book tighter and was thrilled to see the golden glow reach out to her.

"I don't believe you," she told Jake. "I used the magic to heal Ariel." She gestured toward the cage with a lift of her chin. "Look. She'll be able to fly."

Golden sparkles danced all around Ariel. The magic was working. Keelie's heart gladdened despite the dark, icky vertigo that had begun to swirl in her brain.

Elia looked at her, then clapped her hands over her mouth. "Keelie, Jake's right. You didn't save her—you've condemned her. Look at you."

"What?" Keelie felt a little sick, but no different. "You're wrong, Elia. If you hadn't cursed her in the first place, then I wouldn't have had to use the book. She won't die. If your heart is good, then you can control the bad magic. The unicorn trusted me. I'm saving Ariel, and I'll be able to save Grandmother and the Dread Forest."

Keelie felt drunk with the power of the magic. It felt so strong now, flowing through her and making the dizziness ebb away. It was as if her mind was being cleared. She didn't understand why Dad or Grandmother hadn't used the magic before. It was so different from tree magic.

Keelie stepped away from Jake, out of his reach. She looked at Elia, who stared back in shock.

"I have to restore the Dread. The Shining Ones' magic can be used to help others."

Jake edged closer to her. "No, Keelie. You don't understand. It's not a magic book from the Shining Ones.

It's a darkling book filled with the secrets of the Underworld—the dark fairies. It's dangerous, and it's changed you already."

"No it's not. You just want the power for yourself." There was a part of Keelie's brain that was reeling in shock—thinking, "what are you saying? This is not you." But no, the book belonged to her. It was hers. She could use this magic for good. This wasn't like tree magic, or the Dread, or even the charm that the elves used on humans.

She heard the trees calling to her, afraid. *Tree Shepherdess? Tell Dad I saved Ariel. Tell him she can see.*

Tree Shepherdess, your father is…

A loud clanging pierced Keelie's ears. She twisted, trying to get away from the sound. Her head filled with the ringing of hammers on hot steel. Her mind whirled with images of the dwarves' forge. "I can't hear the trees."

Jake frowned. "The Underworld is reaching out, blocking you from the trees."

Keelie shook her head. "Underworld? Dark fairies? This is supposed to be the magic of the Shining Ones. The magic of Einhorn and the good fairies."

"But this is not the power of the Shining Court, Keelie. I told you." Jake lifted his head and listened. "Armored men are coming close."

"I don't understand what you're telling me. If it's not the Shining Ones, who is it?" The clanging made her head spin and a headache pounded behind her eyes. She shifted the book to one arm so that she could rub her temples.

"The dark fae."

The clanging drew louder and Keelie realized that it wasn't all in her head. Panic and nausea hit her like a punch to the pit of her stomach as she realized what she'd done. "I've used the magic of the dark fairies to heal Ariel," she managed to whisper. "How can I undo it?"

"Forget the bird—how can she use the book to help my father?" Elia asked impatiently.

"Your father made his choice and it can be undone no more than Keelie can undo hers." Jake sounded just as tense. "But Keelie can summon the bird to do her bidding. Maybe it can help us."

"We've caught you, vampire!" Three armored jousters sprang from the bushes and surrounded Jake, swords drawn, so that he could not escape. Two more stood on either side of Elia. The armed men wore breastplates and fitted helmets over tunics. They must have dressed hastily.

Niriel strode forward, a lantern in his hand. "Give me the book, Keelie, and don't listen to this creature. He was formed from an act so vile that it tainted his soul and turned him into a vampire. There was nothing evil in what you did, dear child. You merely wanted to save your bird."

"Leave Keelie alone, Niriel." Jake stood in front of her, pushing aside a sword blade.

The elven lord motioned with his hand. "Look at your hawk." He lifted the lantern and Keelie saw that Ariel's eyes were no longer milky white with blindness—they were golden and bright with a ring of black around the irises.

Her red tail feathers had turned black. It was as if Ariel was no longer in the hawk's body, replaced by something dark and sinister.

Wondering if Niriel could be right, Keelie placed her hand against Ariel's cage, her fingers trembling. "What's happened to her?"

"The magic has transformed her," Jake answered. "Even though your intentions were good, the dark magic works unexpectedly."

"I'm sure your transformation was unexpected as well, was it not, vampire? Our forest will soon be cleansed of your presence." Lord Niriel's smile was smug.

Jake lunged toward the woods, but two of the jousters restrained him, holding his shoulders tightly.

Niriel walked past him to Ariel's cage. The hawk watched him intently, head thrust forward, as he unlatched the door's catch.

"What are you doing? You can't let her go in the dark." Keelie watched, dismayed, as he flung the door open.

Ariel spread her wings, then jumped into the doorway and launched herself like a feathered missile into the night sky, disappearing into the shadows of the trees with three fast beats of her wings.

"See, child, the hawk is flying free, isn't that what you wanted? To restore her sight, so she could fly?" Niriel's eyes narrowed with evil pleasure. He brushed his hands together. "Now that you've accomplished that goal, you can give me the book and I will be a character witness for you at the trial. I will tell them that you were distraught about the hawk, driven mad with the goal of restoring her sight. The book called to you and because of your human blood, you couldn't resist it."

"What trial? What are you talking about?" Keelie clutched the book tighter, not trusting Niriel's intentions, especially if he meant to bring her to trial.

"You wouldn't dare bring her before the Council." Jake tried to struggle free of the jousters, but he couldn't break their hold.

"It's really your fault if the Tree Shepherd's daughter is condemned," Niriel told him. "A trial has been called based on evidence that she has concealed your presence from us. Elianard was to be judged, too, but he is in poor condition."

"It's not fair," Elia cried out. "My father was trying to save the Dread. He didn't want to kill Einhorn. He only wanted the horn to renew the magic, and now he's fading and no one will help him."

Jake looked at her, a tender expression on his face. He must love her, Keelie thought. When did that happen? Nothing was going her way this night.

Above, Ariel called out, a joyous sound that rang through the trees. Keelie looked up and saw her hawk, glowing with the power that vanquished her curse. Whatever happened, Ariel would survive.

Emboldened by the realization, Keelie faced Niriel. "Let

them go. You have me and the proof of what I've done. Jake and Elia have done no wrong."

"Tell her, Jake … is that what you call yourself now? Tell our little Tree Shepherdess how you became a vampire." Niriel's smile was cruel.

Jake's expression darkened and he struggled against his captor's grasp. "You were part of it, Niriel. Tell her yourself."

Keelie looked from one to the other, puzzled. "I know what happened. Jake said he used dark magic."

Niriel's smile widened. "And so he did. He killed the unicorn of the Okanogan forest, and used its horn to restore the Dread. Alas, it doomed him."

Keelie looked at Jake. "You killed a unicorn?" Her stomach twisted as she remembered Einhorn, broken and dying, before her magic had restored him. "How could you?"

Jake lowered his head, then met her eyes. "Like you, I thought I could control the dark magic. Elianard, Niriel, and I thought the unicorn's horn could be used to restore the Dread and save our home. It worked—but I spend every minute of every day regretting my decision." Jake looked at Elia with sadness. "I'm sorry." He reached out to her, and she ran to his embrace.

"Elia?" Niriel scowled. "You let this abomination touch you?"

"He is no abomination." From within the circle of Jake's arms, Elia lifted her chin, defiant. "You are. You're the one who urged Father to save the Dread by killing the Wilde-wood unicorn."

"Your father is the one condemned by the magic, not me." They were all included in Niriel's contemptuous stare. "If he had been able to follow the plan we made, he would have remained untouched by the magic. The unicorn's horn would be ours."

Keelie knew what the plan had been. "You were going to kill the Wildewood unicorn and use his magic to save the Dread Forest, and I was supposed to lure Einhorn while you killed him—but Einhorn lived. So why is Elia-nard dying?"

"Because he used the amulet with intent to harm. You, my dear, can use the book and the amulet, too. You will restore the Dread."

"But I'll be cursed," Keelie said. This didn't sound like a great plan.

"You're already cursed," Niriel said curtly. He turned to the jousters. "Let's get them to the Lore House."

The jousters moved forward.

"I won't do it." Keelie held the book high. "The magic of this book was guarded by the tree shepherds, and the amulet was entrusted to me by Einhorn. I'll give them to my father."

Niriel cocked his head and motioned nonchalantly. Several jousters stepped up with swords drawn. "Brave words that signify nothing. You will be held in the Lore House to await the pleasure of the tree queens and the Elven Council."

Jake growled.

Niriel pressed his sword tip into Elia's chest, daring Jake to come closer. "I wouldn't move if I were you. This one's death would spare the Council one decision."

Elia stared at Niriel, unafraid.

The other elven jousters moved in around Jake. He stood still, his eyes on Elia. "Don't hurt her."

"He actually cares for you, Elia. And you care for him. I thought it impossible for someone to break through your icy veneer. To think I even considered a marriage between you and my son." Niriel laughed.

Jake broke free of his captors and one of the jousters lifted a sword in a wide, slashing arc toward Jake's neck.

"Stop." Keelie dropped the book and lunged forward to grab the sword's blade, ignoring the sharp pain as it cut her hand. Her blood sizzled, and sparks shot from the steel as it transformed to wood.

The elf dropped the sword with a startled cry and jumped back.

"Impossible," Niriel hissed.

Everyone stared at the wooden sword on the ground. The jousters shifted uneasily.

"A pretty trick." Niriel motioned for more elven guards. The jousters recovered from their surprise and surrounded Jake, Elia, and Keelie. "Take them to the Lore House."

"The trees told me there was trouble." Zeke walked

rapidly toward them. The jousters stopped, confused at the sight of the tree shepherd.

Niriel reached down for the book, but Zeke's booted foot stepped down on it. "This book is forbidden to you."

Niriel straightened with a scowl. "Tree Shepherd. Of course."

"What goes on here?" Grandmother appeared behind Dad, her eyes wide at the sight of the armed men. "The trees called to me in my sleep. It's been so long since they've spoken to me. They told me my granddaughter needed me."

Keelie was so glad to see them, but she was also frightened and embarrassed to be found out.

Grandmother looked at Keelie, and then her gaze slid to Jake. She lifted a trembling hand to her face, her expression frozen in a mask of disbelief. "Dariel?"

Jake bowed his head. "Mother, Zekeliel."

Mother? Keelie looked from Jake to Dad. Oh yeah, she could see it now.

Dad paled. "Dariel, why have you returned? Leave at once, or you'll be killed."

Keelie looked from Dad to Jake. "What's going on here?"

Dad shook his head. "The trees whispered of this, but I hoped it wasn't true. And if it wasn't, then it was a secret best left in the past."

So Jake was Dad's long-lost brother. This was a family disclosure straight out of *Star Wars*.

"Jake, you could have told me that you're my uncle."

"Family secrets revealed." Niriel sneered at them. "Really, Zeke, you must learn to communicate with your daughter." He shook his head, feigning sadness. "Of course, this changes nothing. I am escorting them to the Lore House, Tree Shepherd. There they will await their trial."

"Ridiculous," Grandmother said angrily. "If anyone is to go on trial it is you and Lord Elianard."

Niriel bowed his head. "But Keliatiel, we have witnessed Keliel's use of dark magic, and she has admitted to aiding the vampire, as has Elia. Our laws are clear and must be honored. You lead us, what say you?" His eyes shifted from face to face.

He's lying, Keelie thought. His plan's been found out and he's making this up as he goes along.

Keliatiel looked from her two sons to Keelie, eyes shining with unshed tears. "I will see you at the Oaken Circle of the Queens, before the Caudex."

seventeen

A jouster stepped forward, dressed in silvery chain mail. It was Tamriel, Niriel's right-hand elf. He always did whatever the elven lord wanted.

He signaled to the other jousters, and they fell into formation, marching four abreast, then parted and surrounded Keelie, Jake, and Elia. Dad joined them, the book held firmly in his hands. Keelie slipped the amulet into her pocket. Once they were surrounded, the troop turned to face the path. Grandmother stood regally to one side and watched.

Tamriel looked down his haughty nose at Keelie. "I will walk behind you," he said in a firm tone.

They had no choice but to obey. Niriel said nothing as the men began to march, herding their prisoners.

Keelie's head rang with a clanging of hammers, and the earth beneath her feet vibrated with energy. From the corner of her eyes, she watched as the *bhata* darted in the treetops as if keeping tabs on her whereabouts. An angry cloud of *feithid daoine* buzzed nearby. She was hyper aware of everything around her.

Most of all, she was aware of the book in Dad's arms.

She wanted it. She felt its power reach out to her. She could use the magic within to restore the Dread. When she restored the Dread, the elves would not put her on trial. They would free her and Jake, too.

Dad reached out and tilted her chin up. "Your eyes."

"What about them?"

"They've changed. They have the look of the fae about them."

"Are they silver like Zabrina's?"

"No, they're green flecked with glimmering gold, like the magic that comes from the book."

Keelie couldn't help it. She glanced at the book.

"It calls to you, doesn't it?" Dad held the book loosely clasped in his arms. He didn't seem worried that she would make a grab for it.

"Yes." Her fingers reached out.

"Keelie, you've got to fight the temptation."

"Dad, you can't let the aunties have it."

"Keep moving," Tamriel commanded.

Dad and Keelie quickened their pace to appease the jouster.

"Don't worry. Once it's in their possession it will be safe," Dad reassured Keelie.

It wasn't the answer she wanted. She wanted the book, but there was more to worry about.

"I'm going to be put on trial. What's going to happen to me?" She slowed, waiting for his answer. "I keep thinking of the Salem witch trials. They ended in a barbecue."

Tamriel pushed her forward. "I said keep moving."

Keelie glared at him until Dad took her elbow and gently tugged her forward. He whispered in a do-it-now-and-don't-argue tone, "Walk with me. Don't make Tamriel angry. He's looking for an opportunity to use his sword."

She complied, matching her steps to his.

After a few minutes, they fell into a rhythmic pace. Dad leaned in closer to Keelie. "Why did you use the book?" His voice was sad.

"I had to heal Ariel—it would be just a little bit of magic. And if it worked, I figured that it would prove to everyone how the book could be used without bad effects. Then we could figure out how to save the Dread. I would have told you. Grandmother Keliatiel wouldn't fade, and you wouldn't tie yourself to the forest."

"The book deceives the user."

"Like Jake? He thought he'd found a way to save the

Dread," Keelie said. "Look at him now. He's a vampire. Why didn't you ever tell me you had a brother?"

Dad lifted his head, his gaze on his long-lost brother. "Some memories and people are better left in the past."

Keelie watched as Jake wrapped his arms protectively around Elia. They were a couple who had possibly found love in the midst of turmoil. Maybe there could be hope for them. She had to hang on to that thought. She had to believe that she wasn't cursed, that she hadn't cursed them all.

"What's going to happen to them at the trial? What's going to happen to me?"

Dad sighed. He pulled her closer to him as if he was hanging onto her, as if these fleeting moments with her were precious and he wanted to keep her close. Not a good sign.

"The trial is overseen by the Council. We haven't had one for many years. If found guilty, you could be exiled, if the Council is kind. Or sent to fade, out in the world away from the forests. It is a painful experience for an elf to fade—or to die, as you know it—away from the forest. Your name will be struck from the lore, and it will be as if you'd never existed."

"Oh!" She found it hard to breathe, imagining the loneliness. Then she straightened. She'd survive. She could make it, even if the elves were cruel and made her leave. There was no way she'd fade—she was half human. She'd come from Los Angeles, and she could go back there. She leaned closer to Dad, letting some of his strength seep into her body.

But the thought of miles of concrete and steel made

her stomach clench and her heart ache. Maybe she was more elf than she thought.

"Doesn't it matter that I wasn't trying to hurt anyone? I cured Ariel. For that they'd kill me?"

"Death is not an option. They will more than likely banish you."

"That means I can't live in the Dread Forest with you."

"Not here, nor anywhere else that the elven have claimed as their own. It means you would never be able to see me again, unless I came to you. If you're exiled, you would be made to forget your past and all in it."

Stunned, Keelie looked up at Dad. "They can't make me forget you."

Dad nodded grimly. "They can. And your mother, and Ariel. That's what happened when they banished Jake."

"But he came back." Her voice was a whisper. She'd thought of all the things Jake had seen, without wondering what he'd lost. And he remembered now, she knew he did.

"It's been a hundred years since I last saw my brother." Dad's voice was sad. "Something must have triggered his memory." Far ahead of them, Jake was walking alongside Elia, now holding her hand. He alone looked happy. Keelie wouldn't have a hundred years to regain her memory.

A commotion behind them drew Keelie's attention. She turned to see Sean striding up to Tamriel.

"Lord Niriel requests that you run ahead and tell the Council to make ready at the Lore House."

Tamriel looked baffled. "But my lord, he has given me no such orders."

"Do I need to tell *my father* you disobeyed?" Sean stood, tall and regal, in their path. He didn't look toward Keelie and she was glad. Right now she wished she were invisible. He must know she'd used the dark magic—the whole world would know by now. Maybe it was imprinted on her forehead. No, it was imprinted on her eyes for all to see: *Dark Magic User.*

Tamriel nodded and sprinted up the path ahead of the others, around Jake and Elia and into the woods.

Sean stepped toward Keelie. She closed her fist, ready to deck him if he got any closer. Instead, he leaned toward her father.

"Everything is going as planned," he whispered. "I've had a message from Knot. He will meet you near the Lore House. Watch for his signal."

Keelie scowled. "You heard from Knot? You don't understand cat."

"Knot has a unique way of communicating." Sean raised his sleeve. Runic scratch marks appeared on his skin. He arched an eyebrow. "Despite the fact that you think I'm a—what is it you called me, a wienie?—I'm not."

Dad put a hand on Sean's shoulder. "Sean has been helping me, Keelie. I'm sorry he had to let you think he didn't care for you anymore."

One of the jousters walked within hearing distance.

"No matter what happens, don't forget how I feel about

you," Sean whispered as he strode ahead and joined the other jousters. He looked like he belonged with them.

Keelie was confused. She didn't know who wouldn't be. She was cursed now. How long before she started craving blood? They were on their way to her trial, where she could be banished and made to forget about her father and the guy she cared about. The guy she thought had betrayed her, but who was now telling her that he cared about her.

She had been through too much for the elves to treat her this way. She'd done so much to help them and had gotten nothing but misery in return.

Knot had tried to warn her. Jake had told her about the dark magic, but she hadn't listened. She had been so determined to save Ariel from blindness that she had blinded herself to the truth.

Dad held the book tight in his right hand and held her hand in his left. They didn't talk because armed men were hovering very close, eavesdropping, as if hoping to pick up some incriminating evidence.

Keelie soaked up the nearness of her father. She had missed this. Just being with him. She leaned her head against his shoulder. It eased the pounding in her head.

On the path, they passed an evergreen with low-lying branches. A *bhata* climbed down onto Keelie's shoulder and patted her cheek and pointed upwards. She looked.

Awe filled her.

The air was thick, a green nourishing soup that glowed all around. Above her, branches larger than many trees' trunks clasped arms hundreds of feet in the air. It was as if they were in a great living cathedral, its canopy filled with *bhata*. Ariel flew by, and a glittering trail of golden magic illumined her wings as she glided through the trees. Her piercing cry rang out over the forest, reminding Keelie that even though she had used dark magic, it had been for a good purpose. Somewhere, that had to count for something.

"Dad, look—Ariel."

"I know." His voice cracked.

Watching the hawk made Keelie's heart soar.

"Your little bird is putting on quite the show." Niriel joined them. "Nevertheless, it's time to break up this happy family reunion. The Lore House is not too far. This is where you will have to part ways with your daughter and your brother, Tree Shepherd."

Dad's expression grew angry. "You told me I could accompany Keelie all the way."

"I've changed my mind."

Out of the corner of her eye, Keelie saw Knot. He motioned his head to the side as if saying, *Come on.*

She didn't need a PhD in cat body-language to understand that it was a signal.

Dad's hold on the book had loosened as he argued with Niriel. "Your word is your bond."

"Not when I'm dealing with prisoners."

Keelie hadn't made any such promise. She saw that everyone was distracted. She leaned close to Dad, grabbed the book and ran.

eighteen

"Stop, Round Ear." A jouster was close behind her. He tripped, and Keelie felt a gloved hand close around her ankle.

Come to us, child, the aunties called to Keelie. Whether in command or invitation, it was her best bet.

She kicked the hand and scrambled away. Above her she heard Ariel's keening cry. The hawk plunged down and attacked the downed jouster, her talons gripping his exposed head. He screamed and swatted at her, but she kept attacking, releasing him briefly, then swooping down to slash at him again. He fell to his knees and cowered, protecting his bleeding head with his forearms and yelling for help.

Ariel circled upwards, and then turned and came in again for another attack. The screaming jouster's mail shirt rattled, but it was his head that needed protection since he wore no helm.

Keelie couldn't believe it. Ariel hadn't flown away—she'd returned to help her. Jake had said that the hawk been transformed by the dark magic, but here she was, saving Keelie, giving her a chance to get away.

Hurry, Keliel. Come to us, now, the aunties urged. But she couldn't. She had to help Jake and Elia.

Ariel screeched as if she were saying, *Go, go, while you can.*

"What's happening?" A deep voice shouted from nearby.

Keelie's heart pounded so loudly she was sure whoever had shouted could hear it.

"Over by the trees. Hurry, get this damn bird off me."

Where could she go? Wherever she went, she'd be found. The elves knew this forest much better than she did.

The three giant oaks, the aunties, beckoned her with their massive branches. *Come, Keliel. Come to us.*

Something furry brushed up against Keelie's ankle. She jumped, looked down, and to her relief saw that it was Knot. "Where have you been?"

The shouts of the jousters were getting closer and she

could hear the pounding of their booted feet, but before she could run, cool greenness filled her, pushing away the darkness, clearing her mind of fuzzy thoughts.

Knot didn't wait. He dashed toward the village green, and Keelie ran after him, freed from indecision. Some elf folk made as if to stop her, and then hung back. Maybe they thought the dark magic that filled her was contagious. She grinned. Yep, they were afraid of her darkling cooties.

Knot disappeared between the massive roots of the giant oaks. It was as if he'd walked into an invisible doorway.

Keelie stopped, wondering what to do next. Knot's head popped back up from behind a tree root. He blinked his eyes, then motioned with his head for her to follow. She swallowed. She had definitely seen that. She clambered over roots until she was at the base of one of the aunties.

"She's up near the circle." She heard someone shout, then heard Tamriel's voice mingling with the others.

Knot meowed and wriggled down a hole next to the root. Keelie stared, dismayed at the smallness of the crevice. She could never fit through it. But as she watched, the root moved, widening the opening. A branch lowered and pulled the book from under her arm. The book vanished up into the tree's high canopy. With the jousters now in sight, Keelie had no choice. She threw herself feet first into the hole.

The soil was moist and cool, and hair-like rootlets hung like untidy fringe from the top of the little cave. Above her the root shifted again, covering the hole and leaving her in darkness.

Tightness squeezed her lungs as the dark seemed to suck the air out of them. Fighting claustrophobia, she thought of open meadows and wide paths through the forest. It was no use. The hole seemed to be tighter, like a grave.

She thought of a mall parking lot. Acres of black asphalt shimmering under a hot California sun. Suddenly she could breathe much easier.

Above her, she could hear the rattling armor of the elven jousters as they surrounded the tree. Heavy footfalls echoed all around her.

Her fingers closed around the rose quartz in her pocket, but she couldn't use it to see by. The light might spill out from around the roots and reveal her hiding place.

Even though the jousters' voices were muffled, Keelie could make out their conversation.

"She vanished in here."

"I saw her."

"She's a tree shepherd. The trees will protect her," a frustrated voice shouted out.

The deep clang of metal hitting something rang out. One of the jousters must have hit one of the aunties with his sword. How dare they! The sound was followed by a yelp of pain. Keelie imagined the aunties swatting the jouster with a branch, like a naughty child being spanked.

"We're not going to find the girl here," Tamriel's deep voice said loudly.

There were mumbles of agreement.

After a few minutes, silence.

Keelie lay in the nest of the roots and didn't dare move for fear of being discovered, but a cool breeze tickled her ankles. She listened again for footfalls and conversation outside the trees. Nothing. She reached out for the aunties, opening her mind to them.

Is it safe?

You cannot go up to the village.

I've got to find my father and help the others.

Your father is safe for now. You must follow the guardian.

Somewhere below her, Keelie heard a muffled meow. Knot! Relief spread through her. She wasn't alone. If she was going to follow him, though, she had to have some light.

She reached for her rose quartz and its soft pink glow illuminated a narrow passageway. She wiggled and dropped a few feet, then stopped. It was like being on an annoying slide that wasn't slippery.

She wriggled her way down the narrow, womblike passageway toward Knot's meow. After a few more feet the space widened and she inhaled cool, earthy air.

Another wiggle and suddenly she was sliding fast. A quick pang of fear was followed by panic as her legs slid into nothingness. Her heart clenched as she flew out into space, thinking in that split second of all the things she'd wanted to do with her life, of her mother and her father, her friends and her new life in the forest, and how at least Ariel would be able to fend for herself now that she could see.

She landed hard on her backside, which knocked her breath away. She sat still for a moment, grateful to be alive, and held the rose quartz high.

The pink light illuminated a huge underground room. It was like an alien airport hangar with limestone stalagmites growing from the ground and massive tree roots hanging down. Clods of dirt fell from the earth ceiling.

Are you safe now, child? She was under the aunties. That meant she was under the village. She didn't think that the elves knew about this cave, or the aunties wouldn't have shown her the way down.

Something moved at the edge of her vision and she turned her head, startled, holding her quartz up like a lantern. She relaxed when she saw that it was a *bhata*, a big one, staring at her with juniper berry eyes. Next to it was another one, and then another. To her surprise, hundreds of them moved into view, a breathing mass of sticks, leaves, and moss. They covered every inch of the floor and the walls, and clung to the roots that hung from the ceiling far above. Keelie moved forward carefully, shuffling gently for fear of stepping on one of the stick fairies.

The *bhata* made way for her. "What is this place?" she whispered.

A meow echoed from far away, and Keelie realized that

this was not the only room. There was another cavern, and beyond it she sensed another. She had the impression of great space above and around her.

"You are Under-the-Hill, Keliel of the Dark Ones," a hivey voice said.

She turned around warily, expecting to see one of the elves. But there was no one there, only the *bhata*. Far ahead she heard Knot's faint meow, urging her on.

Follow your guardian, the aunties encouraged.

The *bhata* parted, showing her a path. She ran to catch up with Knot. The next room was just as large but with less rubble, and the roots hanging from above were smaller.

Here lit torches were set into the walls. Somebody lived down here. She wondered who, and did they possibly have something to do with the disappearing Dread?

Knot led her through cavern after cavern. Some rooms were illuminated, others dark. She tread carefully, afraid she'd break an ankle and no one would ever find her.

After a while, she noted something familiar about the pattern of the caverns' layout. They were spiraling inward, always turning toward the right. It reminded her of the symbol on the book covers—an immense underground spiral labyrinth. She thought about the last time she'd seen the design on the book, and her mind became cloudy with the need to hold it once more.

A soft tapping came from nearby. Somebody was close. Knot had vanished. Afraid to call out to him, Keelie hurried. She didn't want to be alone.

She heard a meow ahead and, relieved, entered the next chamber. It was empty, and completely cleared of the bits of rubble and dirt that had cluttered others. It looked as if it had been swept. On the far side, the opening to the next chamber glowed with warm light.

She glimpsed Knot's silhouette and hurried to catch up with him. She found herself in a room filled with glowing stones set in the spiral pattern. On the far side was a stream, dark and deep, running through a crack in the bedrock outside of the labyrinth. The center of the spiral was below a bare place in the ceiling. Knot sat in the center of the spiral, his tail twitching as if he had been waiting for her for a really long time.

What was this place? The tapping sound became louder, echoing all around. If someone else was down here, she would meet them soon enough.

Knot moved quickly across the room, and Keelie rushed after him. She tried to go across the spirals but was knocked back, as if she'd run into a wall. She reached out, but could feel nothing. Knot meowed. Keelie got up and dusted herself off. Fine, she'd follow the crazy spirals.

"Slow down, Knot! Some guardian you are." The evil kitty was the only one who could get her out of here.

She traveled around the labyrinth, and as she grew closer to the center, a path appeared that led to a small stone bridge that crossed the dark stream. On the other side she could now see a workroom, with stone benches and tables. Three small people, a woman and two men, stared at her from the benches.

Dwarves!

One of the men jumped up and came toward her. He was dressed in jeans and a Flogging Molly T-shirt, and as he grew closer Keelie saw that he wasn't much older than she was. Light glinted from a minute shard of crystal just above his eyebrow.

He grinned. "I'll bet you're that elf girl that Jadwyn's always talking about."

"And you must be the guy who got the silver eyebrow ring from Zabrina."

The little man touched his transformed eyebrow ring, grinned, and held out his hand. "My name is Barrow."

The woman scowled at him. Keelie figured this must be his mother. Mom used to have the same expression on her face whenever Keelie was caught doing something she wasn't supposed to do.

Barrow confirmed her suspicion. "That's my mom, Madalyn, and my dad, Radorak." The elder bowed his head gravely.

Madalyn eyed Keelie. "So you're Zeke Heartwood's daughter?"

"Yes, ma'am."

"How came you here? How did you find us?" Radorak asked in a serious tone.

"I wasn't looking for you, I promise. I got lost when I

stumbled over some tree roots and found my way down here. I didn't know this place existed. Do the elves know?"

The three of them looked at each other. Madalyn sighed. "The elves don't know. They keep to the Aboveworld. But the trees know, and thus the tree shepherds know."

"Or at least, they know of the Underworld. None have been here," Radorak corrected.

"How do you keep an entire world secret?" She wondered how much Dad knew about this place.

"Easy," Barrow answered enthusiastically. "Most people never know what exists beneath them. Look at Portland and Seattle. Dwarves have lived underneath the subways and streets for years and the humans have no idea."

"Oh! I guess you're right." Keelie had lived in L.A. all her life, but she couldn't imagine what was below the sidewalks and streets.

"There are dark things here, too, like the dark fairies, trolls, Red Caps, and such, but they won't bother you unless you aggravate them. Or summon them."

Keelie shuddered. She glanced at the creek's black flowing water. She wondered what was beneath its surface, then decided that she really didn't want to know. But if it flowed to the outside world, it might be her way out. "I need to get out of here."

As if sensing her urgency, Madalyn reached for Keelie's hand and patted it reassuringly. "We'll show you the way to the town. There you can get to safety. We'll help you."

Keelie shook her head. "No, I have to go back to the forest. My family's in danger."

By the flickering firelight of the torches, Keelie saw a look of concern pass among the dwarves. "Zeke is in trouble?"

Keelie nodded. "The Dread has failed."

Radorak frowned. "Jadwyn must know immediately."

"By Jadwyn, you mean Sir Davey?"

"'Sir.'" Radorak laughed. "Gives himself airs Above-world, he does, but Underworld, he's Jadwyn. We'll tell him to meet you at the store."

"What store?"

"We run the hardware store in town."

"I remember it. You've got funky yard art in front and a display of expensive gardening tools."

Madalyn nodded. "Yes, we make the forged-steel gardening tools. Since we're so familiar with the earth, we make excellent gardeners, too. We give good advice, and folks have listened over the years, so we've built up a good business."

Barrow beamed and his chest puffed out. "And our yard art sells very well, too. Especially the one of the water sprite. Lots of people like to buy that one after rafting down the river."

"It would be great if Sir Davey—er, Jadwyn—could meet me at the store. Let's go. The sooner I can get back, the better." Keelie felt as if a weight had been lifted from her shoulders.

"Well, there's a problem. Jadwyn has to get back, first."
Radorak sat down on a stone bench.

"How long is it going to take him to get here?" The
weight returned to Keelie's shoulders.

"He should be here the day after tomorrow."

"That's too late. I have to go back *now*."

"It's too dangerous for you to go alone," Madalyn said.
She blushed. "We hear things down here. We heard about
the book."

"Then you know that I have to go."

Knot meowed.

Madalyn looked at him and her eyebrows rose. "If
that's the way it has to be. If you ask my opinion, she's a
mere babe to be doing such things."

Barrow wrinkled his face. "Mom, are you talking to
that cat?"

She gestured him away. "Never mind that, Barrow.
Keelie, you're going to have to take the stream. If you ask
me, the child needs a cup of hot coffee and a good night's
sleep, but she has to go back Aboveworld…"

Keelie recoiled at the thought of stepping into the oily-
looking black water. The offer of a cup of coffee and a
good night's sleep was much more appealing.

A cool greenness filled her mind, driving away the dark
thoughts. The calmness of the trees and a mental surge of
sunlight warmed her veins. Keelie stretched out her arms
and reached upwards to the roof of the caverns, seeking
the warmth of the sun. There had to be a balance of dark

and light. The elven part of her needed the sunlight—the human part of her needed the earth. But there was still something else she needed ... She didn't quite understand.

The aunties' mingled voices filled her mind. *You are your Grandmother Josephine's child, too. She was half fairy, and her fairy blood gives you access to the Underworld. Find the water sprite. She will lead you out.*

Fairy? So Grandmother was telling the truth about Grandmother Josephine? Is that why Dad said I was under the protection of the fairies?

Yes.

The image of kindly, matronly Josephine in her nurse's volunteer uniform came to Keelie's mind. There wasn't a fairy bone in her grandmother's body. She loved helping people, but that didn't make her a fairy. Then Keelie remembered that Grandmother Josephine never talked about her childhood.

A *bhata* touched Keelie's cheek. Knot rubbed his head against her ankle.

Keelie shook her head as if clearing it. *What's going on above ground? My father? Elia and Jake?*

The tree shepherd and the others will stand trial tomorrow.

Keelie had less than twenty-four hours to save Elia, her new-found uncle, and her Dad.

The *bhata* dropped to Keelie's shoulders and pointed behind her. She turned, as did the trio of dwarves. Hundreds of *bhata* had followed her.

Madalyn placed her hand against her chest. "My word, I've never seen them congregated together like this."

"You must be something special for them to be here." Barrow eyed Keelie with new respect.

Radorak's deep blue eyes held a wisdom matched by his deep voice. "Davey said you were a gift, a rare gift among elves and humans, and now I understand."

Knot rubbed his head up against Keelie's ankles. Then he bit her.

"Ow!"

The water sprite bobbed up from the stream.

Keelie splashed backwards. "Holy cow. How did you get down here?"

"This is the same stream that goes through the forest and down to the river rapids." She giggled. "I told you he liked you."

Knot hissed, baring his fangs.

Keelie rolled her eyes. "He had a bean burrito for lunch. This is just a gas attack." She rubbed her leg. She was going to need a rabies shot, a tube of Neosporin, or maybe a quarantine for cat cooties. She examined her leg. Knot hadn't broken the skin, although it hurt as if he'd taken a chunk out. She glared at him.

He was now washing his tail as if he hadn't done anything wrong. Like *big deal, I bit you—get over yourself.*

"You're a psycho!"

Knot stopped washing his tail and straightened, his spine crackling as he did so. He blinked at Keelie, then purred. He really hadn't had a bean burrito for lunch, but she'd covered for him.

The water sprite shook her head. "You need a tour guide out of here."

"Yes, I do. Can you help?"

"I'm a great guide. I swim down to the river where the humans go river rafting. Sometimes I like to freak out the people as they're coming over a big rapid and I pop out of the water. They're screaming anyway, and then when they see me, they scream even louder."

"Isn't that dangerous, exposing yourself to humans?" Keelie hadn't realized how far the little sprite got around.

"Nah, the only ones that can truly see me are the ones with fairy blood. Anyway, it gets boring hanging out with elves, who can't see me and are too busy playacting the Middle Ages, and with dwarves who are too busy working all the time."

The water sprite sounded lonely. Keelie could sympathize.

Barrow seemed insulted. "I don't work all the time. I do sculpture. I even did one of you. I see you in the caverns splashing around."

The sprite seemed surprised, "Really?" She gazed dreamily at the dwarf. "Why don't you say hi? I could pose for you." She lifted herself up from the water.

"Yeah." Barrow blushed.

A piteous meow broke the moment. Knot was crouched at the edge of the stream, his eyes dilated. He dipped a paw into the water, then looked back at Keelie. She figured he was telling her that it was time to go.

"I'll take you up on that offer of a tour guide." Keelie slipped down the bank into the cold, black water, reaching gingerly for the bottom. To her relief, the water was only waist-deep.

The sprite swam ahead of Keelie.

She tried not to think about anything living in the water as the wetness weighed down her jeans. She would focus on getting out of here, back to Dad and the others.

Knot meowed, pacing along the bank.

"What?"

He meowed louder and moved close to the water, then bounded back.

She couldn't leave him here, although the thought was tempting. Very tempting. She needed him, but she'd at least get something out of this favor.

"I'll carry you, but no more sleeping in my underwear drawer or sticking your face in my oatmeal." She should probably negotiate for more, but she was too worried to think straight.

Knot's tail twitched back and forth and his eyes narrowed to slits.

The water sprite snickered. "He's got it bad for you."

Knot tilted his head, then gave a little yowl and waited for her at the edge of the stream.

She braced an elbow on the edge of the stone bank and reached out for him. He was a dead weight in her arms, at least twenty-five pounds. Keelie's arms were going to be numb by the time she reached the village.

Knot had other ideas. He was not going to get wet. He climbed up her torso as if she were a rock-climbing wall, digging his claws into her skin. When he got to her shoulders he placed his back paws on them, and his front paws on her head. She knew he must look like an Egyptian pharaoh kitty. Her shoulders cramped from the weight.

"You're going on a diet."

He dug his claws into her scalp.

"Ow, ungrateful beast."

Keelie waved goodbye to her newfound friends and slogged forward.

After what seemed like a long time, she saw enormous tree roots hanging down from the cavern ceiling. It had to be the aunties. *Are you there, oh, great trees?*

We're here. You need to go to the treeling. She needs to be with us.

Guilt washed over Keelie. Alora was alone—she had to get back to her. She reached out to her.

The treeling sniffled. *Where have you been?*

Long story. I'll be there soon.

I heard some mean elves stomp into your house.

Meaning that the jousters had searched her bedroom. *Are you okay?*

Yes. But I heard them say that at least you'd gotten rid of the puny plant. I'm not a plant. I'm a tree. I'm Alora, acorn daughter of the Great Tree of the Wildewood Forest.

Relieved, Keelie smiled. *You sure are.* Alora was okay. *I'll be there soon.*

Hurry it up! I'm thirsty.

The sprite stopped. They had reached the first cavern, where Keelie had entered. The underground stream ended here as well, vanishing into the wall.

Knot launched himself off Keelie's head and onto the bank with an elegant jump that didn't do her scalp any favors, but her head and shoulders felt tons lighter. She twisted her neck and hunched her shoulders, trying to re-adjust her muscles. She was going to need to see a chiropractor once this was all over.

Still waist deep in the water, Keelie looked down at the little sprite. "Thanks."

She stared up at Keelie with wide eyes. "You going to be okay?"

"I have Knot."

The water sprite shook her head. "That's not saying a lot."

On the far side of the tree roots, Keelie noticed movement from several *bhata*. They were returning. "I've had help from the fairies, the trees, and the dwarves. I think I'm going to get through this."

"I'll be around if you need me."

"Thank you."

Keelie climbed up the bank toward the tree roots, squelching with every step, and grabbed an exposed tree root to pull herself up. As she touched the root, familiar green energy filled her, as comforting as chicken soup. The queen oak above her sent her strength.

Go to the youngling. She is to play an important role and she needs her shepherdess.

For a second Keelie remembered her old life, when her fate was not manipulated by ancient trees and curses. She sighed. *What about the jousters? Are they guarding you?*

The one named Sean is here. He will help you.

Sean has betrayed me. I don't trust him.

His heart is yours, Tree Shepherdess. He is true.

Tell that to Risa, Keelie thought.

We do not have time to discuss the hearts of humans. You must help the treeling.

Trees. Where was their loyalty?

Keelie climbed up through the roots, working to push her wet clothes through the dirt. She was going to be a mud ball when she got out of here. She broke through to the night air and inhaled the fresh green smell of the forest gratefully. She had come up under a different tree, another of the aunties.

Sean stood under the tree that had first led her to the Underworld. His blond hair moved in a pine-scented breeze and her heart beat faster despite his betrayal.

She was going to have to trust him. She hadn't believed him when he'd said the marriage hadn't been his idea, and his father had turned out to be her family's enemy. But now she was going to have to trust him. The aunties were asking for a lot.

"I need for you to get his attention," Keelie whispered to Knot.

He blinked. *Gotcha*, he seemed to be saying. Or at least she hoped he was.

He sauntered over to Sean, who was looking up into the aunties' branches. Keelie glanced up and saw Ariel perched on a low bough.

"Ow!" Sean hopped on one foot and glared at something on the ground.

"Everything okay?" One of the other jousters shouted.

"Yes, everything's fine."

Keelie shook her head. Had that cat ever heard of subtlety?

Knot sat behind Sean, out of view of the other jousters. He was admiring his paw, claws extended. Sean looked ready to drop-kick the kitty out of the forest. Knot motioned his head in Keelie's direction, and Sean's gaze turned to her. She popped up and waved.

Sean hesitated a moment and then sauntered over, standing with his back toward her. "Where have you been? We've looked everywhere for you."

"I need to get to Alora. It's important."

"Who is Alora?"

Keelie blinked, surprised, then remembered that Sean didn't know the princess treeling. Thank goodness, or the jousters who searched Grandmother's bedroom would have taken the treeling.

"She's a friend." Okay, so maybe she didn't totally trust

Sean, no matter what the aunties said. "She's in my grand-mother's bedroom."

Sean nodded. "So you need to get back to the house? I'll help you."

"How?"

"I don't know. We need a distraction."

As if on cue, Knot sauntered out of the sheltering roots.

"There's that cat," one of the jousters shouted. "Lord Niriel said to catch him."

Knot waited until several men had spotted him, then dashed into the forest.

Keelie ducked back into the roots.

An armored man clattered by. "Stay here and guard the trees, Sean," he said, already breathing hard.

Knot would lead them on a merry goose chase.

When they were out of sight, Sean held out his hand, rough from hard work, and Keelie accepted it. He clasped his other hand over hers and she felt a delicious tingle run up her spine.

A shout went up from behind them. "There she is!"

Sean turned quickly, then looked back at her. "Run, Keelie."

Run? To where? Keelie ran back to the massive tree trunk. *Open the door.* Her mental shout got a quick response. The giant root that blocked the entrance to the Underworld twitched to one side, as if it were a dainty la-dy's finger and not a tree root the size of a station wagon.

Keelie dropped into the exposed hole and slid painfully down the way she'd just climbed out, faster now that she was coated in slick mud. Above, the jousters' shouts grew louder. They'd spotted her escape hatch. Why wasn't the auntie covering the hole?

Her heels hit the bottom hard, jolting her, and she took off, racing down the dark cavern passage. Behind her, she heard the metallic clatter of a jouster falling down the hole.

She hoped he was okay, but she couldn't stick around to find out. Echoing shouts told her that more men had come below ground, and they'd be after her in a second. She ran faster, retracing her earlier route. At her side, a shadow raced. Knot was with her once again.

nineteen

Keelie raced on, passing through the caverns that she'd explored earlier. The labyrinth room was empty, and she crossed the bridge over the silent black river and dashed through the empty workroom, wondering where Barrow and his parents had gone.

She was in unfamiliar territory now and still she sped on, not daring to stop. She passed ruined palaces and places where feeble sunlight shone into abandoned, thorny gardens. After a while she realized that no one was chasing her, and she stopped. Under-the-Hill was enormous, and she had no idea where she was.

She stood at a stone-floored crossroads, the cool, mineral smell of the rock cavern mingling with an earthy scent, as if she'd gone deep into Mother Earth herself. Her pink quartz glowed dimly through her pocket. She pulled it out and held it up.

The light cast tall shadows all around and Keelie quickly dropped her arm. Too creepy. She turned slowly, holding out the light at waist height. Three steps to the right and the light brightened.

She started walking in that direction, thinking that Sir Davey would be proud of her. Before long she heard voices speaking in a strange tongue, and she hurried, spurred on by the fear of being alone.

The passageway curved, and then she was on the outskirts of an underground town. Dwarf homes, their facades cut into the living rock, were interspersed with workshops.

Small, stout people were walking briskly, packages under their arms, while others worked in their shops. Keelie recognized Barrow.

He gave a start when he saw her and hurried over. "Everyone's talking about the elves coming Under-the-Hill. What happened?"

"They were waiting for me when I went back up to—" She faltered, not knowing what word to use to mean her own world.

"Aboveworld?"

"Yes. And I jumped back down, but they followed me.

I'm not sure when they quit chasing me, I was running too hard."

Barrow put a hand on her arm. "I think instead of going back up there, maybe you should come to our hardware store in town."

In town. The elves would never think of looking for her there. She frowned, remembering Dad and Jake and Elia. What would become of them? She had to get back to the village as soon as she could. With Sean and the aunties' help, she could get to the Lore House and free the prisoners hours before the trial was to begin. Then she had to get Alora to the aunties and retrieve the book from them.

Barrow led her through busy market streets. It was strange being two feet taller than everyone else. It was unusual for the Underworld dwellers, as well. They stared at her and whispered as she went by.

They turned down a narrow street, and Keelie slowed. The smooth stone lane ended at the door of a wooden building, the only large-scale use of wood she'd seen so far in Under-the-Hill.

"Here we are." Barrow grinned at her. "It doesn't seem so far, does it? It's like that in Underworld. Don't trust distances, or time either. Both get tricky down here."

He opened the door and motioned her in. She stepped across the threshold cautiously (oak, from nearby, but very long ago), followed by Knot. They found themselves in a narrow storeroom filled with boxes and bins bursting with tools, casks of nails, and folded tarps.

Barrow closed the door behind them. "Go straight up these stairs, Keelie Fae Friend, and you will be back among the humans."

They climbed the stairs, Keelie in front. "Fae Friend. That's a new one."

Barrow took her hand, blushing. "I hope you don't mind. You are a true friend of the fae, Keliel. You treat all creatures alike. I would also call you Dwarf Sister, and proudly."

Tears prickled in her eyes. "Thanks."

They reached the door at the top, and Barrow twisted the knob and pushed the door open. "Well, gotta get back before the old man finds out I've ditched work to bring you here. See you later." He skipped back down the stairs and disappeared into the dark storeroom.

Keelie entered the back of the shop and closed the door carefully behind her. Would this be like one of those magic doors, where everything changes when you reopen it? She opened it quickly and looked. Same dark stairway, same smell of damp stone and rusting nails.

She closed it once more and walked quickly through the shop toward the front door, waving cheerily to Barrow's astounded mother behind the cash register.

"Where have you two been all night? Where is Barrow?"

"All night?" It seemed just an hour or so since she'd slid under the aunties' roots and Under-the-Hill. "Barrow just said 'bye' at the base of the stairs."

"Take care, then. Come by for supper sometime." Madalyn was headed toward the stairs in back—Barrow was in trouble.

Knot waited for her on the sidewalk outside, warming himself in the morning sunshine. Keelie took a deep breath of tree-scented air. All of the town trees spoke her name, and she sent out a warning.

Tell no one I am here.

Tree Shepherdess, the Dread Forest calls for you.

Keelie frowned. She couldn't hear the trees of the Dread Forest. She did have to hurry back, but how? She looked around the quiet streets of the sleepy town. They didn't even have bus service here, and it would take hours to hike up the road to the elven village.

A brightly colored sign drew her eye. Of course. Keelie hurried toward the tattoo parlor.

Through the glass door, she saw Zabrina seated behind her counter, wearing a tank top that read, "Come to the dark side. We have cookies." Her hair was intricately braided and she looked beautiful. It made Keelie very aware that she was scratched from Knot's water ride on her head, and that her clothes were stiff with drying mud.

At least Knot was muddy, too, and his fur was a mess. If he'd used magic to make himself look good, Keelie would have been angry at him. She opened the door and stepped in, noticing a sticky feeling all over as she passed through. Zabrina was sketching in a book, her left hand loosely clasped around a cup of coffee. She looked up quickly and stared, open-mouthed at Keelie. "How did you get in here? That door was warded." She stood up as she noticed Keelie's muddy clothes. "What happened to you?"

"A lot. I just took a tour of Under-the-Hill, thanks to a mutual friend of ours, Barrow."

"You've been Under-the-Hill?" Zabrina gasped. The little fairy tattoo lifted from her shoulder and hovered, wings trembling. "And you walked through my warded door as if it was nothing. What are you?"

Keelie shrugged. "I'm still figuring that one out." She pointed to Zabrina's mug. "You have any more coffee?"

"Sure." Zabrina poured Keelie a cup and handed it to her. "Tell me everything."

Keelie sat on a stool beside her new friend and told her as much as she dared, leaving out the part about Jake being a vampire.

"Time passes differently Under-the-Hill," Zabrina explained. "A few minutes can turn into days Above-world."

That meant Dad hadn't heard from her all night. He was probably frantic. "I need your help, Zabrina. Can you drive me back to the Dread Forest?"

Zabrina grasped the edge of the counter as if seeking support. "I can't go to the Dread Forest."

The tattoo fairy buzzed around the shop, agitated.

"The elves don't want us there. They can't even see the lesser fae, and I'm like, an abomination to them." Zabrina glanced up at Keelie. "And you've been messing with fae magic—very risky. Look at what's happened to you. Look at your eyes. You've changed."

Keelie hadn't been near a mirror, and figured that her muddy clothes drew attention enough. She ducked her head to look into the mirror on the counter by a display of earrings.

Her hair stood out in mud-caked elf locks, and her pointed ear was scratched and bleeding. Long scratches radiated from her scalp, thanks to Knot, but it was her eyes that made her mouth drop open. Their leaf green was now flecked with bright metallic gold, and a wide ring of gold circled her pupils. Would they ever return to normal?

She forced her attention back to the real urgent matter. "I need your help. My father, my uncle, and Elia are in danger."

Zabrina's face paled. Keelie could tell she was on the verge of saying yes, but she was afraid. She put her hand on Zabrina's arm. "Innocent people are in danger. I might fail, Zabrina, but I want to know that I did everything in my power to help them. I'll accept the consequences."

Zabrina sighed. "And I have to live with those consequences, too. You're very powerful, Keelie. Lucky for you, I'm used to bratty girls with lots of power." She reached underneath the counter for her car keys and glared at Keelie. "Didn't you say that your mother was a lawyer?"

"Yeah."

"It must be in the blood. Come on. Do your thing, Molly."

Relief flooded through Keelie as she realized Zabrina was going to help her. Molly, the tattoo fairy, blended back into Zabrina's skin, and they walked out of the shop followed by Knot.

"Hold on while I lock up and reset the wards you trashed." Zabrina grinned at Keelie. "You don't know how powerful you are, do you? Kid, I had the strangest feeling when you walked into my shop. I felt that my life was never going to be the same."

If she had power, Keelie knew that she would need every bit of it to help Jake and her father; against Niriel, Keelie felt that she had only her wits to help her. She hoped it would be enough.

Zabrina unlocked the passenger door of a faded blue Volkswagen Beetle that looked a hundred years old.

Knot jumped in, and Keelie sat on the cloth seat gingerly. There was a hole in the floorboard.

"Oh, don't worry," Zabrina said cheerfully as she jumped in behind the wheel. "Vlad's seen everything. A little mud won't hurt him." She patted the dashboard. "Vladimir's a survivor. Except he sucks oil like a vampire. I always have to keep several quarts with me."

Keelie shivered.

"It's a joke."

Keelie grinned. "Vladimir the VW Vampire. Now I've heard it all."

With a grinding of gears and a belch of acrid smoke, they took off down the street. Keelie prayed that they'd get back up the mountain in time to stop Niriel from poisoning the minds of the Elven Council.

Zabrina turned onto a two-lane highway and headed north. Ahead loomed the Dread Forest, an impressive wall of dense green woods.

Suddenly a gray barrier loomed before them. Zabrina shrieked and wrenched the wheel. A roar filled the air as the VW spun, the world looping around, and came to rest on the black earth at the side of the road.

Keelie closed her eyes, willing the world to stop moving, then glanced at Zabrina to make sure she was okay. Zabrina was staring, open-mouthed, at the massive vehicle that had swooped onto the road in front of them.

"I hate it when these tourists with their castles on wheels think they can hog the road," she said in an angry tone.

It was a deluxe RV, an immense square box on wheels, stone gray. "Sir Davey!" Keelie pulled off her seat belt and flung her door wide.

The door to the driver's side of the RV opened and a small figure climbed down. The man had a neat goatee and luxurious, long dark hair.

His glare turned to surprise and he hurried toward Keelie. She bent down to hug him. "Oh, Sir Davey I'm so glad you're here."

"I had calls from my brother, then from Radorak while en route. What on earth is happening? I ruined two turbocharged crystals getting here, but I made it."

"We don't have a minute to lose. Leave the RV here and come with us." Keelie pulled him across the street toward Zabrina, who was standing next to her car watching them warily.

"Zabrina, this is Sir Davey. Or Jadwyn." She looked down at her teacher and friend. "What do you go by here?"

"Davey will do." He extended a hand to Zabrina. "How do you do? You own the tattoo shop, right?"

"Yes. I think we've met. I've seen you around town, and at the harvest festival too."

"Chat later, drive now," Keelie commanded, and dove into the front passenger seat. Davey climbed into the back with Knot, then Zabrina scrambled in. Vlad the VW was crowded now. They probably looked like clown-car refugees from a circus.

Keelie gritted her teeth, impatient. Who knew what was happening up in the forest? She smacked her hand on the edge of the car door. "The trees!"

Zabrina and Sir Davey stared at her.

"The trees can tell me what's going on."

"Do you have your tektite, lass?" Sir Davey was sitting in the center of the rear seat, hands on the backs of both front seats. Knot prowled the little car's back deck like a pumpkin-colored caged tiger.

"I do, but I don't need it or my rose quartz. The Dread's gone. Totally broken," Keelie told him.

Davey closed his eyes for a second, as if feeling for it,

then his lids sprang open again, framing his eyes against his hairy eyebrows. "How is this possible?" he whispered.

Keelie told her story for a second time that day, this time leaving nothing out. When she got to the part about Jake being a vampire, Zabrina shot her a wide-eyed panicky stare and the car fishtailed.

"Eyes on the road," Keelie and Davey said simultaneously. Zabrina clenched her jaw and leaned forward, concentrating.

The fairy tattoo peeled away from Zabrina's shoulder and fluttered near Keelie.

Sir Davey arched an eyebrow. "That's something I've never seen."

The little fairy turned her head coyly and batted her eyelashes at him, just as she had with Dad.

"She's a little flirt." He laughed.

"Her name's Molly." Zabrina pushed down on the accelerator and Vlad's engine groaned with more effort. The tires crunched on the gravel.

Before them, the Dread Forest loomed, a primeval woodland of tall trees whose uppermost leaves seemed to brush the sky. Underneath the canopy, the air was green and the ground was carpeted with moss and small plants. Every inch of this world was alive.

Keelie rolled up the window to keep out the toxic cloud of burnt oil that roiled around the car like an angry storm cloud.

Molly mimed a small, delicate cough. She fluttered

around Sir Davey's head. He didn't seem to appreciate her, but was tolerating the little fairy's presence just to be nice.

Knot climbed into Keelie's lap. She put an arm around him to keep him from falling off. He snorted, then sneezed on her.

"Do not hork up a hairball," she warned him.

He purred.

They went deeper into the forest, and the tires crunched less as the road turned into softer ground. Keelie opened her mind to the trees. She needed their soothing green presence in her thoughts.

Tree shepherdess, the poison cloud makes us ill. The trees, mostly spruce, that grew along the road spoke in unison.

Keelie glanced behind them at the spinning exhaust plume behind Vlad the VW. Ooops. No wonder they were upset.

The poison cloud will be gone soon. It brings help for the Tree Shepherd.

The trees seemed confused. As Zabrina drove past, Keelie saw the shocked faces in their trunks.

Trust me.

The scent of evergreens filled her mind.

"The Dread is well and truly gone." Sir Davey's voice was thin with awe. "That Zabrina can get this far into the forest is surprising, and you're not feeling the effect at all, Keelie."

"It's far worse than that. ATVs have been getting in. Dad fears it could become like the Wildewood. Look."

Keelie pointed at crisscrossed tire tracks and flattened foliage on both sides of the road, and gashes in the tree bark. She made a mental note to tell Dad and return to heal the trees.

Zabrina shook her head. "That rotten stinker of a mayor. He's been pocketing money from some of these so-called recreational vehicle companies who want him to open up the trails. If I had anything to do with it, motorized vehicles would be banned from the woods."

In between the trunks of two large spruces, Keelie caught a glimmer of silver. Niriel would have guards out looking for her. He wouldn't give up.

She opened herself to the trees. *Show me the location of the jousters.*

Images of armored and searching jousters on horseback came back to her from all across the Dread Forest. Other images flashed across her mind: the village green surrounded; the Lore House protected.

The aunties called to Keelie. *You need the treeling. She will help you save your uncle, Tree Shepherdess. Without her, there is no hope.*

"Stop," Keelie shouted.

Zabrina slammed down on the brakes. Vlad squealed to a stop and they all lurched forward.

Knot flew off of Keelie's lap onto the floorboard. Molly was flung into the windshield. She looked like a parking sticker for a rock and roll concert.

Sir Davey clung to the passenger seat, his knuckles white with fright.

"What?" Zabrina flung her hands up in the air.

"We need to get out. I think the jousters have spotted the exhaust. The trees will cover for Sir Davey and me."

"So, this is where we part ways." Zabrina seemed sad that her part of the adventure was over.

Something thunked the hood of the VW and bounced off the chrome strip in the center.

"What was that?" Zabrina stared at a crease that now ran across the VW's hood.

"It's a lance." Sir Davey said grimly.

The jousters approach, Tree Shepherdess. We will try to stop them, but cannot for long.

Two mounted men in armor appeared around a bend in the road, and another, the spear launcher, came at them through the forest. Zabrina laughed. "What a hoot! This is like at the Ren Faire."

"Yes, but for real." Keelie didn't like the look on the jousters' faces.

"We need to go," Sir Davey cautioned. "When lances are thrown, in my experience, drawn swords aren't too far behind."

"Thanks for your help, Zabrina." Keelie was anxious to reach her father and Jake. "Will I see you again?"

"You know where my shop is. The luck of the forest to you."

"It will be." Through the VW's window Keelie saw the face of a nearby spruce looking down at her. *Protect her.*

She opened the passenger door and stepped out into the green, springy ferns that bordered the road. Sir Davey clambered out, disappearing into the forest. Knot ran after him, as if he'd had enough of Vlad the VW.

From the side of the road, Keelie watched as Zabrina turned Vlad the VW around in a billowing cloud of sooty exhaust. The two jousters on horseback coughed, then quickly reined their mounts around as the VW charged them, bouncing off trees like an insane pinball game.

Keelie caught up with Sir Davey, who was running toward the village. They slowed to a walk. No jousters were in sight. "Sir Davey, before we go to the trial, there's someone I have to get."

"Who?"

"Alora."

"The treeling?" Wrinkles formed on his forehead. Then Sir Davey said in a panicked voice, "Keelie."

A cold point jabbed Keelie's neck. "I found you. If you move, you will feel my blade," a deep voice rumbled behind her.

She recognized the voice. It was Tamriel. He must have used a shielding spell to hide himself.

"Don't move, dwarf."

"Let her go." Sean stepped out from behind another tree.

"Not this time. Niriel will be pleased that I've caught her."

"I'm his son, so what I say goes, too."

"Everyone knows you're smitten with the Round Ear. I listened to you last time. Not again."

Sean's eyes widened with alarm as Tamriel pushed the sword blade deeper into Keelie's neck.

"Ow!"

"Quiet," Tamriel growled. "We will go to the Lore House. You will not speak to trees, nor summon your birds or cats."

Keelie looked at Sean. He sighed, as if he'd come to a difficult decision.

She held Sean's gaze, his green eyes bright with concern and pain. She knew what he was thinking. If he let Tamriel take her, he was following his father's evil direction. If he rescued her, he would be breaking away from his Dad. It was hard to disown his father, evil or not, even though many lives hung in the balance—and possibly the fate of all the elves.

"Tamriel, release Keelie." Sean's voice held no uncertainty.

Keelie cried with relief. She knew she had been right about him.

"What? You would choose a Round Ear over your own father? Over your own kind?"

"Release her."

Sir Davey waggled his fingers. There was a rumble underneath Tamriel's boots, and thousands of earthworms began wriggling around his feet.

He lowered his sword and began hopping out of the

way of the squirming mass. "What in the Great Sylvus is this? A dwarven curse?"

Sir Davey went in for the tackle like a little football player, crashing into the jouster at the knees. Tamriel toppled over.

Sean grabbed Keelie and swung her into his arms. He held out his sword, the blade pointed toward Tamriel. Tamriel glared at Sean. Keelie clung to her rescuer. He wrapped his arm tighter around her waist. She would remember this moment for the rest of her life.

Sir Davey kicked Tamriel's sword away, but Tamriel countered by flinging a handful of earthworms into Sir Davey's face. Davey gagged and staggered in a circle, scraping worms from his hair. Tamriel turned over onto his knees and got up, armor clanging, and ran into the forest.

"I hate to leave you here, but I know you will be protected by Sir Davey." Sean nodded his head toward the dwarf. Sir Davey nodded. "I need to catch Tamriel before he reaches my father, or there will be worse trouble for your family."

Keelie watched as Sean ran after the fleeing jouster. She had no idea how much time she had left, and she still had to get Alora.

twenty

The area around Grandmother's house was deserted, so Keelie ran upstairs.

"Where have you been?" Alora shook her leaves.

"Coming here." Keelie tugged Alora's flowerpot away from Grandmother's now-empty bed. Outside, Sir Davey waited with the cart from the shed. Knot stayed close to Keelie. His eyes were narrow slits as he surveyed the area around him.

"I swear, if this tree were human, she'd look like Laurie," Sir Davey said as he rolled Alora toward the village green.

Alora didn't let up once she started her list of complaints.

I could've died of thirst.

Do you know what neglect is?

Just wait till the aunties find out what you've been up to. You're in trouble.

In the distance, Keelie heard voices, and they were growing louder. They were on the backside of the village now, hidden from view, but still they were taking a chance being so close. Everyone's attention was on the Council, including the guards. A trial was a rare thing for the elves.

Come to us, child, the aunties called.

Sean was on guard near the aunties. As they made their way, hiding behind sheds and large trees, Keelie wondered if Sean had managed to catch Tamriel. She didn't dare make her presence known.

"I guess this is where we part ways, lass. For I need to go and speak with your father." Sir Davey had reached the edge of the green, where the elven crowd had their backs to them.

Nodding, Keelie dragged the treeling off the cart and into the safety of the Auntie's tree root.

You're leaking salty water again. Alora reached up and patted Keelie's cheek with her branch as Knot slipped away.

A ragged jouster emerged behind Sir Davey, his sword drawn, ready to plunge it into the dwarf's back. Keelie recognized him—it was Tamriel. She struggled to get out of the Auntie's root and shout a warning.

"Wait, Keelie," Alora called out.

As Davey ducked, Tamriel whirled and struck out at nothing. He recovered and slashed again. Knot bounced back into view and leaped behind the jouster, who turned, still hacking at an invisible opponent.

Knot turned to grin at Keelie, then leaped onto one of the auntie's roots. Tamriel followed, in furious pursuit. Tamriel was soon backed up against the aunties, and before he knew what was happening, a root lifted and he vanished from sight.

Knot saluted her with his tail, and Keelie bowed her head to him. She was going to have to rethink pushing his plush booty across the floor with her foot. He had hidden talents.

Everyone in the village had gathered around the Caudex. The elegant chairs, which looked like her father's work, were arrayed on the fossilized wood platform. There sat Grandmother, the Lady of the Forest, with several other elder elves, including Etilafael, the Head of the Council. They were an impressive sight.

Niriel stepped onto the Caudex like a plucky rooster. He waved his hand as if he were a politician at a rally.

"Greetings, lords and ladies. We gather here under grim and solemn circumstances, the likes of which we thought we would never face again. We have been betrayed, and all that we are is now in danger. Before you will come those who wish to see us extinguished from the earth, and it would be meet to punish them as they would have us punished. Oh, elevated ones, members of the High Council, you see before you the criminal returned."

Jake was pushed into the clearing. He stumbled, then turned to the Council and bowed elegantly. He seemed not to react to the stony silence that met his flourish, but Keelie noticed his tiny wince, and the worry that clouded his eyes.

Lord Niriel continued. "You have consorted with the unnatural child of one of our own, one who was once your brother. When we capture Keliel Heartwood, she will share your fate." He said her name as if it was a curse.

"If you can't say something nice, don't say anything at all." Her voice rang through the clearing. All faces turned, mouths open, as head held high, Keelie walked into the tree circle.

twenty–one

He'd called her unnatural. Was that because of her human self or her use of dark magic? Keelie stood straighter. She'd show them. The moment she stepped up onto the fossilized wood she felt its hum and stared down, astonished. The tree was dead, but amazingly, its energy lived on.

Lady Etilafael stood, leaning on a tall staff. "Keliel Heartwood, you stand accused of wielding dark magic."

"Yes ma'am. But it's not dark in a bad way. It's just different." Keelie looked around for her father. He stood to one side of Grandmother's thronelike chair, with a clear view of the Council and the crowd. He met Keelie's gaze.

Dad felt the tree's hum, too, but he looked worried. Sir Davey near him, holding a stone and murmuring to it.

She wondered how many other elves could feel the ancient tree's magic, how many had that much tree shepherd in them that they heard the forest speak to them. A quick glance showed that not many did.

Despite Niriel's decree that this was a solemn occasion, many of the elves looked almost darkly gleeful, as if they were happy that she'd been caught doing wrong and would now be cast out. Risa's red hair stood out in the crowd, and Keelie gritted her teeth as she saw the girl talking excitedly with another elf girl, her eyes wide, barely containing her laughter.

Two more of the Council stood, and Grandmother stood as well. Her serious expression did not betray any hint of love or sympathy as she addressed Dariel—now called Jake.

"You were banished from our forest, doomed to forget, and you have returned. You knew that the consequence was death." The members of the Council looked at each other, except for Keliatiel, whose eyes were glued to Jake.

"No way," Keelie muttered. Dad had said that death was not on the table. "It's not his fault his memory came back," she cried out. "And he loves this forest. He was worried because the Dread was failing."

"Silence!" Lord Niriel swept forward. "For all we know, the Dread failed because of the vampire's return. Did he not kill three trees and countless animals?"

All the gathered elves started to speak.

"Silence!" Lord Niriel raised an arm and turned slowly, and the crowd grew still once more. "Your turn will come, Keliel Heartwood. You have no say in this matter."

"I'm a witness. I saw the true vampire, myself. Jake only took a little of the animals' life essence, and he never killed any. He never harmed a tree. "

Etilafael banged her staff against the wood-stone floor. "Enough. Child, you know not of what you speak. Events long ago sealed this one's fate, and now he must pay."

A green-cowled elf brought the Lore Book and placed it in the center of the slab. Next to it he put a silver knife. Not a good sign.

"This isn't civilized. He deserves a fair trial, not a bunch of antique rituals. The trees can be witnesses." Keelie gathered every bit of knowledge she'd gleaned from her lawyer mom. "What real wrong can be blamed directly on Jake? That he returned? He'd been warned against it, but is trespassing punishable by death? Are you going to execute every hiker who wanders up here?"

The elves murmured, and Lord Niriel frowned and walked forward swiftly, the Lore Book in his hands.

The crowd parted and a stretcher was brought to the circle. Lord Elianard lay in it, pale and trembling, his once-beautiful golden hair lank and plastered with sweat against his head. He looked as if he was dying. Elia stood beside him, a hand on his shoulder, the other holding a cloth to her tear-stained face.

Lord Niriel pointed to his former flunky. "Behold another who allowed the darkness to touch him. Lord Elianard is on his way to becoming a vampire, and it is Dariel's doing that has brought him to this end."

Keelie opened her mouth to protest, but Jake's face fell and his shoulders drooped when he saw Elianard's condition.

The gathered elves were silent as Niriel read aloud from the elven law. "Vampires are parasites not to be tolerated. They bring attention to the Otherworld and endanger all by their presence in the human world."

Three elven guards came forth—Niriel's lackeys—and each in turn presented their evidence against Keelie: the amulet she still wore around her neck; that she was subject to the Dread, and therefore human; and that she befriended a vampire and kept his existence a secret.

"I should be allowed to present witnesses for the defense," Keelie argued.

Her grandmother looked at Etilafael, and the elven matriarch nodded.

"I call forth Knot."

Niriel laughed. "A cat?"

Shouts erupted as Knot strode out in his Puss n' Boots garb, sword at his furry side. Keelie stared. This was right out of her dream. She could almost smell the fish sticks. She knew that Knot was more than a cat, but this was a lot more than she'd envisioned.

He raised a paw for silence.

First, he bowed toward the Council, then turned to bow to each of the aunties, the queen oaks.

"Meow am not a public speaker, but meow must come before yeow to defend my Dariel Fae Friend. Meow tell yeow that yeow have falsely accused yeow boy. Dariel of the Tree Shepherds is meow friend. A friend to all fae, a blood bond that meow takes not lightly. Meow is guardian to his kin, meow is bonded to Keliel." He bowed to Keelie, then winked one big eye.

Eloquently, in his kitty accent, he described what happened in the Wildewood, and that the unicorn Einhorn himself gave Keelie the amulet that Elianard had used against him.

Niriel jumped up from the seat he'd taken at the side of the standing crowd. "It is as I said. Nothing has changed. Elianard used the amulet against the Wildewood unicorn, and now Keliel has the cursed thing and uses it in our own forest. Is the Dread not broken? Surely she has done this with the help of her vampire kin."

Knot hissed at Niriel, fangs exposed. "Yeow are the villain in this play."

"The cat is a fairy," Niriel said quickly. "Everyone knows the fae are fickle and not to be trusted."

Some of the elves looked doubtful. They knew Knot, and certainly had never seen him take this shape.

"Would the testimony of a tree help?" Keelie asked. The trees around them murmured.

"Since Zekeliel and Keliel are the only ones who can

hear tree speak, trees may not testify in this matter." Etilafael looked around. The elves nodded. Grandmother Keliatiel looked bemused. For a long time she had heard tree speak only in dreams, but yesterday her skill had returned.

"But there's a tree that can speak plainly for all to hear." Keelie turned to her father. "Dad, get Alora." She turned to the Council. "The acorn treeling will testify."

Dad wheeled out the pot in which the treeling was planted. Alora seemed very pleased with the attention. Keelie was afraid that they were in for some more of her obnoxious dramatics, but instead she just straightened her leaves.

"Do you think you can you make them all hear you?" Keelie whispered, bending low. "Jake heard you, but of course he's a tree shepherd."

"Don't worry, Keelie. I've got Wildewood sap in my trunk. I can make myself heard." Alora waved her branches for attention, then showed her face.

The crowd roared, excited by a sight that they'd only heard about. Dad and Grandmother looked around, astounded. Everyone could see the tree's true face.

"I am the daughter of the Great Oak of the Wildewood," Alora's voice rang out. "Sent to renew our bond with our sister forest. I was entrusted to Keliel Heartwood, daughter of Zekeliel Tree Shepherd. I witnessed the end of the battle, and my parent trees watched as well while Keliel defeated the evil elven wizard Elianard and his daughter Elia of the

Dark Heart. They had used the amulet to drain the Unicorn Guardian's energy and weaken the forest. They took his horn."

Gasps arose from the crowd. Niriel scowled at the treeling, who continued, unperturbed.

"Zekeliel Heartwood himself fell ill from the dark magic. As an acorn, I was entrusted to Keliel's care in gratitude for her service. Now I speak for the Wildewood. Keliel Heartwood is welcome there. She is sister to me. The one you seek is not accused, but I accuse him. Niriel of the Silver Bough."

The crowd gasped and Niriel paled, but stood tall. "This is nonsense. Obviously I am no vampire. Will you listen to a talking tree?"

Keliatiel stood once more. "Our fates are tied to the trees. We are honored that the Princess Alora addresses us."

A branch snaked down from above, holding the book that Keelie had surrendered to the aunties before she went underground. Niriel jumped, trying to grab the book.

A piercing cry from above signaled the return of Ariel, who swooped down, talons extended toward Niriel's face. He ducked and Keelie grabbed the book.

Niriel straightened and adjusted his robes as Ariel perched on a branch above them. "See? She herself proves me right. Her dark magic restored the sight of the hawk, and now it is a darkling beast that does her bidding. She used this cursed book and now she wields it once more."

Keelie turned to Jake. "Tell them the truth. Tell them what happened with you and Elianard and Niriel."

Jake shrugged.

"You can't just give up. Think of Elia. Don't you love her? Do you want to die when her own father is fading, and she will be left alone?"

Jake's eyes flitted to Elia, who stood at her father's side, a faithful daughter even though she knew he'd led her into doing wrong. He slowly met Keelie's gaze, then gave her a tiny nod and smile, straightened his shoulders, and faced the Council.

"Now will I speak of that which took place in this forest long ago," he began. "I killed the unicorn of the Okanogan forest, and used its death to restore the Dread in our forest. For this I was punished, but know that I did not act alone. Lords Elianard and Niriel helped to plan and carry out the act. Together we slew the beast."

The elves roared and angry shouts filled the clearing. Etilafael banged her staff against the Caudex once more, and after a while the crowd silenced.

Lord Niriel was frowning. "How sad that Dariel must accuse the innocent to assuage his own conscience. But surely a life outside of the forest is not worth living? Why fight for more of it?"

"Well, he didn't fade did he?" Keelie shouted. "He was just fine in Seattle until his memory came back. He only came here for justice, and because his mother was fading."

Keliatiel stared at her.

"I'm telling the truth, Grandmother."

"She is telling the truth," Elia said. She pulled a wrapped bundle from her gown and unwrapped the unicorn's horn, its base jagged from where it was broken from Einhorn's head. "Lord Niriel urged my father to do this. And to my shame, I helped."

Gasps, then silence, met the revelation.

"That is mine," Niriel shrieked. He lunged for the horn, but Elia tossed it to Jake. Niriel threw himself on Jake, knocking him to the ground. The two wrestled as the astounded elves rushed forward to stop them. With a shriek, Niriel lifted the horn over his head and drove it into Jake's heart.

Jake stilled, his eyes wide in surprise. Then they closed, as his body went limp. Keliatiel cried out and ran to her lost son's side. She knelt next to him and wept.

Keelie stared at her dead uncle, her friend. It had all happened so quickly.

Elia fell to her knees on Jake's other side, tears rolling down her face. "What have I done?" she cried. "What have I done?"

A moan arose from the forest around them. Above, Ariel cried out and launched herself into the air. Dad grabbed Keelie's shoulder. "Keelie, I want you to go back to California. Davey will take you to Laurie."

"What are you talking about, Dad?"

A ripple crossed the clearing, as if the earth had shrugged, and wind tossed the treetops. "Just listen to me. My mother has surrendered the forest. I must take control."

Keelie felt the green energy building, like surf, rolling in and receding, growing stronger with each pass. "You don't think you're going to survive this, do you? You think it'll kill you. You've tied yourself to the Dread!"

Dad kissed her, holding her tightly against him. "It's the only way, Keelie. I love you." He thrust her away and turned to the trees.

A green whisper floated through her mind and Keelie knew what to do. She threw the book of magic onto the center of the ancient tree's rings, then grabbed Alora by the trunk and yanked her from the pot. The pot crashed to the ground, breaking. Alora's exposed roots wriggled. Keelie lifted the treeling and banged her down over the book, sending her twinkles into a dancing fury. Immediately her roots surrounded the book, pulling it apart as a great cracking was heard. The base of the Caudex split. Alora's roots entered the crevice and, fed by the magic from Under-the-Hill, the treeling began to grow.

The earth heaved as she rose, trunk widening, throwing elves and dwarf to the ground. Like a green tentacle, one of Alora's roots wrapped around Jake's body, pulling it into the roiling earth beneath the trunk, the unicorn's twisted horn still protruding from his chest. Keliatiel and Elia tried to pull him free, but Alora was stronger.

Twenty feet tall now and still growing, the treeling

stretched her branches high and the queen oaks bowed before her.

Dad was laughing as he looked up into Alora's face, now far above them. Keelie wondered if he'd gone nuts, and then it hit her like a runaway school bus, knocking her to her knees. The renewed Dread was roaring through the forest—brought back by the combined power of the Wildewood's gift and the fae magic released by the book's destruction.

Sir Davey pushed his stone into her hand. "Here you go, lass. I figure you'll be needing this."

Keelie stood up, a little wobbly but able to breath without throwing up. The Dread was back—so the forest was safe, and so was her father and her grandmother.

But Jake was dead. She sobbed as she realized that she'd never see him again.

Quit crying, Keelie. That salt water is bad for my roots. Alora lifted one of her roots. *See?*

The *bhata* swarmed up from below her, filling the forest with their chittering and the ticking of their sticks. They carried the wooden sword, which they brought to Keelie.

Keelie picked it up. "Gee, thanks." What was she supposed to do with it?

On the other side of the clearing, Elianard stumbled from his cot and staggered toward his weeping daughter. He fell to his knees beside her. "Elia, I have failed you. I wanted the forest to be whole for you, for your future, but I have doomed us."

Keelie remembered Jake's words, that to not help someone was to curse them. She looked at the sword and felt the amulet's cold kiss against her skin. Why had Einhorn given it to her? What use would it serve now?

She pulled the cord over her head and walked to Elianard, who looked up at her, pale and shaking, his face creased with pain and sorrow.

"I am sorry, Keliel Heartwood. I have wronged you and your father, and all the forest guardians. I am so sorry. I deserve my fate." He glanced at his daughter and his pain lifted momentarily, showing tenderness. "Will you be a friend to Elia?"

Forgiveness. It was tougher than retribution. Keelie held out the cord with the thorn-wrapped silver acorn dangling heavily at its end. "I give this to you, from Jake. From my Uncle Dariel the Tree Shepherd."

Elianard stared, transfixed, at the amulet that had been his undoing. Keelie watched him put the cord over his head. He seemed to think this was part of his punishment.

Another green whisper and Keelie looked over to Dad, who winked at her and motioned to what she still held. She offered the wooden sword, hilt first, to Elianard as well. "This seems to be for you."

Puzzled, he took the hilt, then jerked back as he was hit with a jolt of green magic. The wooden blade sizzled and sparked, and from its tip smoke curled as the process reversed itself and it once more became steel. The green magic that had made it wood was seeping into Elianard's arms.

Elia stumbled to her feet as Elianard stood, healed. He threw his arms around his daughter and held her tightly.

How about that, Keelie thought. Elia had been right—she *was* the one to heal Elianard.

Above them Ariel cried out a warning, and Keelie saw that Niriel had turned to run.

Zeke stood in Niriel's path. "I am the master of the forest. Your fate is to wander the earth, forgetting your heritage. Remember us not. And return on pain of death." Dad raised his arms and the trees swayed. The Council assembled beside him, Grandmother included, although she looked heartsick. Together they raised the magic that would send Niriel away, as Jake had been sent away a hundred years before.

Niriel stood tall, but Sean cried out and begged them to stop.

"Father, I love you." His words were lost as a wind whirled into the circle. Niriel's robes lifted, the edges trailing away into dark fog. The change had begun.

Niriel's eyes were focused on his son, as if he would try to remember this one thing forever. Keelie's chest grew tight. She couldn't bear to watch. Niriel's love for his son was in his eyes, even as he surely felt the magic tear his memories away. Was this how Mom looked just before the plane crashed? Had she tried to take the memory of Keelie with her to the other side?

Niriel's robes were almost all fog, and his fingers had lengthened strangely, the tips fading, but the rest of him was here. Keelie hadn't been able to stop the plane, but maybe it was not too late to stop Niriel's destruction.

"Stop!" She put all of her power into her shout. The trees listened, the earth shivered, and the fae stood still. "Stop the spell." Keelie lowered her voice to address the Council. "If Elianard can be forgiven and healed, then why not Niriel? The elves must change. Vengeance is not the answer, nor is a punishment that harms the innocent." She pointed toward Sean's grief-ravaged face.

The Council members looked at each other, then at Grandmother, who had hidden her face in her hands. They nodded at Zeke, who dropped his arms. The wind died down. The spell was broken.

Green shot through Keelie as the trees cried out to her, and she saw Grandmother raise her hands, amazed, reaching up toward the high canopy above them. The trees were talking to her once more.

Keelie opened her mind and heard them. Despite Jake's death, there would be much rejoicing tonight, for the forest was restored.

Zeke scratched the earth at the edge of the great clearing, and Niriel was free. Sean, who had stood outside the circle, shoulders bowed and looking sick and very alone, ran into his father's arms. Keelie felt Dad's hands on her shoulders and turned to hug him tightly. "It was Mom," she said. "I thought that maybe Mom felt like Niriel, just before the end."

Dad kissed her hair and said nothing, but she felt a

tear hit her neck and tightened her arms around his waist. Knot rubbed against Keelie's leg, kitty-sized once more, and she heard him speak again. "Alora wants yeow."

She stared down at the cat. Maybe hearing him talk was not such a good thing. She let go of Dad. "I'll be right back."

He nodded, and as she returned to the now huge treeling, her father and Sir Davey went over to Sean.

"So what do I call you if you aren't the bratty treeling any more?"

"What are you talking about, Keelie? Of course I'm still the treeling. I just need bigger twinkles. And more of them. Now."

The aunties laughed in her head. *She is the Queen Tree of the Dread Forest, Keelie. Our own Great Tree.*

Keelie shrugged. She wasn't up to laughing right now. Poor Jake. He'd come home to die. She wondered if she should hug Grandmother. A scary thought.

"What's the matter, Keelie? Didn't everything turn out the way you wanted? You are safe, and the Dread is back. I'm in charge, as the Wildewood and the Dread Forest meant it to be. Your father is the Lord of the Forest. What more can you want?" Alora seemed perplexed.

"My uncle died. I know that for trees it's different."

"We'll have a Lorem for him."

"Not the same. I'll miss him. Elia will probably miss him more. She loved him. And he loved her." Keelie wiped fresh tears from her eyes.

"Stop it with that salt water thing. I warned you. Very well, this will stop it."

A grinding sound filled the clearing, and all laughter stopped as Alora's roots gave way, exposing a dark corridor under the now-massive tree. "Now you can go Under-the-Hill whenever you want."

"Thanks." Keelie tried to sound enthusiastic.

A flutter of movement near the dark opening revealed a swarm of *feithid daoine*. Then the darkness vanished in a blinding glow of white and the clatter of hooves on stone.

The elves grew close, shielding their eyes from the brightness that filled the clearing. When they could see again, a unicorn stood before Alora, its long horn a slender spiral of glimmering silver.

Awed, the elves bowed in reverence as the unicorn walked around the circle, looking at each of them. It stopped before Zeke and touched him with its horn, then it did the same to Keliatiel before going to Keelie.

"Oh, Alora, thank you." Keelie looked into the unicorn's soft green eyes, so beautiful that she wanted to weep from the joy of having him near her.

The unicorn bowed its head to her, touching his horn to her heart. A bubbly happiness fizzed through her, erasing the pain of Jake's death. She frowned. She didn't want to forget Jake, but the unicorn had moved on to the other side of the clearing, where the crowd of elves reached out to touch him.

He tolerated their hands, but pushed them gently aside until he reached Elia. The elf girl looked frightened, as if he would stab her with his lethally sharp horn, but instead he looked at her long and lovingly, then he shimmered and dissolved to silvery mist.

A cry of disappointment went up, but from the mist stepped a white-robed man, tall, handsome, and sharp-earred ... and very familiar.

Elia cried out, holding her hands to her hide her face. He pulled her wrists down and kissed her lips.

He turned to look at Keelie, and winked a bright green eye.

She gave him a thumbs-up. "Welcome back, Uncle Jake," she whispered, and went to hug a sparkly tree.

epilogue

Keelie sat against the big pine on the ridge and watched the forest below. Gone was the earth-moving equipment, and even the bare dirt. The magic that had flowed down the mountain five months before had erased all signs of human work. Spring was just around the corner, and buds were starting to appear in all of the forest's trees.

Ariel had caught a thermal and was just a hawk-shaped speck in the sky. She was still dark, but so beautiful that she made Keelie's chest ache. Her joy in flying and hunting was wonderful, except for when she brought Keelie torn-mousie love presents. Only Knot enjoyed those.

Keelie wondered how the elven spokesmen would explain the forest's change to the town. Of course, with the Dread's effect working full force, it was unlikely that any human would want to build this close to the Dread Forest ever again.

She scratched her arm, dislodging the *bhata* that clung to her sleeve. The fairies really had a thing for her now. They were everywhere, too. Who knew there were this many stick and bug people? The forest was crawling with them.

A giggle sounded from the other side of the tree. Keelie rolled her eyes. Elia and Jake were all over each other again. She couldn't bring herself to call him Dariel, although he sure looked different now that he was the unicorn lord of the forest.

She will bear a child, a voice whispered in her head. She looked at the *bhata* that was climbing up her jeans leg, its holly berry eyes intent on her face.

Really? The thought of Elia as anyone's mom was pretty scary, but it would make her a local hero, and Elia loved attention.

It hit her that she would be Aunt Keelie. She smiled. She kind of liked that. No, wait. If Jake was her uncle, then his baby would be her cousin. Not as cool. She'd hold out for being called Aunt Keelie.

Aunties are cool. The voices of the oaken aunties, the Queens of the Dread Forest, trilled at each other.

I want to be an auntie, Alora said. *When are you going to have an acorn, Keelie?*

Not for a long, long time.

The *bhata* nodded in agreement.

Leaves crunched under booted feet, and Keelie watched as Sean jumped over the stream, then waved at her. He wore a Silver Bough Jousting Company jacket, since they were working hard for the upcoming Renaissance Faire season and he was now in charge. Since the trial, Lord Niriel had kept to the forges, working the fires and twisting steel into beautiful new swords. Recently he'd gone to Germany to work with the Black Forest elves on a swordsmith exchange. A new swordmaster would soon take his place in the Dread Forest.

Some of the Dread Forest elves thought that pardoning Lord Niriel had been a mistake, but Sean was so happy and relaxed these days that Keelie knew it had been the right thing to do. For right now, at least. And since Risa's father didn't want his little girl involved with Niriel's family, the wedding was called off. Risa didn't speak to Keelie, but she had seen the elf girl watch Sean, her face full of yearning. Risa kept busy with her gardens, drying herbs and bottling herbal elixirs. The rumor swirling around the village was that Risa would soon be joining the faire circuit, starting with the Juliet City Shakespeare Festival in California. Keelie suspected that Sean's relief at being off the hook would soon be ended.

Keelie was going to be at the High Mountain Ren Faire

with her father in May, and she knew that her grandmother had plans for them to visit several failing forests. Keelie was now considered an expert in forest renewal. She was going to hold out for getting a driver's license first, since she'd been taking lessons with Zabrina—a few more dings on Vlad the VW didn't seem to bother her new friend.

She lifted her hand to return Sean's greeting, then stood up and brushed off her jeans, deliberately shutting out the tiny voice of the prophetic *bhata*.

Whatever the stick fairy had to say about her and Sean would have to stay a secret. She ran down the hill toward him. She couldn't wait to find out on her own.

About Gillian Summers

A forest dweller, Gillian was raised by gypsies at a Renaissance Faire. She likes knitting, hot soup, and costumes, and adores oatmeal—especially in the form of cookies. She loathes concrete, but tolerates it if it means attending a science fiction convention. She's an obsessive collector of beads, recipes, knitting needles, and tarot cards, and admits to reading *InStyle* Magazine. You can find her in her north Georgia cabin, where she lives with her large, friendly dogs and obnoxious cats, and at www.gilliansummers.com.

Keelie's adventures continue!
Watch for Book I of the Scions of Shadow Trilogy.